Within A Captain's Power

A Captains of the Scarlet Night Novel

Lisa A. Olech

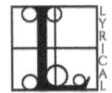

LYRICAL PRESS
Kensington Publishing Corp.
www.kensingtonbooks.com

Lyrical Press books are published by
Kensington Publishing Corp. 119 West 40th Street New York, NY 10018

First Electronic Edition: April 2017
eISBN-13: 978-1-5161-0078-1
eISBN-10: 1-5161-0078-6

First Print Edition: April 2017
eISBN-13: 978-1-5161-0080-4
eISBN-10: 1-5161-0080-8

Printed in the United States of America

Never underestimate the power of a pirate . . .

Captain James Steele is duty bound to capture the privateer Scarlet Night and bring her rebellious crew to England to hang. Then he will leave his majesty's service, make an upstanding marriage, and join the landed gentry. But the winds of fate are blowing the straitlaced commander utterly off course.

Once aboard, James comes face to face with a pirate boy who is in reality fierce, desperate—and gorgeous—Samantha Christian, on the run from a sadistic Virginia plantation owner. With her identity unbound, the good captain dutifully takes her under his personal command, whereupon decorum goes out the porthole. But while his heart is lost to Samantha by the time they reach England, her noose still awaits. Now James's sense of duty will be severely tested. As for Samantha, she has a plan, and a duty, of her own . . .

Books by Lisa A. Olech

Captains of the Scarlet Night
Within A Captain's Hold
Within A Captain's Treasure
Within a Captain's Fate
Within A Captain's Power

Published by Kensington Publishing Corporation

To Bob – Another fine captain.

Acknowledgements

I wish to thank all the hands who have lovingly brought my pirates to life upon these pages. Thanks to Amanda, my editor; Dawn, my agent; and the fine folks at Kensington Lyrical and Blue Ridge Literary Agency.

Thanks, also to Kathy, and the Plot Bunnies. I couldn't have done this without you!

Chapter 1

Pleasant Ridge, Virginia — 1715

"Are you trying to get yourself killed?"

"I'm buying myself some time." Samantha Christian whispered behind her fan.

"You're buying yourself another beating." Her companion, Rebecca Whitmore, whispered back.

"As long as I know it will be the last, Wessler can do his worst."

The air in the Whitmore's ballroom was stifling. The room was packed with an overabundance of Virginia's beautifully dressed elite. Plantation owners with their gossiping wives and pampered daughters wearing their latest Parisian fashions. Political bigwigs vying for attention, and high-ranking British military in crisp, sharp uniforms. All these, and Samantha—in the ill-fitting, cast-off gown of Damian Wessler's deceased wife. She did her best to blend into the silk damask wallpaper. A mighty challenge wearing the color puce.

It was the annual harvest ball. An anticipated favorite in the surrounding community. It would be social suicide not to attend, which is why Wessler agreed to allow Samantha to come, even though he despised her burgeoning friendship with Isabelle Whitmore and her daughter Rebecca.

"Fine. We'll go. But I won't be spending my money on some foolish new gown. One of Marlene's will do." He snatched at her upper arm and gripped it viciously. Samantha shook with the effort not to cry out. "And if I catch you talking to those blasted Whitmore bitches, or you embarrass me in the slightest way, you'll live to regret it." He spit between his clenched teeth.

It was his favorite expression. *"You'll live to regret it."* There was much Samantha regretted, but it did her little good to go back and try to undo what had already been done. Her only other option was to put her plan in action to leave the vile prison she found herself in, regardless of the unavoidable risk to her health. Wessler's beating tonight would happen whether she followed his strict dictate or not. She might as well earn it honestly.

Samantha fanned at her cheeks. She and Rebecca stood tucked in amongst the huge floral arrangements decorating the room. Magnolias and dogwood perfumed the space. She caught Wessler glaring at them from across the room and massaged the nauseous pitch and roll of her stomach with gloved fingers.

"Mother has sent word, but if the *Scarlet Night* has moved on from their hiding place..." Rebecca clutched at Samantha's wrist. Pale eyes, wide with concern, met hers.

Samantha smiled, trying to reassure the girl. "That's a chance I'll have to take." She closed her fan with a snap, kissed Rebecca's cheek, and shot a defiant smile in Damian Wessler's direction. "Now, why don't you introduce me to the handsome Captain Steele?"

Captain James Steele of the Royal British Navy was among the guests at tonight's ball. He cut a dashing figure in his dress uniform of navy and cream. Broad shoulders filled his gold-trimmed coat. Brass buttons winked in the flicker of the hundreds of candles lighting the room. He wore no wig, choosing to club his hair. The color was a rich auburn that shone to a light ginger in the candlelight. It made the blue of his eyes all the more striking. Taller than the majority, he was by far the most noticeable man in the room.

After the proper introductions, he swept her onto the dance floor. "Have you lived in Virginia long, Mistress Christian?"

Her gaze darted from Wessler's livid glare to the handsomeness of Captain Steele. "Six months. However, it feels more like six years."

He grinned. The curve of his mouth revealed a slight dimple in his left cheek. "Do you miss your home so much?"

"I do, and my family most of all." She tried to concentrate on the steps of the dance and boost her fortitude.

"I, as well, but soon I'll happily set sail with orders bringing me back to England. I'm looking forward to autumn in Weatherington."

"Weatherington? Is that where you're from?" She dared another glance in Wessler's direction. His glower caused her to falter and step on the captain's polished boot. "I-I grew up not too far from there in South Oxbridge."

Captain Steele never missed a beat. "You don't say. I know South Oxbridge well." He spun her to the music before dipping his head and dropping his voice almost to a whisper. "I must warn you, my lady, there is a gentleman standing off my port side who has the most disagreeable scowl directed at us."

Samantha could almost feel Wessler's eyes burning holes through her back. She forced a grin. "Does he resemble an overfed hound dog in a wig?"

The captain threw back his head and laughed. The sound warmed her clear through and somehow gave her a necessary measure of courage. "Why, yes, now that you mention it, there is something a bit hound dog about him. Who is he? A suitor perhaps? An overprotective uncle? By his expression, perhaps he is your betrothed?"

She lifted her gaze from his pristine silk neckcloth. The Captain's eyes were impossibly blue. They were the sky on a brilliant summer afternoon. "No, he is not my betrothed. He is more my jailer."

Captain Steele laughed again. "Isn't that somewhat the same thing?"

"Spoken like a man who is either terminally single or unhappily betrothed."

"Betrothed, but not unhappily. Impatient. I'm to be wed as soon as I return to England."

Samantha blinked at the quick rush of unexpected disappointment. "Congratulations, Captain. Your fiancée is a lucky woman indeed."

"Thank you. Lillian is lovely. We're well matched."

"Will you wed in Weatherington?"

"Unfortunately, no. Lillian lives in London. She does not share my love of the country. A bit too rustic for her tastes."

"I'm a true country girl, I'm afraid," Samantha lifted a shoulder in a slight shrug, "but I've always longed to see London."

His rust-tinged brows rose. "You didn't sail from there?"

"No, Portsmouth." Turning once more in the dance, Samantha caught Wessler heading toward them, only to be intercepted by one of the other local plantation owners. He acknowledged the man with a civilized nod. The tolerant set of his jaw told Samantha he'd been caught in conversation. He shot her another dark scowl.

"Well, if you ever find yourself back in England, you must allow me to show you London."

Captain Steele's warm voice softened the edge of Wessler's threat. "Won't your Lillian mind?" She blinked up at him.

The dimple in his cheek flashed once more. "I suspect she'd frown like your guard dog."

"I can certainly understand why. You are quite handsome." A darting look told her Wessler still watched. Samantha laid her hand on the lapel of the captain's jacket. "What is it about a man in uniform that is so appealing?" She traced the gold braid.

"I wouldn't know. I'm surrounded by men in uniform every day. I fail to see the allure."

Samantha's laugh sounded tinny and forced to her ear. Their dance ended. Couples began to clear the dance floor. Wessler finished his conversation and seemed intent on making his way through the crowd toward them once again.

"Captain, I do beg your pardon, but I am suddenly feeling a bit…It's so terribly warm…" She feigned a stumble.

He caught her arm. "Are you unwell?"

"Air." She lifted a shaky hand to her throat. "I'm desperate for a bit of air."

The orchestra began another lively tune. New dancers crowded the floor and blocked Wessler's approach as Captain Steele guided her quickly in the opposite direction toward the French doors leading to the back veranda.

The night breeze was a blessed relief after the heat of the ballroom. Moving them into the shadows, Samantha pressed a hand to her ribs and drew in several deep breaths. She lifted the back of her hand to her cheek.

Captain Steele gave her a worried frown. "Are you all right?"

"Yes," she nodded, "I believe so." She shot a glance over her shoulder.

"Can I fetch you some water, perhaps?"

"No, thank you. I'm feeling much better." She laid a hand on his sleeve. The lights from the ballroom filtered through the sheer fabric adorning the doors and accented the attractive angles of his face. "Are you always so kind, Captain?"

He gave her another small grin. "Unless I'm ordered otherwise."

"You *are* in His Majesty's service." Samantha responded coyly and curtseyed.

"Aye, and loyal to king and country." He inclined his head in a small bow.

"And steadfast in your duty?" she teased.

Captain Steele stood tall. "I know of no other way."

The doors to the veranda flew open. Music and the hum of conversation tumbled out as Damian Wessler rushed from the ballroom. He stood for a moment at the railing, peering into the shadowed pathways of the Whitmore's formal gardens.

Blood rushed in Samantha's ears. Fear and panic caused her to clutch at Captain Steele's sleeves. "Forgive me, sir." she whispered before rising on tiptoes to crush her mouth to his.

"Madam—" Captain Steele put his hands to her waist and gently tried to push her away.

Samantha heard Wessler's curse behind her. She tightened her grip. "Please, Captain, I've no time to explain," She rushed. "Play along." She slipped her arm about his neck, angled her mouth, and kissed him again.

Wessler's boot heels punctuated each stride as he marched toward them. He wrenched her out of Captain Steele's grasp. "What in the bloody hell—" he snapped. His eyes held a murderous rage as he growled into Samantha's face. His jowls trembled with barely contained fury.

Samantha wiped at the corner of her mouth. She flashed Wessler a coy smile. "You can't blame me for stealing a simple kiss." She shot a nervous glance at the Captain. In the dim light, she couldn't read his face, but the increasing bite of Wessler's fingers interrupted all else.

She faked a small stumble and a tiny burp. A forced giggle through her gloved fingertips capped her performance. "Whatever was in the punch? I'm so lightheaded."

"You'll pardon us, sir, but Mistress Christian," he jerked her to his side, "and I need to bid you a good eve." As he spoke, his grip continued to tighten. "Come along, my *dear*," he snarled as he jerked at her arm. "Didn't I warn you not to drink too much this evening? Time to get you home."

Samantha pushed at his punishing hand. "We shouldn't be rude to the Whitmore's distinguished guest." She shot Captain Steele an embarrassed glance. He was watching the exchange between her and Wessler. A frown knit his brows. "Another dance, Captain?"

"We're leaving," bit Wessler.

"The spirits were rather potent tonight. Perhaps, Mistress Christian simply needs a bit more air, Mister...?" Captain Steele held out his hand.

Damian had to release her arm to return the Captain's handshake. She couldn't stop the small gasp that escaped her. Her fingers wrapped around her battered skin.

"Wessler. Damian Wessler. I own the Blackwater Plantation. Mistress Christian is in my employ, and she can be rather wild. Undisciplined.

Ignorant to social protocol. Almost defiant." The last words he directed toward her as he reached for her once more. "If you'll excuse us."

Samantha started to thank the captain for his kindness, but Wessler jerked her away. His vise-like fingers left little room for argument. He dragged her back through the crowded ballroom and past a horrified Rebecca.

"We—we need to t-thank our hosts." She resisted the strength of his pull, casting a pleading glance back at Rebecca. She'd rushed to Isabelle's side, and now both women watched their hasty departure, concern etched on their faces.

"And give you yet another opportunity to humiliate me?" He wrenched her arm, causing her to gasp as he snarled into her ear. "Shut your fucking mouth and keep moving, or—"

"Or what? I'll live to regret it?"

Chapter 2

Samantha pulled the hood of her black wool cloak low to conceal her face. Ahead of her, through the gloom of a murky night, her rescuer urged her to hurry. She stumbled upon an upturned root, and her guide cursed.

"Damn it, hurry. The tide will be turning soon. If we are not away, we won't be able to leave 'til dawn."

"I'm moving as fast as I can." She quickened her pace as best she could. "These shoes are too big. They keep slipping from my feet."

Less than an hour had passed since Captain Tupper Quinn alerted Samantha of her arrival by tossing small pebbles at her bedroom window. Now was the time. It was tonight or the opportunity—and her savior—might be lost.

At the first sound of those lifesaving pebbles, Samantha had raised the window, then caught the knotted rope tossed to her before securing it to the heavy post of the bed. Moments later, Tupper swung over the sill to drop into the room.

The wild-haired woman in breeches and boots wasted no time with pleasantries. "Put these on and be quick about it. If he catches us, we won't get away without a messy fight."

In the pack Tupper tossed at her, Samantha found a pair of mud-brown breeches and a shirt of coarse linen, together with a long, wide strip of muslin. Stockings and buckled shoes finished the outfit, along with a wide, thick leather belt.

Stripping off her dressing gown, Samantha winced against the ache in her ribs. She heard the sharp intake of breath behind her and turned to find Tupper's narrowed eyes upon her.

"He put those marks on you?" Her breath hissed through her teeth.

Samantha nodded, clutching her gown to her chest. Tupper brushed the hair away from her face, before tipping it to the light. Samantha couldn't hide the dark ugly bruise marring her cheek. "He prefers to inflict bruises on his staff none can see, but his anger often gets the better of him."

"Lowlife son-of-a whore bastard," Tupper grumbled, releasing her chin. "Best be quick, before I change my mind about leaving and choose to end his miserable life instead."

"I'm tempted to let you."

Tupper nodded to the muslin. "Bind your chest. Make it good and tight."

Samantha began to wrap the fabric about her, flattening the fullness of her breasts as best she could. She donned the strange-feeling pants and finally slid her feet into shoes two sizes too large.

"Now your hair," Tupper instructed.

Samantha smoothed a hand down its long length. "My hair?"

"You're passing as a lad. It has to go." Tupper pulled a short dagger from her boot.

"All of it?" Clasping a handful, she held it to her heart. She always kept her hair long, but knew the cost of her freedom this night. She didn't need to hear Tupper's answer. Samantha closed her eyes and nodded.

The honed blade made short work of the task. Tupper began cutting through the thick shanks of hair. Soft brown locks fell in curled fistfuls at their feet. Samantha felt tears prick the backs of her eyes, but as the first length of hair fell, she knew there would be no turning back. Soon she'd be free of this hellish existence, and by the grace of God, she'd be saved.

* * * *

Later, as she struggled to keep pace with Tupper, the cold dampness of the night air upon her neck felt strange and only added to the surreal scene in which she found herself. How they found their way through the moonless night, she could not say, but soon her feet hit the sandy soil that harkened their arrival upon the shore.

A small skiff with four large men waited. Tupper helped her into the boat, retrieved the shoe that dropped into the water, and swung in to join the rest.

"Make haste, gentlemen, the tide won't be waiting."

The skiff jerked as each man tugged sharply on the oars. It took only a moment for them to find their synchronized rhythm.

The coal-black outline of the land against an ebony sky was Samantha's last sight of Virginia and hopefully the last she would ever see of Damian Wessler and his evil children.

Samantha held her sodden shoe in her hands. The men made short work of bringing the skiff out to a tall, three-masted sloop anchored not too far off shore. There had been no conversation. Tupper sat facing her but paid her little attention, concentrating instead on the men behind her. One of them hummed to himself, pulling at his appointed oar in time to the song he sang only in his head.

When they reached the ship, a rope ladder lowered and soon the small party was climbing swiftly up the side of the dark ship. Samantha struggled to keep her footing. Her shoes making it near impossible to navigate the shifting rope in the darkness. Once she decided to shove them into her belt and make her way without them, it was much easier going.

Tupper pulled her over the gunwale and called out. "All set, gents, let's weigh anchor and be off."

Shouts and a flurry of activity erupted around them. The ship was dimly lit with a handful of low lanterns, but the crew worked as if by feel and instinct alone. Three men circled a pegged wheel of sorts. Its brass cap catching the low light as they turned it round and round. Heavy chain coiled around its center post. As they began to move, the ship creaked and popped. The deck beneath Samantha's stocking-covered feet began to rock.

Overhead, the sails snapped as they caught the night's breeze. Samantha stumbled and grabbed hold of the thick-tarred rigging as the ship came to life and began its leap across the water.

"You, lad," Tupper called out. Samantha looked behind her, until Tupper stepped closer and jostled her shoulder. "*You*, lad, follow me."

Samantha trailed her across the deck, moving between men of every shape and description. Some pulled at ropes others climbed up wide rigging into the dark of the night. She slowed her stride to watch, but a bark from Tupper had her rushing to catch up.

"I'm not a patient soul, boy. Move yer arse." Laughter rose around her, and someone close to Samantha gave her a mighty shove in Tupper's direction. She didn't dare turn to see who had pushed her. Their coarse laughter followed in her wake.

Tupper disappeared down a stairwell, and Samantha hurried to follow. The passageway was dark as a tomb. She groped her way along the rough wood walls. Ahead of her, a door opened, and a blade of blessed light lit her way to the rear of the ship. She stopped in the doorway of a large, impressive cabin.

"If you're waiting for a personal invitation, you'll be standing there quite some time. Get in here and shut the damn door." Behind Tupper, a ragged black bird squawked from atop an iron perch. "Hush, Leviticus."

"Oh, I'm sorry." Samantha scrambled into the room and shut the door.

"Pay no attention to him. He's a crotchety old bird who's long past the age of dying but too damn ornery to give in and keel over." Tupper removed her hat and tossed it into a chair. A fine-tooled leather baldric soon joined it. Turning to look at her, Tupper ran a hand over her head, smoothing the stray hair from her face. The light from the lanterns caught at the wide streak of silver running through her long, dark hair. Piercing eyes of green appraised her as Tupper moved to stand behind a large oak desk.

Opening a drawer, she pulled a crystal decanter and two glasses from what looked to be a special carved niche designed to hold the delicate items. She poured a healthy draft of the liquor into each glass and handed one to her.

Samantha eyed her over the glass as Tupper tossed back the entire contents of hers in one swallow. She repeated the action and paused to refill Samantha's glass, only to find it still full.

"Drink up."

Samantha mimicked Tupper's actions, and soon realized what a mistake she'd made. The drink burned her throat and stole her breath as it burned a fiery path into her belly. Tears filled her eyes as she coughed and sputtered, and tried in vain to breathe. Tupper filled her own glass again, smiled, and sat down.

"Have a seat." Samantha did as she was told, wiping the tears from her eyes. Tupper frowned. "Are you all right?" She couldn't answer but nodded her head. "Another?" Tupper held up the decanter.

"No," rasped Samantha, "no, thank you."

"More for me and the bird." Tupper dipped a slice of cut fruit into her glass and fed it to Leviticus before downing the drink and pouring herself a fourth. She and the bird must have stomachs like iron pots. Maybe that's the reason the bird refused to die.

Pulling a small pipe from another cubbyhole, Tupper packed the bowl and lit it before leaning back in her chair. Drink in one hand, pipe in the other, she rested her boot heels on the corner of her desk and locked eyes with Samantha.

"Now would you like to explain why I've been dragged into your particular mess in the middle of the night? I receive a frantic message from Isabelle Whitmore and, fortunately for you, I was close enough to port to be of some assistance. All I was told was, I had to get you away from a man named Wessler, and Virginia, as soon as possible."

"I...I will be forever grateful to you and the Whitmores."

"Isabelle is an old, trusted friend. If she went to all this trouble, the situation must have been dire. Your bruises have already told me as much." Tupper blew a cloud of smoke toward the ceiling. "So can I assume Mister Wessler is at this moment sailing out with the authorities to meet us?"

"You needn't worry. I still have two days." Samantha ran her thumb over the intricate cuts on her crystal glass.

"I don't understand. Two days?"

"When I got the news you were coming, I picked a fight with him. Openly flirted with an English naval officer at a party we attended night before last." Samantha's mind flashed back to her stolen kiss in the dark with the handsome Captain Steele. The dip of his dimpled cheek, his warm smile, the feel of his lips against hers. Perhaps it was the rush of nerves that had sent the heated flush through her when they kissed? What did it matter now? It was unlikely she'd ever cross his path again. She shrugged. "It cost me another few bruises, but I was guaranteed four days of being locked away as punishment. Wessler won't even open the door unless his cock decides to work, but I wouldn't count on it."

Tupper gave a snort of laughter. "What about when they bring your meals?"

"No meals."

Tupper's eyes narrowed. "He doesn't feed you?"

Samantha notched her chin and held Tupper's gaze. The last thing she wanted was her pity. "He believes it will break me."

"Well, at least Isabelle didn't exaggerate the situation."

"I know I put her in a precarious position, but I had little choice and an even smaller chance."

Tupper held her gaze as she set her pipe aside. "You're tough, I like tough. A good thing, too, because I'm not about to play nursemaid to you. But understand, you've put *me* in a rather precarious position as well. With my crew. I've never lied to them before and don't particularly like doing so now, but the situation here is quite simple. I'm the only woman currently allowed upon this ship. The fact I've been Captain now for more years than I can count makes it an indisputable fact. Hell, I doubt if many of the crew even notices I am not a man, and frankly, that's the way I like it."

She slid her boot heels off the desk and leaned forward. "You, however, are a different story. From the moment you climbed out your window and down the rope at Wessler's estate, until the time we deposit you wherever it is we are to deposit you, you are my new cabin boy. Samantha is now Sam, and you will do nothing to raise questions beyond that fact. Clear?"

Sam nodded. "Yes, of course."

"You will put your mark to the ship's Articles on the morrow and follow all the rules. You'll be assigned duties and responsibilities to pay for our generous hospitality, and you shall do nothing to disrupt the running of my ship. Do you understand?"

"Yes, Tupper."

Tupper pointed a sharp finger in her direction. "Nay, you say, 'Aye, Captain.'"

"Aye, Captain."

Tupper gave a smart nod and sat back. "Now, about your final destination..."

Samantha pulled a deep breath. "Take me anywhere."

"Back to your family in England, I assume?" Tupper relit her pipe.

"No." She turned the glass in her hand. "They don't know the truth of what's happened since I've been here, and I don't want them to suffer for my shame. I'll send word when I'm able, telling them I am safe and well. They do not need the disgrace this would bring them."

"The only shame and disgrace is Wessler's."

Samantha gave a bitter laugh. "He doesn't know the meaning of those words." She pushed her glass across the desk. "Could I get a bit more of whatever this was?"

"It's fine, sweet Jamaican rum. My personal favorite." Tupper grinned as she lifted the bottle and filled both their glasses again. Her sharp green eyes sparkled, adding softness to her weathered face. "I'm beginning to think having you aboard may be all right after all." She pushed Samantha's drink across the desk. "How are you at shooting a pistol?"

Sam tossed back her drink and coughed. "If I were any good at it, would I be here?"

Chapter 3

Captain James Steele gave the order for full sail, as a rush of men scrambled up the rigging with practiced precision. Soon the pride of King George's fleet, the newly appointed frigate HMS *Lion,* pounced like its namesake over the waves. The ship had been made flush for speed and power. Even with a company of more than three hundred men and fully armed with sixty cannon, the golden *Lion* could attack out of the blaze of the sun and seize her prey with speed and might. Perfect for her new assignment.

With the fresh rank of Post Captain, James Steele stood in the bow with his hands upon his hips and his legs splayed as he rode the ship through the wide-open waters. Salt air cooled his face. The wind lifted the tails of his heavy woolen coat.

As James marveled at the beauty and strength of the new warship, he couldn't help but wonder what his father's reaction would be to the news of his commission. Securing such an important post after only three years of captaining the *Carlisle* came as a surprise. As did his orders.

His father had passed along the seawater flowing through James's veins. A marquee now, but a captain once himself, Captain Jaxon A. Steele had been the pirate of a great ship called the *Scarlet Night*. He'd argue that, added to the seawater pumping through James's heart, there was pirate blood as well.

James smirked. *Oh, beg pardon, "privateer" blood.* In the years leading up to the decision to leave his lawless way of life, his father held tight to his Letter of Marque and Reprisal making him a privateer. A great distinction once. The ultimate honor among thieves. But now, that lofty distinction wasn't worth the parchment it was written on.

A frown tugged at his brows. James pulled a great breath of crisp air into his lungs. His new orders weighed heavy on his head. His loyalty to his father was strong, but his sworn oath to king and country must overrule his nagging conscious.

James was to take the *Lion* and her seasoned crew, prowl the seas, and capture pirates. Six months past, the Crown had revoked all the Letters of Marque. Privateers who had fought and pillaged the Spanish, French, and Dutch in the name of Britain were once more labeled criminals and charged with crimes against the king. Treason was now their offense. Death, their ultimate fate. Their choices were few. They could surrender, whereby they'd be transported to the nearest British prison to be hanged. Or they could ignore the king's call for surrender and await capture before meeting the same end. Either way, they would all die a few inches taller wearing a hemp cravat.

The once golden age of piracy had tarnished like brass in the salt air. With more sea traffic came more protection and less opportunity for these thieves. Their time of pillaging for profit was over. James's duty was clear. The list of criminals, their ships, last known locations, and preferred routes awaited him in his quarters. He'd receive a healthy bonus for each capture and, if successful in bringing the most notorious to trial during this sweep of the Atlantic, he would be elevated to the rank of rear admiral of the blue. His career would be secure. He could return home a hero. Wed his fair Lillian. There, at least, he hoped to emulate his father by knowing a great love and ending up happily married.

"Bloody hell, James. You certainly sucked a juicy tit this time."

"Damn it, Dunbar, you can't talk to your captain like that." James hissed as Lieutenant Richard "Ducky" Dunbar moved alongside him.

"No one can hear us, you great prig." Ducky issued a crisp salute before James noticed he only used one finger in the sharp execution of said salute together with a puckering of his lips to complete the rude gesture.

"One of these days you'll push our friendship too far and land us both in the brig." James returned the proper statute of salute and headed toward the aft of the ship and his quarters.

Ducky fell into step alongside. "Oh, pardon me, sir. A thousand lashes for me, sir. Feel free to keelhaul my sorry arse."

James shook his head. He and Ducky had served together since their first day of training. They had both been lieutenants upon the *Carlisle* until James's rise in the ranks. When appointed captain of the *Lion* and asked which officers James might want to accompany him, Ducky had been first on the list.

Even given his cheek, Ducky Dunbar was a fine seaman and a good man to have around when the fighting started. They had protected each other's backs on more than one occasion. Ducky was his best mate. He was to stand up for him at his upcoming wedding, too.

"I've never seen a more impressive ship, you lucky sot."

James led him into the rich appointment of his quarters. He hung up his hat and baldric as Ducky helped himself to a brandy and flopped into the nearest padded leather chair. James snatched the etched crystal bottle from his greedy hand and corked it. "I'd like to think luck had little to do with it. I've worked hard for this."

Ducky raised his glass. "Far harder than I, for sure, and yet..." he glanced around, "here we both are, walking her fine decks, lounging in the richness of the captain's quarters, drinking fine brandy."

"If you drank a bit less brandy, you could have your own ship."

Ducky only smiled. "True. But if I were captain of my own tub, I would carry all the burden and headache. And I wouldn't get to see your ugly face every day." He lifted his feet to rest upon the corner of James's desk.

"Please." James shoved his feet off their perch. "A little respect."

"Fine. Your ugly face, *Sir*." Ducky swirled the amber liquid in his glass. "I should thank you, I suppose."

"For your new assignment?"

"Nay, for getting me away from Virginia's shores....and Justine's claws."

"Justine?" James searched his memory. Ducky's list of female admirers was larger than his good friend's ego. "I don't remember a Justine."

"Of course you do. Met her at the Harvest Ball last week. Red hair, pink gown, overflowing corset." Ducky's hands indicated an abundance of breasts. He propped his heels back on the desk. "Never fails. Give a woman more than one night of pleasure, and they're ready to grab a fistful of flowers, find a preacher, and march you down the nearest aisle."

At the mention of the Harvest Ball, James once more thought of Samantha Christian. The surprise of her heated kiss, followed by her blatant lie about being drunk, had thrown him. *Forgive me.* She had worried his mind for days. He couldn't make sense of what happened, nor could he stop thinking about the way that Wessler cad had physically dragged her from the ball. The hostess, Missus Whitmore, had been most distressed after they left. James had been filled with the uneasy feeling that Mistress Christian was in need of his protection. He was tempted to inquire as to the whereabouts of Blackwater Plantation and visit to ease his concerns; assure himself she was well. But business with the admiral precluded any such plans. Days later they'd set sail.

Lisa A. Olech

Still, Samantha flitted into his thoughts with surprising regularity. Her kiss had jolted him in more ways than one. He could still taste the sweet fullness of her lips. Remember the narrow span of her waist between his hands and the smell of magnolia in her hair. There was something unique about her that was difficult to name. She was an amazing contrast in contradictions. A gentle Northern English woman with a headstrong American independence. She hid a sharp, delightful wit behind those soft doe-brown eyes, and a decided vulnerability beneath a tempting bit of bravado. An honest truth under the disguise of an unskilled lie. He'd never met anyone like her before.

"Hello, James? Did you hear what I said, or are you dreaming of the fair Lillian and your own imminent death march down the aisle?"

James glared at Ducky. He couldn't help the twinge of guilt at hearing Lillian's name. Shouldn't it be her kisses filling his mind? "I was thinking about the night of the ball."

"Exactly. I asked about the girl you were dancing with. The one in the hideous mud-plum gown. Dark hair. Slight build. Lovely mouth."

Were his thoughts that transparent? Ducky had an infuriating knack for reading his mind. "Mistress Christian." James fingered the sealed document containing his list of conquests. He should forget her and get back to what was important. Ducky's conversations never strayed too far from some mention of women, however.

"Was that her name?" Ducky cocked an eyebrow. "Caused quite a stir, you dancing with her." He tsked. "Whatever would Lillian have said?"

"She would have said we have more urgent matters to discuss than balls." James scowled at Ducky's adolescent snicker before breaking the seal on the new orders.

Beyond the high windows, the day darkened behind a cloud. James raised the wick of the lamp to read the list before him. The roll of names filled the page, but one stood out, blurred the rest, and caused his stomach to lurch. He lifted the sheet closer to the light and pressed his fingers to ease the crease in the parchment. Perhaps he had read it wrong.

He hadn't. "Bloody hell."

Ducky rose and came behind the desk to help himself to more brandy. "What is it?" He peered over James's shoulder.

"Is this someone's idea of a joke?"

"Doubt it. The British Navy is not known for its humor. What are you finding so funny?"

James handed him the list and poured himself a finger of brandy. "Third line."

"Bloody hell..." Ducky repeated. His eyebrows reached for his hairline. "Isn't that...?"

James nodded as the liquor seared a path into his belly. "It is. Father's old ship. We've been ordered to capture the damned *Scarlet Night*."

"You know, I heard she's captained by a woman. This gives the name *T. Quinn*." Ducky handed James back the missive. "What does the 'T' stand for, I wonder?"

James scowled at the page. "I don't know. Father passed command of the ship on to a Captain Gavin Quinn decades ago, but I understood he was lost in the earthquake of ninety-two, which brought down Port Royal."

"So this would be his kin? Sister, daughter, wife?"

"Wife, I imagine. Jamaican, or African. Quinn had strong ties to the African coast. He was a fierce objector to the slave trade. The report says they still frequent the gold coast."

"Must be a hardened ox of a woman to take command of a ship of thieves."

"She'd have to be tough, but wives taking their husband's place are not unheard of. It's up to the crew to decide if the woman is worthy."

"The *Scarlet* has a vicious reputation along the southern routes. T. Quinn's made quite a success at it. What more do we know of her?"

"Nothing short of her cunning. Over the last few years, she's been caught dead to rights on numerous occasions, only to slip away at the last moment. The ship is a sloop. Small, but lightning fast. Flaunts red sails and smoke. Crew can't number more than sixty, but the reports tell of a fierce loyalty. Once they set upon a prey, they're relentless. I've not seen any accounts of outright barbarian behavior unless forced. But once provoked, they give no quarter."

"Well, she's never faced down the *Lion*. I'm almost anxious to see her—the captain and the ship. Isn't the *Scarlet Night* where your parents *became* your parents? Ah, if only those deck boards could talk." Ducky settled back into his chair.

It was true. His parents told the tale of their meeting and hasty marriage often. As a young lad, it had embarrassed him to no end to hear the story, but now on the threshold of his own marriage, he envied them their romance. He and Lillian's courtship had been rather cool by comparison, with proper introductions and protocol. His parent's story was more something of an epic tale, with stowaways, heated passion, evil villains, and heroic ends. Evidently, had it not been for brave "Aunt" Alice, none of them would be alive today.

James proceeded to tell Ducky the tale of Alice Tupper and her brave rescue of his parents one fateful day in a cave along the north shore of Jamaica.

"Growing up, my sister Alicia would beg to hear the story of her namesake." Alice was a treasured friend from his parent's tumultuous past. James was convinced, however, the details of her heroism were largely exaggerated for their childish amusement as all fairytales were embellished. Never once could he remember meeting the mythical Alice. He was told she'd sailed off to the colonies when he was still in nappies. To what end, none could say. Aunt Alice had never been heard from again.

Looking at the name, the *Scarlet Night*, brought back all the stories. Whatever would his parents say when they learned about this? He could almost hear his father's heated objections.

"Imagine your father's reaction when you tell him." Ducky read his mind once more.

"What he has to say is irrelevant. I am an officer. An order is an order. He, more than anyone, drilled a sense of responsibility into me. It is not in my power to do anything less. Nor would I. It is my duty."

"Brings an interesting question to mind. If your father's name was on your list…" Ducky pointed with his brandy glass.

James set aside the dictate and gathered the ship's log to make his daily entry. "Why must you always play devil's advocate?"

"Because I know you so well. A man more black and white, I have yet to meet." Ducky returned to his chair. "Perhaps I'm hoping one day you'll surprise me."

"Then you know my answer." James dipped his quill. "No one is more grateful my father is away from that life."

"You'd arrest him?"

James lifted his gaze. "I'm honor-bound to do my duty." He swept a hand in Ducky's direction. "Dammit, I'd arrest *you* given the order."

"Bloody hell." Ducky jerked as if slapped. "Would you be standing there watching when the noose was fitted over my head?"

"I couldn't go against a command, so yes, I would arrest you." James held up his hand to stop Ducky from leaping to his feet. "But once done, I would move heaven and earth to earn your release. I'd defend you with my last breath. Cite your loyalty and upstanding character."

Ducky bit out a sharp laugh. "And you believe that would save my neck?"

"Wouldn't it?" James went back to his writing.

"What if it didn't? What then?"

James set aside his quill and rubbed his forehead. "You're giving me a headache."

"You're sending me to the gallows. Answer the damn question."

"Fine. I would throw myself upon the mercy of the court, and if that failed, I would stand beside you and we could swing together." Ducky didn't respond. James held his gaze. "It's my turn to play the devil and spin the table. Would you arrest me given a direct order to do so?"

Ducky snorted. "No. Of course not."

"You bloody liar. You're telling me you would defy the king simply because I'm your friend?"

Ducky scowled and shook his head. "I wouldn't need to defy orders. Sainted James Samuel Herbert Steele would never do anything to earn an arrest decree from the king, so the question is moot."

James grimaced at Ducky's memory. He regretted telling him his full name all those years ago. Ducky threw it at him often, like a mother scolding an errant child. "This entire conversation is moot."

"Nay, I find it rather enlightening." Ducky leaned back and continued to sip at his brandy. "You remain true to character. There is no gray with you, James. Something is either right or it is wrong. Your military career is your highest priority, and you have worked hard to make yourself one of the finest captains in the fleet." He lifted his glass in salute. "I have much less drive and ambition. However, I respect you highly for your level of commitment, even if it may get me strung up like a butcher's ham."

"You make me sound like some coldhearted tin soldier who would hang his own mother."

"I never said you would hang your mother. God forbid, not her. I've carried impure thoughts about that beautiful woman since the day I met her. Hang your father and me perhaps, but, please, never such a stunning creature." He swirled the brandy in his glass and held it up to the light. "I can't drink brandy without thinking of her golden eyes." Ducky took another long, savoring sip. "Now that I think on it, go ahead and hang your father, but pray, spare me. Then I could live out my fantasy and have her all to myself."

James shook his head. "She'd rather you hanged."

Chapter 4

The creak and sway of the bed cut through the fog of Samantha's mind. As she opened her eyes, pain shot through her skull. She slammed them shut, groaning. Had Wessler beaten her again? No, she ran a cooling hand over her aching forehead. This was a different kind of pain.

Another sway of the bed had Samantha's memory flooding back. She was aboard the *Scarlet Night*. Cautiously cranking open one eye confirmed she was still in the captain's cabin. The slight roll of the ship echoed in her belly, and her head cursed at her, but still a small smile tugged at the corner of her mouth as she shielded her eyes against the morning's bright assault.

She was away from the devil named Damian Wessler and his feral spawn.

Samantha wasn't ignorant to the fact that she was far from safe aboard this ship, but having escaped the hell she'd been in, made everything else pale in comparison.

Rolling to one side, she noticed things in the light of the new day, which she had missed last night.

A bank of diamond-paned windows across the back wall of the cabin sparkled in the sunlight and flooded the well-appointed room with a morning filled with blue skies and calm seas. Beyond, a wide frothy wake spread behind the ship like a fine lady's train.

Tupper was still asleep in her chair behind the beautifully carved oak desk. Her hair unbound, its silvered streak fell in a shimmering wave from root to tip. Her bare feet poked out from beneath the rough wool blanket wrapped around her. She snored. Her ancient crow was awake, however, and pecked at the stale bread on her plate, glaring at Samantha with one glassy eye.

Empty bottles rolled against one another following the sway of the ship. How much had they drunk last night? With a slight groan, Samantha ran a hand over her face once more and pushed her fingers into her shockingly cropped hair. A quick frown creased her brow. The shortness of her hair was a ragged reminder of her current predicament.

Samantha recalled the sight of her dark tresses fluttering to the floor as Tupper cut them away. Spotting a looking glass secured to one wall, she rose. The image staring back made her gasp. Uneven dark hanks stuck out at odd angles. Their ends had started to curl in the humid sea air. She plucked at them in dismay.

Samantha ran her fingertips over her cheek and down her neck. How thin she appeared without her hair. Shadows stood out beneath her eyes and made her look haunted, drawn, beaten. Dark purple bruises along her jaw and cheek had begun to fade yellow at the edges. Her own family would not have recognized her. She couldn't have looked further from the girl that left them a short time ago with high hopes and fanciful dreams. She'd been a fool to believe Wessler's blatant lies and nearly paid for it with her life.

Perhaps she had. After all, Samantha Christian was no more. Her name…correction…*his* name was now Sam. Not waiting until morning, Sam Christian signed his name to the Ship's Articles last night. Looking back in the mirror, it struck her again. Samantha was indeed gone.

Had it truly only been a few days since she'd spun in the arms of the handsome Captain Steele, her hair piled high upon her head? She looked down at her new breeches. Perhaps a puce gown had not been so ugly after all. *Stop.* Now was not the time for regrets or reconsiderations. What was done was done, and regardless of what was to come, it was better than dying by Wessler's hand.

The pinch of tears behind her eyes threatened to undo her, but there was no place for tears now. Weeping was what weak women did. Men did not cry, and she was a man now…or at least a boy.

"Ye look like shite." Tupper's graveled voice sounded almost pleased. It startled Sam and made the crow fluster away from its stolen breakfast. Tupper coughed."Ye need a bit of lamp black to dirty ye up a bit. Hide who ye be." She scrubbed at her face before giving Sam another look and jerking a chin in her direction. "Make sure you keep those bindings on your chest good and snug." Tupper began tipping empty bottles, one by one, to drip into her glass before tossing them aside. "We may just get away with this."

"And if we don't?"

Tupper gave her a bleary look. "You don't want to know." From a cupboard behind the desk, she retrieved another bottle. The cork squeaked on its way out of the bottle's neck. Tupper splashed a measure into her glass. She held the bottle out to Sam. "A bit more shine on the ole' cannon ball?"

"No." Sam grimaced as her stomach rolled at the thought. "Thank you. And you're mistaken. I do want to know."

Tupper stowed the bottle. "They'd kill us both. And not quick, mind ya."

"But you're their captain. Doesn't that count for something?"

"Not here." Tupper began plaiting her hair. The gold ring on her right hand caught the light with each turn of her wrist. "Things don't work like that aboard a pirate ship. Every member of this crew has a say and a vote. We've a crew of fifty-five at present. They may look motley, but you would be wise not to underestimate them. They are the most feared crew on the Atlantic and get paid highly for their skills. Happy when their pockets are full and the rum ain't watered." She lifted her glass and drained it in one swallow.

"They adhere to strict rules, and if broken, they see ye pay the consequence. It's as simple as that. I've lied to my crew by bringing you aboard. It's not something I've dared do before now. They don't take kindly to deceit. A broken trust is never forgiven. I doubt their loyalty to me would prevent them from issuing swift justice. 'Course, they could be in a good mood and only maroon me on some Godforsaken island with no water and a loaded pistol."

Tupper shrugged. "More likely they'd hang my head from the bowsprit and toss the rest over the rail to feed the sharks."

She fit a wide belt about her waist. "And you…. Well, I'm afraid there are many unpleasant ways to kill a man…or a woman. The woman parts of ye may humor them for a bit, but its fair te say we'd both be begging to die at the end."

Samantha's head went light as all the blood seemed to leave her brain. She dropped to the side of the bed. "Didn't think it possible, but you've made me rather miss Damian Wessler."

"Too late to be missing the bastard now. There ain't no turning back from here. That's why ye're to do as I say. Keep yer head down and yer mouth shut." Tupper slipped her feet into tall boots before pointing a finger at her. "Folks see what they expect te see. Play yer part well, and we'll both live to tell the tale."

Sam let out a great breath. "I'll try."

"Ye better do more than try," Tupper warned. "Keep to yerself. Work on becoming invisible. I've still got to figure where you should quarter. Can't be putting you in with the men. There's a sliver of space in one of the holds, but if I put you in there it would arouse suspicion. For now we'll just ride the tide. Hell, they could figure you from the start and we won't live long enough to worry about where ye'll be sleeping tonight."

A knock sounded at the door. The crow gave a halfhearted sweep to his perch. In the light of day he looked more moth-eaten than he had last night. How old was he? Tupper adjusted her baldric. "Come."

Sam crossed her arms over her chest and fixed her gaze on the wide floorboards. When no one entered, she shot a nervous glance toward Tupper.

"It be Bump." She stomped on the floor sharply with her heel. "He's deaf."

Sam hid her surprise as a tall, bronze-skinned man entered the quarters with a trencher of bread and cheese, and what she suspected was a pitcher of ale. His hair was fashioned in thick dark twists that hung oddly past his broad shoulders. It reminded Sam of long wool roving. When he turned intense pale eyes in her direction, she ducked her chin. He faced Tupper and jerked his head back toward her.

"New boy. Sam." As Tupper spoke, she made several odd gestures with her hands.

Sam held her breath and prayed to be inconspicuous. Everything seemed impossible all of a sudden. They'd never get away with fooling the crew into believing she was a cabin boy. *Bet the sharks have already begun circling the ship.*

To her staggering relief, the man called Bump simply nodded, before gathering a few discarded things from Tupper's desk and leaving.

"I'll never survive." The words left her in a rush. "We'll never get away with this."

"You did fine." Tupper tore the end off the loaf of bread and tossed it to Leviticus, who nearly fell from his perch to catch it midair in his wide black beak.

"Getting by a deaf man perhaps." Sam gestured weakly toward the door.

Tupper glared at her. "Bump may be deaf and dumb, but he is far from stupid." Her anger was swift and heated.

The reprimand stung. Sam rushed to explain her misjudgment. "I didn't mean—"

Tupper jabbed a sharp finger toward the door. "That man is the finest seaman on this ship. He's been a member of this crew longer than I have, and he's more intelligent than the rest of the lot put together. I'll not have ye speak ill of him, not one word, or I'll throw ye over the rails myself."

"I'm sorry. I take it back. I just thought—"

Tupper's voice rose. "I know what ye bloody well thought, and ye thought wrong."

Sam hurried to defend herself. "When he came in... It suddenly hit me how dangerous my situation is. I panicked."

"That's a fine way to end up dead," Tupper snapped. "And me with ye." The crow squawked at her as well when Tupper shouted, flapping his wings in agitation.

Sam held up her hands in defense. "I truly am sorry."

Tupper huffed. The crow flew awkwardly to her, as the room pulsed with tense anger. Samantha searched her mind for something to say. She was ashamed at her own rush to judgment. After a strained moment, she asked softly. "Is it hard for him? Being aboard ship and not being able to hear?" At Tupper's glare, Sam was quick to continue. "I only mean, if it were me, I couldn't imagine such an insurmountable challenge."

"Bump handles the challenges of this life as well as any man. He came aboard as a young child. He knows no other way."

"Is Bump a surname?"

"He has no surname. His given name is William, but I'm sure I'm one of the few alive aboard to remember. He earned the nickname Bump his first days on the ship. He's smart like I said, but it took him a bit to get used to things and develop a set of eyes in the back of his head. Couldn't hear the warning shouts when a loose block got to swinging or when a boom went rogue. Had his head near cleaved in two a few times. Hence the name. But he's a sixth sense about things now. There are those who looked out for him growing up, served as his ears. Sent him into the rigging when the fighting started. Taught him how to protect his back during a battle."

"What were you two doing with your hands?"

"He uses a finger alphabet to spell words. We've adopted other gestures over the years to communicate. A Spanish monk put it all in a book." Tupper moved to the built-in bookcase and slipped a well-worn tome from its slot, holding it aloft. "We...*acquired* a copy from a Spanish merchant ship." Tupper met her gaze before opening the book and flipping through several dog-eared pages. "Lad learned it all. Faster than Gavin and I."

"Gavin?"

Tupper returned the book to the shelf. "Captain Gavin Quinn. My late husband."

"I'm sorry."

Tupper waved away her condolences. "I've no time for this chitchat. Last thing I need is some quaint sewing circle on board this ship. Ye'll do well to remember I am neither your friend nor your mother. There'll be no gossip sessions. No trading fashion tips or fussing with each other's hair." She swept the end of her braid back over her shoulder. "I'm the captain of this ship, and yer just another member of this crew."

"I understand."

"Good. Grab yerself a bite to eat and prepare te meet me on deck." Tupper donned her hat and adjusted the wide leather belt over her chest before fitting two pistols into its holsters. "Be quick about it and..." Tupper notched her chin. "Good luck to us both."

Samantha's stomach turned at the thought of food. Between sheer nerves and too much rum, she decided another morning without food wouldn't kill her. Hell, had she not fled, there'd be no breakfast for days. She'd joked about missing Wessler, of course, but had she escaped one danger at Blackwater Plantation only to be in worse peril upon the *Scarlet Night?* There was one small difference, however. Death was a guarantee at Wessler's hands. Here, death was merely a distinct possibility. That ribbon-thin scrap of hope was all she had to hang on to, but it was something.

Sam pulled the glass chimney from a brass lamp, dirtied her face and neck with lampblack, then bound her chest as tightly as she could bear and practiced an angry set to her face. Overhead she could hear the footsteps and shouts of the crew as they began their day. Tupper was right, there was no turning back. Sam put a shaky hand on the door's handle. Forcing herself to stop trembling, she took a deep breath and stepped out into the galley way heading toward the steps leading above deck.

A heavyset bald man carrying a small barrel under his arm strode toward her, knocking her into the wall as he passed. "Out of me way, whelp."

Sam gripped at the rough wood behind her as she watched him move on. Her heart threatened to break out of her chest, but she straightened and continued on. "One down...fifty-four more to go."

Chapter 5

Samantha shielded her eyes as she stepped into the bright sunlight upon the gently swaying deck. She had the distinct feeling of being a fat steak tossed into a pack of rabid wolves. Any moment she expected someone to turn her way, point a fated finger, and begin screaming "Woman!" With the charade over, the feeding frenzy would begin.

Blood rushed in her ears as she moved through the crowd of coarse-edged pirates going about their duties. Eyes down, sneaking furtive glances, she made her way toward the bow of the ship in her quest to find Tupper.

Moving along the deck, Sam passed a small orchestra playing a lively tune. A group of men mended sails. Others coiled rope and polished rails. Men bathed, some cleaned their weapons, sharpened blades, and several played a game with bone dice. The organized chaos on deck was impressive. Even more impressive, Sam felt practically invisible. No one stopped her or gave her much notice at all. Occasionally, she was told to move or watch out, but none gave her even a second glance. Maybe the sharks would have to look elsewhere for their dinner today.

* * * *

From high on the quarterdeck, Tupper watched Samantha wade through a sea of pirates. Tupper scanned the crew for even the slightest sign of curiosity. To her relief, there was none.

What had she done? She could almost hear Gavin's reprimands. He never would have tried to deceive his crew. They may have voted her in as captain after Gavin's death, but she was not arrogant enough to believe she was a worthy replacement. In fact, she had doubted the sanity of their decision on more than a few occasions. Still, the girl needed help. Gavin would have wanted Tupper to go to her aid. He hated slavery on any level, and from what Isabelle had written in her note, Samantha was as much a slave as those working Blackwater's tobacco fields. But her lot included Wessler's *personal* attention. The thought made Tupper's jaw tighten. She'd crossed paths with men like Wessler before. Most saw the blade of her cutlass. It was a mistake bringing Sam aboard, but it was an equal mistake leaving the bastard alive. Maybe she was getting soft in her old age? Tupper hoped it wouldn't bite her in the end.

"There be the Queen of the May. Are ye receiving homage from the lowly peasants this morn?" The *Scarlet Night's* gunnery master, Malcolm MacTavish, scowled at her from under his grand bush of eyebrows. These days, there was more gray than red in his braided beard.

MacTavish had been a member of the crew when Tupper first came aboard. Crusty as week-old bread and a right pain in her arse, but they'd seen each other through more than their share. He'd been there when Gavin died. A good man. He knew every kind of weapon ever made, and could fully arm a cannon single-handed and sharpen a blade that could split a hair. MacTavish held the secret of the *Scarlet's* red smoke that plumed from their cannons when they attacked. It was a secret he only shared with one other. Her.

"What are ye spouting off about now, old man?"

"Ye leave us with our kilt flappin' in the night's breeze while ye run off te find some green-eared lad te shine yer boots? Do ye ken the risk ye tuk?"

Tupper watched the "lad" in question skirt past the men laying a fresh coat of tar on the rigging. "Of course I knew the risk." Tupper spread her arms. "We're away, aren't we?"

"Weel," MacTavish crossed his arms and cocked his head. "while ye were dashin' off into the dark, we had ourselves a wee visit."

She glared at him. "Why am I just hearing this now? Who?"

MacTavish huffed. "Yer *ladyship* didn't stay on deck long enough te give ye the news. It was Jefferies. *Skull's Cross.* "

"Lying sack of shite." Tupper brushed off the name with a wave. "Always scheming to fill his pockets. What was he trying to sell ye now?"

"Weren't sellin' nothin.' Came te warn us."

"The last time we took a warning from Jefferies, we ended up sailing into a bloody hurricane. Bastard doesn't know east from his arsehole."

"Said there be a whole new storm a'brewing. Royals be out in force. Makin' it so crews be clawing for scraps these days. Plus, King's tired of waitin' fer us to come in flyin' the white flag. There's a new hunt and our name be on the list of prey."

Tupper shook her head and scoffed. "What else is new? We've been hearing the same tale for months. They've always been thick patrolling the coast. Now's no worse than before."

"That's where ye be wrong." MacTavish leaned closer, lowering his voice. He smelled of sulfur and smoked herring. "According to Jefferies, they've unleashed the *HMS Lion* te move in fer the kill. Ship's a monster. Outguns us six te one. Full crew. Three hundred men or more."

"So? It's a tub. You worry like an old woman."

Bump's arrival momentarily blocked Tupper's view of Sam. He'd be waiting for her to order a new heading. Tupper still hadn't decided in which direction they should set course. Sam's rescue put them a hundred miles away from where they'd planned. Time to study the charts with Bump and make another plan. She slapped MacTavish on the shoulder and moved to leave. "We can outrun any ship the navy sends our way."

"Not this one," MacTavish called after her. "New hull. Beast's got enough canvas to wrap the *Scarlet Night* like a Christmas gift fer the king."

She stopped and scowled over her shoulder at the big Scotsman. "And where did Jefferies say they were headed?"

MacTavish lifted a meaty hand. "Said they were doing a sweep to catch those bloggers heading south te put up for the winter months."

Tupper held his gaze for a moment, considering. This could be another one of Jefferies tall tales, but if it were true…. She cocked her head. Her crew could fight better than any they'd ever crossed, but six-to-one were odds too steep even for them. Tupper figured they had one clear option.

She looked back over the ship. Sam had reached the ladder way without a single notice. Tupper would be on high alert with her aboard. The girl might be tough, but she was no pirate. Even if she had made her mark on the Articles. Never would be. That was plain to see. There were too many risks. The sooner she got her off the ship, the better. Like it or not, the best place for Samantha Christian was back with her family in England. She'd deal with their shame far better than she'd deal with cannon fire and British patrols.

Tupper nodded toward MacTavish. "Ye've given me a grand idea. Maybe we should forget sunning our decks this year and consider a late crossing to the north. Get the *Night* into port before the harbors freeze over. Curl up by a nice peat fire and feast on lamb and ale stew. Fine whiskey instead of rum. I could finish up a bit of unexpected business. After, ye could hang up yer fightin' kilt once and for all."

MacTavish's eyebrows brushed toward his hairline. "Ye be setting me off ship? Takin' me home? Te Scotland?"

"Why not? Yer older than dirt now. Ye've filled yer pockets with enough gold to see ye through more years than ye got left. Should have sent you ashore ages ago."

He smoothed a hand over his beard and beat on his chest. "'Cept ye couldn't stand the thought of not seein' me purty face every day."

Tupper scoffed. "Nay, it was more the smell of ye kept the rats away."

She nodded again as the plan fully formed in her mind. Best idea all the way 'round. Drop the girl and take the *Scarlet Night* to tuck in up north. "Those navy bastards would never think we'd dare head in that direction. Not this late in the season. The *Lion* can chase its tail all it wants through the Caribbean. They'll never find us."

"Home. Te me bonny Scotland." MacTavish laid a wide, gnarled hand over his heart.

Bump watched them intently, as was his way. Tupper would have to explain things to him...well, not everything. Sam came up behind him as Tupper jerked her chin to send him on to her cabin.

Turning, Bump clipped Sam and knocked her to one side. He caught her by the scruff of her neck and glared into her face. Sam flinched and cowered under his stare.

MacTavish laughed. "Need to teach the lad he can't be coming up on Bump's blind side. He'll end up getting' knocked on his scrawny arse."

Bump didn't release Sam. Instead, he turned a heated gaze on Tupper. Her stomach dropped into her boots. *Dammit all to hell...he knew.*

Tupper stood her ground as Bump's anger pinned her to the spot. He let go of Sam's collar. She righted her blouse and took a step closer to Tupper, eyes as wide as cannon barrels.

"First day," Tupper reminded MacTavish as her breathing kicked up a notch. "He'll learn." Her mind scrambled with what to do. Would Bump betray her? How the hell had he figured it out? "Are we primed and ready for a fight in case things turn to shite?" She directed her words once again toward MacTavish, even though she held tight to Bump's glare.

"We've enough powder and shot to blow ourselves to Kingdom Come twice over if need be."

"Let's hope it doesn't come to that." She jerked her chin once more in the direction of her quarters. Bump didn't hesitate, pushing several aside as he marched down the ladder way and along the crowded deck. To Sam, Tupper snapped, "You come with me."

"Did I do something wrong?" Sam fell into step and hurried to keep up with Tupper's stride.

"No, I did." Tupper followed in Bump's wake.

"I don't understand."

"We'll discuss it in my quarters."

* * * *

Bump waited large and angry in the middle of the room and jerked a sharply angled hand in front of his mouth. *'Lie!'*

Tupper held up her hands in surrender. "I had to."

Bump shook his head and slapped his chest with the palm of his hand, *'Not to me.'*

Behind her, Sam gasped. "He knows."

Tupper put her hands together in front of her and twisted them outward, making the question. "How did you guess?"

Bump tapped his nose before rubbing his fingers together, shaking his head.

"Son of a bitch," muttered Tupper. "Only you would notice such a thing."

Sam looked back and forth between the two of them. "What? What did he say?"

Tupper sighed. "He says you don't smell as dirty as ye look."

Sam raised her sleeve and sniffed before lifting wide eyes to her. "Oh, God. We're done for. I-I don't want to die."

"No one's dying. Not yet."

"But he'll tell the rest of the crew."

"If you hadn't noticed, he's not a big talker." Tupper put a fist to her heart and drew a circle. "I'm sorry."

Bump set his jaw and glared. She repeated the motion and apologized again. Through the hand gestures they both knew, Tupper tried to explain. Bump was furious. She'd never lied to him before. She needed him to understand she did it to protect him. If the rest of the crew discovered the secret of Sam's identity, she didn't want his neck on the chopping block as well.

"Maybe it's a good thing you know the truth." Tupper put her fist in the palm of the other hand and lifted them both. *Help.* "You can help."

Bump narrowed his eyes.

Tupper's hands relayed her words. "With the patrols coming down hard, even changing our track won't keep us out of trouble for long. This time of year, a northern cross will be rough. Storms will be rolling off the north African coast. Watch her back. Keep her out of harm's way. Just until we reach England."

Sam followed the exchange intently, focusing on their hands. She lifted startled eyes to Tupper. "England?"

"Our next stop. You're going back to your family."

"But—"

"I know you said you didn't want to go to them, but I'm making the decisions here. Unless you'd like to swim back to that Wessler bastard in Virginia, where do you suppose I'm to drop you? You aren't staying aboard this ship one second longer than necessary. If it means you swallow your pride and return to your family, too damn bad. Least you have a family to go home to."

Tupper rubbed a hand over her aching forehead. "If it makes you feel any better, there's a good chance none of us will survive getting there." She snatched at a fresh bottle of rum, and squeaked the cork from its neck with her teeth before spitting it to the floor. "Here's hoping." She took a pull straight from the bottle.

Sam opened her mouth, but shut it again.

"Good. We'll scrape you a dry corner of the forward hold. I want you to limit your time on deck, and stay out of sight as much as possible. Not hidden away, as they've all seen ye, just not under any other keen noses like this one." She jerked a thumb in Bump's direction. "And you," she pointed to the charts littering her desk, "we need to be findin' a route to keep us away from the claws of a bloody *Lion.*"

Chapter 6

Sam tucked her knees to her chest and tried to still the racing of her heart. Tupper and Bump were bent over their maps and sea charts. Every few minutes, they would exchange the odd motions of their hands in a silent conversation. She wished she understood what they were saying. For all Sam knew, they were devising a plan to hoist her naked up the flagpole.

Tupper was bringing her to England, but that didn't mean she was going back to South Oxbridge. At the Whitmore's ball, she'd mentioned her desire to see London to the handsome Captain Steele. Didn't he say he was due to be married there soon? His new wife would be lucky indeed. If Sam closed her eyes, she could still see his beautiful eyes and hear the richness of his laughter. He'd been gentle and kind. She wished she'd had time to explain using him the way she did. Perhaps, if she looked him up when she reached London, he'd know of a position. She could begin again. Lose herself in the city. Give herself time to decide how and when to face her family.

Her father and three sisters had been overjoyed when she'd left for Virginia. After their mother's death and father's accident, news of a prosperous marriage had been their saving grace. Even if it had all been a lie.

As the oldest it fell to her to take care of the family, and when Damian Wessler's letters began to arrive, it seemed an answer to her prayers. Initially, he had advertised merely for a governess for his two small boys, Stewart and Bradley. Soon, the letters hinted at Wessler's heartfelt invitation to more. With the prospect of marriage came the promise of a substantial allowance to her family. All Samantha's travel expenses would be covered. A new wardrobe awaited her. She would be a woman of prominent standing in Virginia. And while he could not guarantee a match filled with love, it was his hope that she might come to feel for them what he had already begun to feel for her.

Sam shuddered as she recalled the beautifully written letters, and how they had filled her poor maiden's heart with an overflow of joy and anticipation.

She closed her eyes. The full extent of Wessler's deception was realized the moment she disembarked onto Virginia's shores. They were nothing as he'd described. The children were much older than she'd been told and unruly to the point of being wild. Damian was far from the tall, fair, gentle man he'd proclaimed to be. The small, exquisite portrait he'd sent her was of a stranger. He'd purchased it from the estate of a dead man. His home was in such a state of filth and disrepair, she had nearly wept when she first saw it. It was once through those doors, however, the nightmare truly began.

When she dared mention the obvious fabrication of lies contained in his letters, Damian had stuck her with such force, she thought he had broken her cheekbone. In a heap upon the floor, lights dancing behind her eyes, she struggled to remain conscious.

Wessler raged at her. Informed her he had paid a hefty sum for her and she thereby *belonged* to him. He now owned her like he owned the darks working his fields. If she didn't want to keep seeing the back of his hand, she would do well to shut her stupid mouth and follow his dictates.

The weeks following were hellish. Beatings became regular and for little cause. The boys were their father in miniature. Stewart delighted in spitting on her whenever she passed, and on more than one occasion Bradley lit her skirts on fire, blaming her ignorance in standing too close to the hearth. She became teacher, housekeeper, cook, and whore.

There wasn't to be any marriage. Wessler's late wife Marlene's will stated if he remarried he would no longer receive her family's monies. But that didn't prevent him from coming to Samantha's bed and forcing his perceived rights.

All the while, through the months of sheer torture she was enduring, Damian Wessler's letters of lies sent glorious reports to her family. Sharing the idealic bliss of their new life together. His sweet sons' instant love for their new stepmother. Thanking her family for blessing him with such a fine, beautiful wife. And he held their fate over Samantha's head like a sword. If she said one word, hinted at anything different, or continued to displease him, he would cut off his support and see her beloved father and her sisters evicted from their home to fend for themselves in the streets.

Samantha brushed at an angry tear. Wessler had made one crucial mistake, however. He'd underestimated her. In her silence, she'd made notice of everything. The moment she discovered the hidden letters from her family, read how her father had regained enough strength to begin work again, and how her two oldest sisters had found themselves lovely, advantageous matches, Wessler's threats were also a lie. Her family wrote about how they understood now she and Wessler were expecting a babe, he was unable to keep sending the money he originally promised. But she shouldn't worry and risk this baby after the loss of her first. They were fine now without it. What mattered was her continued health and happiness. They were praying the specialist Wessler claimed to have hired would help bring even more blessing to their picturesque life and let her give birth to a strong babe this time.

That afternoon, she thanked the good Lord she'd never conceived Wessler's bastard. Hope resurrected, she devised a way to contact Isabelle Whitmore, spit back at Stewart, and began her search for a way out of hell. She didn't care how it came to be.

It was a true stroke of luck that she found the charming Captain Steele to help her break free. She could still see his face the moment after she'd dared to kiss him. He'd been shocked, of course, but there was something else in his gaze. A smolder of intrigue perhaps? Samantha doubted many women had been as bold with him. To her, he seemed a man who was accustomed to taking the lead in such things. After the scene with Wessler, he probably dismissed her as some drunken flirt in a hideous gown and did not waste another thought on her.

The roll of the ship rocked her back into thoughts of her late-night rescue by Tupper Quinn. Tupper and Bump were still bent over their charts. The black bird sat on Tupper's wrist, pulling the ruffle on her sleeve before plucking at the shine of her ring. Sam had to remind herself once more this was not a dream. Her prayers had been answered by strangers. Pirates. Risking their own lives to get her away. Holding her fate in their hands. Scary as that was, it still gave her hope.

As if he sensed her gaze, Bump lifted his eyes to hers. The intensity was still there, but some of the anger seemed to have ebbed. She wished she could thank him. Tupper had showed her the book they'd used when Bump was young. Perhaps she'd let her borrow it.

A pounding at the door snapped her out of her thoughts.

"Come," Tupper bid, lifting Leviticus to his perch. A burly man wearing a striped headcloth and ragged trousers entered.

"Ship, Captain. Off the starboard. Looks fat. Flying for Spain."

"How long to reach her?"

He scratched at his chest. "Hour, maybe more. Sea's up."

"Once we're in range, have Peters put one over her bow. Drop the reds. Send her our dance card."

"Aye." The man left as quick as he'd come.

Turning back to Bump, Tupper traced a path on the chart. "After, we'll follow this route."

"After?" Sam rose.

Tupper looked at her as if she'd forgotten she was there. "Shite." She dropped a fist on the parchments before moving to open a drawer in her desk. She withdrew a small, pearl-handled pistol. "I've no time to give you a proper lesson." Tupper pulled the flint portion of the gun back until it clicked, then pushed the gun into Sam's hand. She gestured to Bump. "See her to the space we talked about." To Sam she said, "When the fighting starts, I want—"

"Fighting?" Sam looked at the pistol as if it were a coiled snake.

"Well, we could invite them te tea, and ask pretty please for all their gold and silver, but I doubt they'd oblige," Tupper scoffed.

"I-I can't fight."

"No kidding." Tupper shook her head. "That's why yer gonna stay below. The pistol is in case someone speaking Spanish finds you. Meaning we lost. You've one shot. The pistol is half-cocked. Move the hammer back all the way to fire. Don't point at anything you don't want to kill. Squeeze the trigger, don't pull. And if you don't want the flash to burn your cheek, or knock out a tooth with the kickback, keep it away from your face when ye shoot." Tupper held her arms straight out in front of her to demonstrate.

"But—" Sam's stomach rolled along with the pitch of the ship.

"Follow Bump. He'll show you where you're to hide 'til it's over." She gestured and added, "I'll be on deck." She grabbed her own weapons and was out the door before Sam could, "but—" her again.

Samantha put her hand to her throat and turned to watch Bump follow Tupper out the door. He turned back and gave her a look that could only mean, *"What the hell are you waiting for, follow me."*

Holding the pistol with two fingers as one would handle a soiled nappy, Sam had no choice but to follow the broad back of the silent man. He traveled the entire length of the ship from tail to tip in long strides before opening a wide-planked door. Pulling a lantern off a nearby hook, he raised the wick and led the way into the darkened space.

Inside the hold smelled of spice and old wood. Above the waterline, this storage must have remained dry, and as a result, was where things prone to water damage were stored. Canvas, rope, and crates of various sizes and descriptions cluttered the space. Sam could only guess at their contents. Perhaps silks and other exotics like peppercorns, cinnamon, and cardamom.

The ship dipped into a deep trench as Bump secured the lantern and began stacking the crates into a wall. With the sea beating upon the sides of the hull, Sam gripped at the doorframe with one hand to steady herself. Overhead, heavy footsteps sounded, followed by shouts and a rumbling of undetermined source. Sam could only hold tight and pray she didn't drop the gun and accidentally shoot herself in the leg.

Bump swept a hand toward the makeshift space he had miraculously transformed simply by arranging some crates. It was small, but with a pile of folded canvas sailcloth on the floor, it looked almost comfortable.

Bump indicated she should enter her new quarters with a distinct point of his finger. She hesitated, wishing once again she knew how to say thank you.

Before the wish could fully take shape in her mind, an explosion rocked the ship. Sam screamed, and in a panicked reaction to cover her head, dropped the pistol. The gun's resulting discharge brought the bulk of Bump's body on top of hers, crushing her against door and knocking the air out of her lungs.

Oh dear God, I shot him!

He was off her a second later, turning his head toward the shot's true victim. Sam hadn't shot Bump, but she had shattered the corner of a crate. He glared down at her. Fury set his face. His hands flew in a rush of silent words she didn't need translated to understand. Anger radiated from him like the sun.

Sam flinched, screwed her eyes shut, and threw her hands up once more to protect herself. When the blow didn't come, she peered at him from beneath her lashes.

His hands had stopped 'yelling' at her. He'd quieted them to fists by his sides. His chest still rose and fell in a rapid cadence, but the expression upon his face no longer looked murderous. His brows were drawn together, but was it curiosity or pity that described his look?

Remembering one of Tupper's signs, Sam put a fist to her chest and made a small circle. "Sorry? I'm so sorry." He jerked as if surprised by the gesture. Was Tupper the only one to speak to him this way?

Once more, Bump pointed into her new quarters as the ship rose and fell in the building seas. Sam ducked and skirted past him. He retrieved the smoking gun from the floor. From his own supply of shot and powder, he reloaded it before holding it out to her. She shook her head. "I don't want it."

Bump shoved the pistol into her hands as another explosion sounded from somewhere beyond the ship. Sam trembled with a fear reaching clear to the soles of her oversized shoes. Bump pointed a finger toward the center of her chest before indicating the floor at his feet. She didn't need a book for this sign either. He wanted her to stay put. She nodded, and he was gone.

Part of her wanted to chase after him, clutch at his arm, and beg him not to leave her alone. Another part of her wanted to pull her crated walls down over her head and hide for eternity.

Distant cannon fire could be heard. Samantha braced herself for the impact that never came. The Spanish had returned fire and missed.

A hellacious roar of the *Scarlet's* cannons had her screaming from her space. The smell of sulfur seeped through the boards above her and stung her nose. At least she kept a firm grip on her gun. Overhead, screams from the crew tumbled down. They were not screams of fright but heated cries of battle. Horns blew, drums beat. Shouts and hideous wails directed toward their foe. Warning them. Preparing them for the onslaught of this barbarian crew. She'd never heard anything as chilling.

In response, the other ship fired again. This time, however, they hit their mark. The resulting blast rocked the *Scarlet Night,* followed by a crash as something heavy fell to the deck overhead. The shrieks above her now were of death and pain. Sam imagined half the ship had been blown to bits. At any moment, the sea would pour into its shattered hull and drag them all to the bottom.

She had to get out of there. Bump's glare flashed in her mind, giving her pause, but another roar of the cannons propelled her forward. She wasn't going to die down here in a heap of sailcloth and pepper, or wait until the seawater rose above her neck. If she were going to die today, she wanted to look the devil square in the eye.

Chapter 7

Unleashed chaos greeted Sam as she fought her way toward the open deck. The scene before her more gruesome than she had imagined. A portion of the front mast had been brought down by the other ship. Wood, sail, and yards of rigging obscured the deck. Wounded bodies were being pulled from the wreckage. Men raced in all directions.

"Fire!" Tupper ordered.

Cannons ignited. Another blast threw Sam against the rails as iron balls and thick, bloodred smoke burst from the guns, obliterating her view. The concussion made her ears ring. As the smoke started to clear, Sam could see the volley hit the other ship along its aft rails. Wood shattered like glass. Bodies flew.

Around them, the ocean churned, and the sky took on an ominous pallor, as if the entire world was locked in battle. The *Scarlet Night* maneuvered closer to their prey. Her crew fired pistols and squat muskets across the water. Some hurled smoking pots of sulfur to billow and poison the other deck. The Spanish crew still fought, but it appeared they couldn't recover from the onslaught of the *Night's* crew. The men of the *Scarlet Night* were too honed, too relentless, too practiced.

A heavy hand clamped onto Sam's shoulder. She fumbled with her gun, but a second hand grabbed for the barrel, pointing it away. Sam raised a terrified gaze to find Bump glowering at her. He lifted her as if she were a child's toy and shoved her up into the closest net of rigging. Shots fired from the other ship. Lead balls whistled past. A quick push to her backside propelled her higher. She scrambled to hang on to the thick roping and still hold on to her pistol.

The battle waged on. From her vantage point, she could see boarding ladders reaching across to the other ship. Some of the crew didn't wait and swung out on ropes to drop into the fight on the far decks. As men from the *Night* flooded their deck, several of the Spaniards made an equal showing and invaded their decks.

The ring of cutlasses joined the blasts of firearms. Below Sam, Bump positioned himself against the strength of the main mast. Keeping his back to the wood, he kept the enemy at bay. Cutlass in one hand, dagger in the other, he was a fierce killer. Two men fell at his feet. The stench of blood made Sam retch, but she couldn't turn away from the scene beneath her.

A third man approached Bump from the left. Sam called out a warning, but the man was on Bump before the useless words were out of her mouth. Steel rang as the men's blades met. Bump lost hold of his dagger and it dropped to the deck. Good God, Bump would be killed.

Sam wrapped a steadying arm through the ladder of rope and raised her pistol. Her hand shook, not only in fear, but she couldn't aim the heavy weapon with one hand. She had no control. If she pulled the trigger, she'd risk killing Bump herself. Firing a pistol twice at a man, who had done nothing but try to protect her, seemed wrong. Hysterics threatened the edge of her sanity. Samantha looked in vane at the gun and back to the scene below. She had to do something to save him.

Hurling the weapon, it spun on its decent. The butt of her pistol made a hideous crack as it creased the attacking man's forehead, stopping the final swing of his sword mid slice. Bump was quick to deliver a fatal slash across the man's throat and shove him aside before lifting incredulous eyes in her direction.

Sam gave him a sheepish shrug before another explosion from the other ship had her tightening her hold on the rigging. The blast hadn't come from their cannons, however. Something had exploded on their decks. Smoke began to billow from the Spanish ship. Tongues of flame could be seen through the smoke.

Members from the *Night* fled back to the safety of their own ship. Tupper shouted the order to abandon the attack and be away. Ladders pulled back and all haste was made to get away from the burning ship before the growing flames reached the *Scarlet Night*.

They'd ignited the other ship's tarred rigging close to the magazine. The Spanish crew scrambled to put out the fire, but it spread too quickly up to the sails and over the tinder-dry decking.

Turning away, the *Night* bucked against the rough seas. Black smoke mushroomed into the sky behind them. Bump climbed up, plucked Sam from her position, and dropped her none too gently onto the deck before grabbing her shirt at the shoulder and yanking her toward the ladder way.

It was there they crossed paths with Tupper.

Hair flying, sleeve torn, Tupper's throat was smeared with grime and her eyes flashed bright with battle. Her cutlass, edged in blood, gleamed in the dull light. Of all the sights Sam had seen today, this was the one she would remember for the rest of her days. The woman was a warrior.

Then the warrior turned her wrath on Sam. "What in the name of bloody hell are ye doing topside?"

Sam stood slack jawed. "I-I…"

"Are you determined to get yourself killed?" Tupper bellowed.

Sam looked to Bump, but any hope of a kinship with the man had come to an abrupt end. His anger only exceeded Tupper's.

"I've no time to deal with the likes of you. If you can't follow a simple order to stay below, I'll cut ye down myself and be done with all the trouble." Tupper jerked her head at Bump. She narrowed her eyes at Sam. "My cabin, and stay there."

"Aye-aye, Captain."

The fire on the Spanish ship reached their store of black powder at the same instant Sam reached the ladder way. A huge ball of fire engulfed the ship, blowing the sails off the masts, setting the entire ship ablaze, and extinguishing all who remained aboard. The force of the blast punched Sam in the chest. Once more, Bump curled over her, shielding her.

Burning debris rained down and floated in the waves, but she didn't witness any more as Bump dragged her below, shoved her into Tupper's quarters, and slammed the door behind her.

* * * *

A sick coil in James's belly rolled through him as he watched his men finish the processing of the newly captured prisoners. They resembled rag-draped skeletons more than men. "Once they're away, set us a northeast course."

"Aye, aye, Captain Steele." His helmsman, Michaels, issued a sharp salute.

The last of the supplies were transferred down to the *Flying Cutlass*. They had seized ship and crew this morning, and James ordered them back to trial in Virginia rather than carry their ragtag crew all the way to London. He released a dozen of his men to accompany the prisoners back to the authorities. The whole business left a sour taste in his mouth. There was no honor in arresting these pitiful men.

Ducky came alongside. "Did you note the looks of relief on their faces at being arrested? They almost seem happy with their fate. How long do you suppose they've been without food?"

"By the look of them, more than a week. Perhaps two." The *Flying Cutlass* hoisted what little sail they had and moved off.

Ducky shook his head. "Should have sailed past the poor bastards and saved the crown the cost of good rope."

"Hold your tongue." James turned away and headed toward the galley.

"James, they were half dead already. We're going to feed them and build their strength just so we can hang them? How sporting is that?"

Leave it to Ducky to put James's thoughts into words. The truth of them grated against him. "It is hardly my fault the *Flying Cutlass* was more of a floating butter knife. This is war, not sport. The ship is listed amongst those charged with treason. I'm following my orders."

"Don't know if you could call it a war when you only needed to fire one shot across their bow before they tossed up their hands in surrender. They were out of fit ammunition. Did you see what they'd stuffed into the cannon barrels? Chain links and cutlery."

"I saw."

"So much for the golden age. Guess not all privateers were as successful as your father."

"Leave my father out of this." How many times had James thought of him in the last few weeks? He'd certainly have a thing or two to say about what transpired today. Hell, the puce-wearing Mistress Christian could have captured the *Flying Cutlass* and not broken a nail.

"So you're not sailing into London the battle-worn concurring hero. Lillian will be happy you didn't damage your bonny face."

Lillian. A quick wave of guilt flooded him once again. He should be thinking of his betrothed, not some woman he shared a single dance with…. and a stolen kiss…. lest he not forget that single kiss. Concurring hero, indeed. Lillian wouldn't attempt to capture anything greater than his passing attention. He scratched at his jaw to cover his sudden smirk at his errant musings. "Lillian did threaten to end our engagement if I came back sporting an eye patch."

"Then she needn't fear. You've barely needed to draw your weapon."

"I've no blood lust, but it's all been rather too easy. We should have found more ships. I'd like one more sweep before heading for home. However, if we're to report on schedule, there's no time." James opened his spy glass and peered through. "Someone's tipped them off. Word got out ahead of us, I'm sure." He scanned the crests of the waves. "They're out there. I can feel it."

"Then they've done a grand job of slipping past us."

"I'll not concede." James snapped the glass closed.

"Forget it. As you said, you've run out of time." Ducky slapped James on the shoulder. "Time we were heading back to London. You've a wedding to attend."

"Don't remind me." James's lack of enthusiasm was worrisome. Weeks ago, he'd been impatient. Eager with anticipation. He gave himself a mental shake. Wedding jitters perhaps?

"What kind of best man would I be to let you forget your last days as a free man? I have my duty as well. I'm to carry the rings and be a constant reminder of the limited time remaining until you're fitted with your husbandly yoke and plow."

James could feel the weight of that yoke all ready. Perhaps it wasn't simple jitters. He brushed away his thoughts. Lillian was lovely. Wealthy. They were well matched. The only reason he was remembering another's kiss was because Samantha Christian had caught him off guard. He much preferred a more predictable woman. Lillian would never dream of stealing a kiss from a total stranger. Hell, he imagined she'd never attempt such a thing after twenty years of marriage. His brows knit at such a disheartening thought.

"You did manage to find a ring, didn't you?" Ducky pulled him out of his pondering.

"Not yet. I wanted to give Lillian a ring like my mother's signet." James pictured it. Handwrought, hammered gold. A fine scripted "A" for Annalise holding a diamond in its tail. "I thought to have one made with a sweeping 'L' for Lillian, with a sapphire perhaps, or a ruby. But when I suggested it to her, Lillian's taste was for something more…"

"Expensive?"

"Traditional," James corrected. "Refined. Elegant."

"Same thing." Ducky laughed. "She'll 'refine and elegant' you straight to the poorhouse."

"I'm not exactly a pauper. I can well afford a wife."

"I've seen women of her like before. Wouldn't dare spend a farthing of their own money, but drain their poor husband's wallets with a careless ease. Best watch out. You'll end up stuffing cutlery in your cannons."

"Very funny. Lill—"

"Captain!" A call came down from the forward crow's nest.

"Yes, Mister Upton, what is it?"

"Smoke, sir," the man pointed. "Off the port bow."

James once more lifted the glass to his eye before calling the order. "Michaels! Fifteen degrees to port!" He handed Ducky the glass. "Let's see what burns."

Chapter 8

"Three dead, four wounded, and not so much as a copper te show fer it." MacTavish rubbed a filthy hand beneath his nose. "Waste o' good powder, if ye ask me. Nice blaze te warm our hands, tho."

"Shut up, ye tartaned ape." Tupper seethed as she stood in the fantail of the *Scarlet Night* and watched their Spanish conquest go up in flames.

"Fought like the devil. What ya suppose they carried?"

"Doesn't bloody matter now, does it?" Smoke and flame billowed from the burning hull. The muscle in her jaw threatened to crush her back teeth. "Maybe if ye didn't cut those sulfur wicks so damn long—"

"Ye better not be blaming me fer this? I'm not the jackass who threw a smoke pot into the riggin.'" MacTavish held out his hand. "Found this scrapin' across the boards. Yours, I believe? Not the only thing half-cocked today, eh?"

Tupper glared at him and snatched the pearl-handled pistol from him. *Son of a bitch!* "Cabin boy trying to get himself killed."

MacTavish laughed as he walked away. "Off te a good start."

Her fingers curled around the butt of the gun until her knuckles shown white. Maybe there was truth to that old superstition. It *was* bad luck having a woman aboard. Sam had to go!

Tupper raised the pistol and fully cocked the hammer. In a final salute to dispel some of her anger and frustration, she shot at the flaming ship behind them. Ironically, the bowsprit of the Spanish ship fell sputtering into the waves. Tupper gave a short bark of laughter before shoving the pistol into her belt. You'd have thought that might make her feel better. It didn't.

Tupper inspected the ship's damage and put the proper men to task. The Spaniards had only clipped the topmost section of the forward mast, but the damage could extend all the way down the shaft to the deck. It wasn't safe to test its strength with the remaining sail. They could manage with two masts, but it would slow them down until they made land once more and repaired the damage.

She checked on the wounded. Doubled the watch in the nest. Made arrangements for their dead, and set the new course. Tupper was on her way to talk to Hornbach in the galley. He was in charge of food and drink. Slower speed meant more days at sea. The food they could ration, but Lord help them if the rum ran dry.

Speaking of rum, she needed a drink. And a smoke. And a wee chat with a mule-headed cabin "boy" who needed a strong lesson in obeying orders. Talk about going off half-cocked.

Passing Bump on her way to her quarters, their gazes locked. She didn't blame him for Sam's stupidity. *'I'll deal with the situation below,'* she signed.

Bump shook his head, frowning. *'Go easy.'*

Tupper narrowed her eyes. Not the reaction she expected, but the man turned away before she could question him further. She could only deal with one thing at a time, and now was the time to set her new crewmember straight.

Sam was sitting on the edge of Tupper's bed reading when she entered her quarters.

"I can tell Bump 'thank you' now." She held up the leather-bound book of hand signs.

"How nice for both of you," Tupper snapped. "Have you learned how to tell him you're deaf as well?"

"Excuse me?"

"Or perhaps your ears just flap over, or you're too damn stubborn to obey orders." At the rise of her voice. Leviticus joined in the fray. She broke off a bit of bread and tossed it at him to keep him still. "What the hell were you thinking up there?" Tupper slammed the pistol she'd given Sam onto her desk and reached for her rum.

Samantha hugged the book to her chest. "I thought you'd be happy."

"Happy?" Tupper stopped pouring mid-glass. She couldn't have heard her right. "Do I look happy to you?"

Sam pointed to the gun. "If I wasn't there, Bump would have been killed." Sam relayed the scene with the attacking man.

"You don't understand, do you? If you hadn't come on deck, where you shouldn't have been, Bump wouldn't have had to lift you into the rigging, and been trapped against the mast to protect you." Tupper emptied her glass in one swallow, then slammed it onto the desktop next to the gun. "You may believe you're strong enough to live in this world, but I've been walking this deck for more years than you've been breathing, and I'm telling you, you're not. Or perhaps your life means so little to you that you can be careless. But you aren't going to put any member of my crew in danger again."

"I'm sorry. I was only trying to help." Sam set her jaw and crossed her arms over her chest. As Tupper glared at her, the chit had the nerve to notch her chin.

Tupper's anger ebbed. In its place frustration remained. And something else. A reminder of herself when she first came aboard the *Scarlet Night*. The first battle she'd witnessed. Bump was a child then. It had been him in the rigging. She'd been the one to try to save *him* then. Gavin had been furious. When he railed against her, she notched her defiant chin, just as Sam had done. No wonder he had been hell bent on getting her away.

Tupper glanced at Gavin's hat, which still hung on the hook by the door. *Is this your way of paying me back?* She snatched at the rum bottle once more, but set it aside without adding any more to her glass.

"Grief is an odd thing. You think you've beaten it. Somehow gotten through those days when you couldn't see past the darkness." She opened the bottom drawer of her desk and ran gentle fingers over a fragile set of letters. Gavin's letters. Old and brittle, ink long faded. She didn't dare open them again for fear they'd fall to dust at her touch. She didn't need to. She knew every line of every page by heart.

"Think you're strong enough to make it through a single day without dissolving into useless tears." She traced the black ribbon holding the stack of letters together. "Then you realize you haven't thought about them for an hour. Two hours. A day. A whole week goes by and life pulls you back amongst the living. The sun still rises. The tides still move. The raw sting of loss loses its fiery edge. And somewhere along the way, you start fighting to live again. You come to respect how precious life is, and how it can end too quickly."

"Why are you telling me this?"

Tupper slammed the drawer shut. "Because I was like you once. Stubborn. Headstrong. I thought I was invincible. Death couldn't touch me. But this life we lead out here is death's playground. It surrounds us on all sides. Toys with us like a cat with a mouse. You may believe you're strong enough, but I've three bodies to slip into the sea who thought the same thing when they awoke this morning. And they weren't foolish enough to take heedless chances."

"Did they sit by and cower in a corner? Or hide in a hold?"

Tupper flicked her hand. "Of course not."

Sam held her gaze. "Would you?"

"Never."

She cocked an eyebrow at Tupper. "Then why would I?"

"Because you're not a pirate."

The girl jumped to her feet and held her arms wide. "Look at me. Look where I am. I am a pirate." Sam dropped the book onto Tupper's desk. "You've risked everything by bringing me aboard. Hiding my identity. I'll never be able to pay you back for all you've done. I am forever in your debt, but that's where your duty to me ends. You're right, I was unprepared for the reality of this life, but could you imagine it if you've never experienced it before? The noise, the sights, the smells? The sheer power of it?"

Samantha couldn't hide the tremor in her hands. "Were you fully prepared your first battle? Were any of these men? Did the first blast of the cannons make you scream? Did your blood run as cold as mine did today? Your first sight of a maimed body and blood on the deck make you retch? Do you suppose death will spare me because I'm ignorant? I don't need a nursemaid. You can't protect me any more than you could have protected those three men who died, and I'm not asking you to."

"You needed to be rescued, but you didn't ask to be a part of this life."

"Did *you* ask to be?"

Tupper flashed back to Gavin's letters, tucked forever in her drawer and her memory. "Yes, I did." She admitted before shaking her head. "But there was no other life waiting for me. I had ruined any future set out for me. It's not too late for you."

The room got quiet. Sam pulled a deep breath before lifting her eyes to Tupper's. "You talk of grief, and how it made you value life. You must have known great love to grieve so profoundly. I hoped for that kind of love when I left everything I knew to sail to Virginia. I imagined meeting my life's love there. What I found was pain and humiliation. I've given up naive daydreams of anything more. Nothing awaits me."

"That's where you're wrong. You have family."

"Samantha Christian had family." She brushed at the thigh of her breeches. "Sam Christian is a pirate."

Frustrated, Tupper wondered if she had ever been this bloody infuriating. Time for some harsh reality. "Well, Sam Christian, pirate, come with me. Time you prepare yourself for what fate awaits us all."

Three shrouded bodies lined the gunwales, waiting for their final slip into the sea. "Good men, these," Tupper informed Sam. "Thirteen stitches close their sailcloth tombs. The final stitch goes straight through their nose to assure we haven't attached cannonballs to the ankles of a man still living." At least the stubborn girl had the good sense to pale at her words.

Tupper gathered the rest of the crew and said the final words over each man before they were lowered into the waves. After the short ceremony, the men returned to their duties. Sam Christian assumed her role as cabin boy and went off to the galley to fetch Tupper a tankard of ale. Tupper didn't care what she said, or how adamantly she declared it, Samantha was not one of them and she did not belong on this ship. She still kept an eye on her as she moved through the rest of the crew. Sam may believe her newfound battle knowledge had changed her situation. That her brave fortitude could see her through, but the facts had not changed. Her biggest threat was still these men walking this deck. Tupper wasn't about to lower her guard.

Only one other person shared Tupper's keen interest in a "boy" fetching her ale. Bump. Tupper caught his watchful gaze following Sam as she made her way aft. It wasn't his watching that struck Tupper as odd. It was the look upon his face. A brief glimpse of unguarded emotion skittered over his features and stopped Tupper in her tracks. It was obvious he was beginning to have feelings for the girl. And not angry feelings. *Bloody hell! That's all I need.*

She called out an order. "I want every inch of sail we can muster, gentlemen." The sooner this crossing was over—.

The alarm bell rang out from the crow's nest. "Captain! Ship! Huge frigate. Running full sail, moving like the devil. Flying a Jack."

"Glass," demanded Tupper.

MacTavish answered the call. "Who be it?"

Tupper focused the glass. The hair on the back of her neck stood as the ship came into sight. They were headed straight for them at top speed. The prow of the ship carved through the waves, splitting the water, sending a mighty spray high to bathe the feet of a golden figurehead. As the figure came into view, Tupper's gut dropped into her boots.

"Good God, it's a lion."

* * * *

"Ship off the bow, sir!"

"What be she?" Called Captain Steele.

"Sloop. Moving at half speed. Rear sails only. Red sails, Captain. They're flying black bones."

James focused his scope on the horizon. "I'll be damned..."

Ducky lifted his own glass. "Who is it?"

James lowered his glass and called out an order to the gunners. "Hold until I give the order. We're going to send them a single shot over her bow. Let's try to keep her in one piece."

Lowering his glass, Ducky gave James a knowing smile. "Taking home a souvenir?"

"Father might want to see her one last time before she's stripped for scrap." James raised his glass again. "The *Scarlet Night* is a beauty, isn't she? I don't have the heart to scuttle her."

"You're being sentimental. You might not have a choice."

"True. Captain Quinn might have other ideas." James tried to assess the other ship's condition. "Doesn't look as if the smoke came from them. I see no fire damage, but they are limping a bit. The floating debris we found came from another ship. A skirmish gone bad? Still, it would be foolish to underestimate the fight in them." He turned to Ducky. "Man your stations, but hold until I give the word."

"Aye, aye." Ducky took one last look through his glass before smirking in James direction and heading off to obey his order.

James watched the ship get larger in his sight. At this speed, they would be upon them in no time. Sentiment aside, he'd do whatever was necessary in bringing the crew of the *Scarlet Night* to justice. If it meant blowing them out of the water, then that was what he was prepared to do.

Chapter 9

As Sam left the galley with Tupper's ale, she heard the alarm go up. The rush of heightened energy spreading through the crew.

"All hands!" The call passed from one man to the next.

Tupper positioned herself on the quarterdeck. Men jostled one another in the chaos. Behind them, the a huge ship raced toward the *Scarlet Night*. Sam pushed her way through the crowded deck to join Tupper.

"Run us due east. Catch all the speed we can." Two men pulled on the heavy oak wheel. Tupper planted her hands on her hips. The muscle in her jaw flexed. "Won't help, but it might buy us some time. We can't out run them," She confided to the large burly man in the filthy tartan.

"When have we ever run from a fight?" he countered.

Tupper shook her head. "Never. But we usually had some sliver of hope of surviving. No sliver this time. Not even a thread." She grabbed at the tankard Sam held and took a deep swallow. Handing it back, she held Sam's gaze. "Stay close."

"Men gather round!" Tupper called out across the deck. The crew pressed in closer below her on the main deck.

She pointed behind them. "The ship heading toward us is the *HMS Lion*. Means to take this ship and the lot of us back to the fair shores of England and stretch our necks by an inch or two.

"Unless the good Lord sees fit to drop the beast into a sudden hole in the sea, we can neither out run nor out fight her. They'll blow us out of the water with three broadsides before we can return a single round."

Men cursed and railed, raising fists and weapons into the air. Several peered back at the approaching *Lion*.

Tupper swung her arms wide and yelled over the din. "Now I'm all for fighting 'til I can't fight no more. If it were just me, I'd rather die upon the decks of the *Scarlet Night* than stand before some moldy judge in a flea-ridden wig so I can die at the end of a rope. But it ain't up to just me. We've always done things by the vote. I'm calling for it now. We can drop the bones and raise the white flag, drop our trousers and ask them English bastards over for a quick fuk. Or...we raise every inch of red we have, load every gun, sharpen every blade and fight like the bastards we are. Fight 'til the last man...or woman...stands. Remind them who the crew of the *Scarlet Night* be. Keep our blades singing 'til the decks run as red as our sails."

A cry started with one small group of men and spread through the crowd, growing louder and stronger. "Fight! Fight! Fight!" The crew fired their pistols, waved their cutlasses, and rent the air with their battle screams.

Into the fray, Tupper Quinn yelled, "No quarter! We fight to the end! Fly the red and double the smoke! Load both port and starboard guns! Godspeed, men!"

A frenzied cheer rose from the crew as they scattered in every direction.

Tupper slapped MacTavish on the shoulder. "Ye didn't want to hang up yer kilt and grow old by some flaming peat now, did ya?"

"Fuk, no."

"Pull everything we've got. Might as well go out in a blaze o' glory." She slapped his shoulder again and sent him hurrying toward the ship's magazine.

Sam's heart slammed behind her ribs. The ship bearing down on them was bigger than any she'd ever seen. After such a show of bravado before, she could scarcely jump screaming into the waves. "I-I believe I'll need my pistol back."

"Nay, ye don't. Ye just became a prisoner." When Sam started to question, Tupper grabbed the front of her shirt. "Don't argue. Listen to me, and you might just live to see another day. No cause for you to pay for our lifetime of crimes. Go below. Stay there. When it is all over, and they find you, tell them who you are. Tell them I kidnapped you. Forced you aboard."

"What about you? I can't let you die. Not after you saved me. There has to be some way—"

"My fate was sealed long ago. Hell, surprised it took this long. I'm sure to be damned te hell, but I won't go alone."

Tupper's gaze shifted to something over Sam's right shoulder. Sam turned to see Bump, his expression hard as stone. "And you." Tupper pointed to him and made a few quick hand gestures. "Stay behind me. I'm not looking back. Not this time. I'll not watch you die."

The thunderous crescendo of activity crested around them. "Remember what I told you," Tupper reminded Sam before she released her grip on her shirt and jerked her chin, asking Bump to bring her below.

* * * *

Back into the hold, Sam's body shook with panic. This couldn't be. It couldn't end like this. Not for Tupper. Not Bump. Not when they had taken such a risk to help her. There had to be something she could do. She owed it to them to try. If only she could calm herself to think. She held her forehead and began to pace.

Bump stayed to one side. She stopped as she passed him a second time. "I'm afraid for you." He watched her mouth. "Tell me what to do."

The sound of cannon fire signaled the beginning of the end. Sam raised frightened eyes to Bump. Damn it, there were things she wished she could say to him. At a loss as to what more she could do, Sam wrapped her arms around Bump's waist and held him. The solid wall of his rigid chest cradled her cheek. For a breath he simply stood there, allowing her to hold him. His heartbeat sounded strong and hurried to her ear. Then something shifted. Softened. As if Bump gave into the moment and wrapped Sam in the brief protection of his strong arms.

They stood locked together until the report of another cannon made Sam's heart skid in her chest, making her break their connection. "They're coming. I'll never see you again." She took a small step back and used her hands to say the one thing she remembered from Tupper's book. Putting her fingertips to her chin, she moved her hand forward. *'Thank you.'*

Bump's fathomless gaze held hers. Hands shaking, she made the sign again. And again until he caught her hand, silencing her. Sam's tears pinched the backs of her eyes. She wanted to weep. For him. For Tupper. For them all.

Lifting her fingers to his mouth, Bump kissed the back of her hand before the roar of the *Scarlet Night's* cannons caused the ship to shudder around them. He held her gaze a moment longer, lingering over her face as if trying to commit her features to memory. Bump laid a gentle hand on her cheek before leaving her and rushing out to join in the fight for his life.

Sam looked helplessly around the hold. She couldn't stay here doing nothing. She couldn't leave these people to be captured and die. She had to fight.

Hurrying back to the captain's cabin, Sam found her pistol where Tupper had left it earlier. It took both hands to pull the hammer back all the way. She had one shot. It wasn't much, but she didn't feel quite as helpless with the gun in her hand.

Above, more cannon fire came from both directions. Sam debated her sanity. She should be finding somewhere to hide and following Tupper's orders. Not going topside and stepping into a certain hell.

It was then she noticed Leviticus. For the first time, he didn't glare at her with his black shoe-button eyes. He wasn't ruffling his feathers in agitation. The bird lay close to Tupper's logbooks. Still. Quiet.

"Oh no..." she sighed.

The quick pace of boot heels echoed down the galley way had Samantha scrambling behind a stack of trunks.

Tupper slammed into her quarters. Donned a second baldric over the one she already wore. Pulled pistols from their holsters and loaded each with quick practiced precision. She yanked open a desk drawer and pulled out a black leather shot case before coming up short.

Sam knew the exact moment she saw Leviticus. Tupper made a sound as if she'd been punched. The box of shot dropped from her fingertips to the floor. "No, no, no... Not today, ye b-bloody old bird." She braced her arms against the side of her desk, hung her head, and curled into herself. Sam couldn't see if she cried. She fought the urge to go to her and offer her comfort. With commotion raining down from above and a battle beginning to wage, Tupper stood stone still for a long moment.

Finally, with a slowness born of what appeared to be a great weariness, Tupper retrieved something from another set of drawers built into the side of the ship. Sam couldn't tell what it was. A bit of cloth, or perhaps an article of clothing? Tupper lifted it to her nose and breathed in its scent before gathering an odd collection of items: A man's straight razor, a book, a stack of old, yellowed letters. Stroking the bird's feathers, she shook her head and sighed. "Best you died before falling into the hands of the bloody British. They'd have likely baked ye into a damn p-pie." Her voice broke. "Ye were a wretched old beast. Ye'd be tough as shoe leather."

Tupper lifted the bird's body and laid it in the middle of what Sam could now see was a man's linen shirt. "It's time, ye know, to say the goodbyes. Long overdue." She gently added each item before wrapping them in the shirt along with the bird's body. "If it be true, and yer waiting for me...doubt ye'll be waiting long." Tupper secured it all and lifted the bundle, holding it close to her chest before crossing to the windows.

Sam's view was blocked by Tupper's back, but she heard the dull scrape of the window latch. Sounds of the fight and the force of the sea filled the cabin. Tupper said something Sam couldn't hear, before dropping the parcel into the ship's wake.

The latch scrapped again, muffling the sound. Tupper returned to gathering weapons. Face set. Methodical. She tested the edge of an extra blade before slipping it into her boot. Making sure her pistols were snug in their holsters, she added another pouch of powder to her belt. Tupper seemed satisfied and pulled in a great breath. She scanned the room. Did she believe she was seeing it for the last time? She stopped as if something caught her eye. Reaching over, Tupper picked up something from her desk.

A single tail feather. Long, sleek, and shining black. Holding it by its shaft, Tupper twirled it slowly between her fingertips before retrieving an old, faded hat from the hook by the door and adding the feather to the banding. Tupper pushed the hat firmly upon her head, gave another look around her quarters, and left.

Chapter 10

The *Lion* pounced. Returning to the deck, the sight of the huge war ship bearing down on them sent ice down Tupper's spine. Five masts reached into the clouds. Brilliant white sails contrasted against the overcast sky. Miles of pristine rigging webbed the beast. The warship sported three decks. Each contained ten guns, both port and starboard. With its three ten-pound forward cannons, the *Lion* was a killing machine with a long reach and sharp claws.

Tupper grabbed an ax from a pile of spare swords, daggers, and the like dragged from the magazine by MacTavish. Testing its weight, she shifted it to her left hand. Tupper dripped weapons like a fine lady dripped jewels. If they were to lose today, she was sure as hell taking as many of the *Lion's* men with her as she could.

Bump came to stand next to her. She held his gaze. There was so much she wanted to say to him. As if reading her mind, Bump nodded. He knew. Or she prayed he did. Either way, it didn't matter anymore, there was no time.

Tupper jerked her chin and Bump moved off to his battle position at the rear of the ship, where he could protect his back against the bulkhead during the fighting. She steeled herself. No matter what happened, she would not turn around. As hardened as she'd become, after all these years of watching men die not only at her own hand, but all around her. Battles more than she could count. Burying men. Mourning Gavin. Even losing an ancient, moth-eaten old crow. Through it all, she'd become immune to more than a fleeting sadness where death was concerned.

But Bump was different. From the first moment, when he was a babe of four, those all-seeing eyes looked into hers, and he forever held a part of her heart no other human being had touched. He was her child, as surely as if he'd come from her body. No, she would not look back. She couldn't bear the thought of watching him die. Tupper lifted her gaze to the sky. "God, if you're listening, I've only one thing to ask...let me fall before him."

The *Lion* made a wide sweep to port. Cannon doors open, their three decks of cannon lining the starboard side were set in position. The upper level fired a crippling blast. Ten fiery cannons exploded at once. The cry went up around Tupper as her crew braced themselves for the attack, but the *Lion's* guns overshot. Each ball landing in the sea. Perhaps they were choosing to ignore the *Scarlet's* warning flags flying overhead? Maybe they were sending their own warning? Giving the *Scarlet Night* a chance to surrender?

Fools. There would be no surrender. The crew was ready. Powder monkeys ran armloads of black powder sacks. Quick matches were lit and poised over touch holes waiting for the order. Battle cries rose to fevered pitch. The fight was on. The *Scarlet Night* gave the *Lion* her reply.

"Fire the port side!" Tupper ordered over the din.

Red smoke billowed from the blast and swirled at their feet. The cannon had been loaded with chain shot with hopes of taking out rigging and sail. The *Lion* was too large a vessel, even bringing down one mast wouldn't slow them much, but if they could aim for the center mast, bringing it down might cause another to topple.

Their shot sliced through the *Lion's* rigging. Sail rippled behind the impact. Chain snapped a great yardarm, sending the weight of wood and canvas plummeting to the decks.

In response, a mighty blast from the *Lion* blew through the gunwales of the *Scarlet Night* and turned gun barrels and the capstan into splinters. Three men were blown from the deck. The brass cap of the capstan became a flying claw from the attacking beast and slashed through another man. His screams, inhuman. Two port cannon had been blown across deck. Crushing anything and anyone that got in their way.

The rugged crew was quick to pull clear the wounded and dead. The gunners used all their strength to get the guns reloaded and struggle them back into place. Huge ropes made slings where needed to replace the damaged gun locks.

Tupper wasted no time. "Fire!"

But the *Lion* was upon them. Had them in her grasp. At this range, the *Night's* shot took out one of the English guns and blew a tidy hole in its rails, but it did little else other than to anger the beast.

Seamen by the score began swinging out from the warship on long ropes to drop upon the *Night's* deck in a hail of pistol fire, killing a good number of Tupper's crew instantly. Smoke and chaos erupted. More soldiers crossed the span on rope and wide boarding ladders. The deck of the *Scarlet Night* became choked with men and arms. The bitter bite of sulfer and the tange of blood choked the air. A vicious battle raged.

Tupper fired three of her pistols. Three fewer British seamen would be making the journey home. The deck beneath her feet became slick with blood. Men swarmed in her direction. She battled hard to keep them at bay. One man would carry a nasty scar for the rest of his days as a reminder of her. Another became home for her ax.

Pulling a fresh pistol from the crossed baldric at her chest, Tupper raised the barrel. From behind, a strong pair of hands grabbed her, viciously twisting her arm behind her back. Her weapon clattered to the deck as another pair of hands kept her from reaching for the knife in her boot. The heavy-handed grip nearly crushed the bones in her wrist. Two were joined by a third.

Kicking and screaming, Tupper thrashed about, trying to wrestle away from them. A quick turn and a well-placed knee, and the three were two once more. If she could get a free hand, she could even the field, but in her struggle she lost her footing on the slick deck.

Soon they had her face down on her own deck. "Hold her arms," snarled one. Her weapons were seized, and while the two held her down, the third, nursing a bruised...ego, cursed. "Bloody bastard!" He lashed her hands behind her back. As payback for her knee, he bound her ankles as well.

Hauled unceremoniously to the far rail, they threw her alongside several of her men already captured. MacTavish soon joined her. Cursing a blue streak. "Get yer fukin' hands off me!" His face florid. His kilt torn from his shoulder.

Six uniformed soldiers stood over them with cocked pistols. "Shoot any of these bastards that even dares to move," ordered one young corporal.

Outnumbered four to one on deck, the remaining crew of the *Scarlet Night* fought valiantly but the odds were far too great. One after another met a similar fate and joined those captured along the rail

Tupper saw her then. *Sam.* Poking her head up from below like a rabbit coming out of a hole. *Bloody hell!* She crept on deck, holding a pistol with two hands. *Where the hell...?* If that was the gun she'd given her when they'd engaged the Spanish ship, it was empty. Unless Sam had taken a quick lesson in loading a gun, she was heading into battle with nothing more than a vacant barrel and a prayer.

Sam raised her arms and took aim. Even from a distance, Tupper could see the tremor in her arms. The British soldier she was aiming at turned as she pulled the trigger, and caught her across the hip with a low slicing swing of his cutlass. At the same time, another man stopped her with a fierce blow to the back of her head. Sam crumbled at their feet. *No!*

Tupper wasn't the only one watching in horror as Sam was taken down. Bump, fighting his own battle stepped away from his post and was distracted for a single critical moment. Plenty of time for his opponent to crack his skull with the pommel of his sword.

Fury and rage pumped through Tupper as Bump was bound and thrown into the growing pile of prisoners. Unconscious, he fell like a sack. Blood coursed from the gash above his eye.

Tupper struggled against her restraints, "Let me loose, ye bastards!" The coarse rope ripped at her wrists and ankles. "Ye fukin' limey sons o'bitch—"

"Shut your mouth." The corporal stood over her, pistol in hand. "Or I'll shut it for you." He raised his arm.

"Corporal!"

The man lowered his hand and snapped to attention at the approach of two officers. Both young. Green. One, a fair-haired dandy. A lieutenant by his uniform. The other, a higher rank. Tall. Broad in the shoulders. He scowled at the corporal.

"Sir."

"We do not beat unarmed, bound prisoners. Is that clear?"

"Aye, Captain."

"You can be flogged for such behavior." The man turned his scowl on the prisoners. Ice-blue eyes captured Tupper's. "You there, does your captain live?"

Tupper glowered back. "Aye." She pushed to a more seated position. "*I* am captain of the *Scarlet Night.*

"Quinn?" The man before her appraised her more closely.

"Aye." She narrowed her gaze. It was oddly disconcerting to hear this British whelp use her name. More prisoners were hauled to the ship's side. The battle was lost. "I'd offer ye a proper salute, whoe'er the hell ye are, if I weren't trussed up like some bloody Christmas goose."

The lieutenant covered his laugh with a cough. "Fascinating."

"Release Captain Quinn. I see no need for restraints just now, Corporal." The young captain addressed her directly. "Do I have your word, Captain, that we can discuss our business in a civilized manner?"

The corporal bent to cut the rope at her ankles. She stood the moment her hands were freed. Rubbing her wrists, Tupper needed to raise her chin to glare at him. She straightened her hat. "Given the chance, I would drop you where you stand."

He stared her down and moved his hand to the hilt of his sword. "Then I'll see to it you don't get the chance."

"Bloody hell, I think I'm in love," the lieutenant muttered under an amused grin.

"Lieutenant, I'll leave you in charge. Transfer the prisoners, see the wounded to the surgeon, cover the dead, and assign a detail to secure the *Scarlet Night* and her goods. Captain Quinn, you'll lead me to your quarters, where I will take formal command of this ship. If you're foolish enough to make good on your declaration, my men have orders to kill the remainder of your crew."

She notched her chin. "You're planning to kill them anyway. What difference does a few days make? Save your empty threats."

"You'll soon learn, my threats are never empty."

"And neither are mine," Tupper countered. Around them, the British seamen snapped into action, following their orders. The wounded, Bump and Sam among them, were moved away first. "I don't know who you are, Captain, but I've been fighting better men than you for more years than you've been in long breeches."

"And yet, I'm the one who bested you." He took off his hat. His hair caught the light. "The name is Steele. Captain James Steele."

The air left Tupper's lungs in a rush. *Bloody hell.* It couldn't be. Surely there were plenty of men named James Steele. A common enough name. A coincidence. Yet, as she tried to deny the possibility, the truth of it stared back at her. *James Steele.* The resemblance to his father was undeniable. His height and build. The blue of his eyes. He carried a fair amount of his mother's genes as well. The red hair, blazing proof, even though it had darkened some since he was a babe. She flashed back to a sunny nursery another lifetime ago, rocking a sweet-smelling bundle with downy ginger hair.

Tupper blinked away the image of the child. The grown man now stood before her. Captain Steele walking the decks of the *Scarlet Night.* Jaxon Steele's son. The irony was not lost on her. Did he have any idea of his connection with this ship? Perhaps he didn't. For all she knew, he was never told of his heritage. His parents could have denied their past, lived their new life and never spoken of it to their son. They could be dead. She didn't dare ask. The thought brought a deep ache to her chest.

Dammit, she could use a drink. Tupper moved past him, cursing the slight tremor in her knees. Make that two drinks. Or six. "You mentioned wanting to see my quarters, Captain Steele."

Chapter 11

James followed the infamous Captain Quinn as she led him below. Accompanied by two of his men, he couldn't help the slight surreal feeling. This was the *Scarlet Night*. It was smaller than he'd imagined. He had to duck his head to enter the Captain's quarters. His men flanked him, guarding him.

The woman, Quinn, moved to the desk and retrieved a fine bottle of sweet rum. "I'll be damned if I leave this to wet the whistle of one of your crew." She lifted it toward James in invitation. He declined, "I'm on duty." James watched as she downed one shot, followed closely by another.

"Might as well take my chair. It's yours now." She waved her glass toward the chair behind the desk before pulling over a flat-topped trunk to sit.

He paused to take in the beautifully carved oak furnishings. The expanse of leaded windows spanning the back wall of the cabin, and a crafted niche containing the bed. He gave a silent thanks Ducky was above deck seeing to duties there. Although he could almost hear the jibes on his behalf. This was where his parents were wed... by a one-legged cook if the stories were true.

"Handsome quarters." He set down his hat and sat behind the desk, running his hands over the smooth rich wood. Was it the same desk Father had used, he wondered? Best to forget all that and remember why he was here. With a nod to his men, they stationed themselves on the other side of the door.

"Now then, as I've said, I am Captain James Steele of the *HMS Lion*, and I have been charged with returning you, as captain of the *Scarlet*

Night, and your men to London to await trial for treasonous offenses against the king."

"Treasonous offenses?" She cocked an eyebrow.

He lifted the ship's log and glanced at its pages. "Piracy."

"Wasn't treasonous when we were filling the royal coffers."

James shook his head. "Unfortunately, the political climate has changed. You're to surrender your ship, along with any and all cargo aboard, and be brought back to English soil to face the charges set before a magistrate."

"Where my crew and I will be found guilty and sentenced to hang in the gibbets lining the Thames." The woman spoke into her glass.

"That is the punishment for the crime committed, yes." James waited for her reaction. Stone still, she held his gaze. The damn woman never blinked. Didn't plead her case. Rail against the injustice. Bargain for her release. She was the picture of quiet resolve. It was most unnerving.

"I'll need to confiscate your logs, and the signed Ship's Articles. Your dead will be identified and receive a proper burial. Your wounded are being attended to by one of the finest medical crew to sail the Atlantic. Once the remainder of your men have been transferred to the *Lion*, they'll be held in our brig. The best I can do for you, given your rank... and gender, is to accommodate you in a cell by yourself."

"I'm in no danger from my men, Captain Steele."

"Desperate men are unpredictable."

She laughed and sipped at her rum, holding out her pinkie. "So are desperate women."

"Touché," he nodded. "Each member of your crew will be interviewed and processed, have the charges against them read and signed. They will have the opportunity to defend or deny their actions at that time."

"Doubt any will deny they're pirates." She leaned forward. "I'll need to demand one concession, however."

James narrowed his gaze. "You're hardly in a position to make any such demands."

"Very true, but there is a member of my crew who won't answer your questions without my presence. My first mate."

"Absolutely not. I can't allow your coercion."

The woman crossed one leg over the other. "Wouldn't dream of it. The man I refer to is a Jamaican. He's among the wounded." She pointed to the area over her eyebrow. "One of your men tried to split his skull. He's deaf. Speaks only with his hands." She frowned. "Now I think on it, it's probably best he's unconscious. Having his hands bound is akin to gagging him. He doesn't take to that well. I'd hate to see his obvious panic misconstrued as aggression."

"I see." He nodded. "In his case, I'll agree to your request and make what allowances I can."

"What about the ship? Will you scuttle the *Scarlet Night*?"

He scanned the room before answering. "No, she's still a fine sloop. It's my plan to include her in the store of bounty."

"Ah, a gift for the king." She cocked her head, holding his gaze. "Or is it more a gift for your father?"

The question caught him off guard. She was shrewd; he'd give her that. She played her cards close to her chest. Ducky was right, she was intriguing.

James sat back and crossed his arms over his chest. "You know of my father's association with this ship, then."

She gave him a smug smile. "Of course. Captain Jaxon Steele was well respected by this crew."

"You joined the ranks after he'd left, am I correct? I'm curious to hear how you came to the *Night*."

She paused to pour another drink. "That's a long tale. I dropped onto her decks close to a year after your father turned over the ship to Gavin Quinn."

"Your husband." It wasn't a question.

"Not immediately, but yes. Gavin and I married. That day I signed the Articles and became a full member of the crew."

"And you chose to assume the position of captain after his death."

"Again, not immediately. He died in the earthquake of ninety-two. Yet another long tale." Captain Quinn emptied her glass and reached for the bottle once more.

A flash of gold caught his eye. Her signet ring. Handwrought, hammered gold, with a fine-scripted "A" holding a tiny pearl in its tail. It looked exactly like—he grabbed for her wrist before she lifted the bottle. The logic of what he was seeing escaped him.

His eyes snapped to hers. "Where did you get this ring?"

Unblinking green eyes fixed on him. The corner of her mouth lifted in a grin. "It was given to me by the finest woman I've ever known. I believe she's your mother. Does she still wear its twin?"

Her words punched him in the chest. What was she saying? "W-who the hell *are* you?" He still held tight to her wrist.

"My crew calls me Tupper." She shrugged a shoulder.

"Dear God...*Alice* Tupper," he breathed.

"Alice Tupper Quinn," she smiled. "Sounds odd to hear the old name. Few have called me Alice since Gavin died." She tugged at his hold upon her wrist.

James released her arm and dropped back into his chair. Tupper finished pouring her drink and offered it to him once more. "Yer lookin' a might pale. Sure you don't want a quick one? You can be off duty as well as on. I'll never tell."

He shook his head. His mind reeled. "It's been thirty years."

Tupper sat back and crossed her legs once more. "Aye, sounds about right. So, you've heard tell of me, have you? You were just a wee babe when I left."

"You saved them," he blurted incredulously. "My parents. *Me.* I grew up hearing the tale. *Aunt* Alice. My younger sister carries your name. She's called Alicia. We all believed you to be dead. How can you be here? Without a single word from you that you're alive? After all these years?"

Tupper shrugged again. "Hardly worth it now. Thanks to you, I'll be dead again in a few short weeks." She leaned forward as if confiding a secret. "I'm not actually your aunt, you know." Smiling, she added, "You have a sister, Alicia. How sweet. I imagine had I ever been blessed with a daughter—"

"Bloody hell!" he burst.

Tupper continued as if she hadn't heard him. "Moot point, I know. Gavin and I were never blessed with children. I had a bird, a crow, but he's dead. Now *your* name." She pointed at him with her glass. "James Samuel Herbert Steele. Herbert *was* an uncle of yours. A great-uncle, I believe. Did they ever tell you where the 'Samuel' came from? This very ship. He was the cook. Samuel 'Cookie' Burrows. Grizzled, I'm told, but kindhearted. Loved your father like a son. Had a peg leg." The liquor had loosened her tongue. "Tell me about your parents, are they well? Still residing in Weatherington?"

"Yes, of course, but…"

She patted her heart. "I'm so glad to hear that. I was almost afraid to ask."

The conversation went on as if they were at a dinner party. Captain T. Quinn was Alice Tupper! The more he ran over it in his mind, the more unbelievable it became. Yet here she was, sitting across from him, across from his father's old desk, swilling rum as if it were weak tea and honey. Alice Tupper. Her mother's best friend. His sister's namesake. And *he* was the one assigned to bring her to justice? *To hang?*

"I want your word as an officer and a gentleman, you won't tell your mother you found me."

He jerked back into the conversation. "Wait. What? Why the hell not?"

"I have my reasons, and if she believes I'm dead already, why change that only to have me die all over again for her. It's kinder this way, don't you think? I never wanted any of this life I've led to tarnish my relationship with her." She pointed at his chest. "You have to promise me you'll say nothing."

"How am I to do that? I have to tell them about the *Scarlet Night*."

She waved his concern away with a flick of her hand. "No matter. Make something up. Who did you suppose I was?"

"Captain T. Quinn. I knew you to be a woman, Gavin's wife. Possibly Jamaican? But in all my imagination, I couldn't have guessed this."

"So that is who you'll say you brought to trial. Gavin Quinn's wife. A lusty Jamaican with long, dark shining hair and beautiful tanned skin."

"I can't possibly lie."

"Of course you can. You must." She slammed her glass to the desktop with a crack. Her rum-induced glibness dissolved. "I'm not asking you for lenience. I'm not asking you to go against your orders. In fact, you'd not be your father's son if you defied your responsibilities. Hell, I'd stripe your back myself if you even suggested it. I won't fight you. Shoot me, hang me, burn me at the stake. I don't care. All I'm asking is for you not to tell your sainted mother our paths crossed. A simple lie of omission. Save her from more pain."

"Seems you're still saving her."

She lifted a shoulder. "I love her. I've loved her since we were children together. Let the story they told you be my legacy." Tupper gave him a saucy grin and cocked an eyebrow. The glibness was back. "It's either that, or I tell your entire crew how I used to change your nappies."

His eyebrows pushed toward his hairline. "That's blackmail."

"That's correct. Is it a deal?"

"I know better than to deal with pirates."

Alice lifted a hand. "Call it...my final wish."

She had him there. Who was he not to honor the final wish of the woman who literally saved his family? She'd freed his father from certain death, and rescued his mother from the hands of a madman? Nursed her through a horrible sickness on their voyage back to England. Was present at his damn birth! "No mention of nappies?"

Tupper shook her head. "None."

"You have my word."

She drained her glass and stood. "Good." She smoothed her hair away from her face and pushed her hat back upon her head before recorking the near-empty rum bottle with a sharp squeak. Tupper wobbled slightly. "Isn't it time you ez-corted m-me to my cell?"

Chapter 12

James hit his quarters like a rogue wave. Dropping himself into his chair, he tossed his hat to land wherever it chose, tore loose his neckcloth, and ran his hands over his face before vaulting to his feet again. *Captain Tupper Quinn is Alice.* The circling of that singular thought was sure to drive him mad. He paced the floor, wearing a path along the rich carpet.

Tupper had the right idea when she began downing close to a full bottle of rum. He stopped pacing long enough to pour himself a healthy measure of brandy. The liquor burned his throat and blazed a trail into his belly. Perhaps it would numb his mind to the impossibility of the situation he found himself in.

What could he do? Nothing. His hands were tied, and with his promise to the outrageous, outspoken Captain Quinn, he was gagged as well. Did he actually think he could keep his word and not tell his family? He had to tell them eventually, but how?

James could picture the scene. Dinner in the grand dining room at the estate in Weatherington. His mother, looking radiant as always, dressed as his father often requested, in a gown of gold. Alicia would rush in, pink cheeked from some late afternoon social engagement. His father, still a picture of health and vitality in his evening attire, tugging at his neckline while complaining about the need for formal wear simply to eat his meal.

Would James break the news to them all during the sherry? "Oh, by the way, you'll never guess who I hanged last week." Or, "Father, I found your ship, killed the crew, but they had nothing but good things to say about you."

Perhaps they could play a guessing game after cigars and brandy. "You're allowed to ask twenty questions. If you can name the woman whose life I've ended, you win a prize."

A quick knock to the door brought Ducky Dunbar into James's quarters.

"I have the report concerning the capture of the *Scarlet Night*. Quite the fine feather in your cap, old boy." He read from the pages in his hands. "A score plus six dead. Eight, ours, eighteen theirs. Another two dozen wounded. Four ours, twenty theirs. Seven critically. All theirs. The rest have been moved into the main brig with minor incidence. Captain Quinn was just locked in the cell across from her crew."

"Captain Quinn…"

Ducky shook his head. "Can you believe the cheek of the woman? Not to mention the sight of trouser-clad legs in those impossibly tall boots? Pistols smoking. Blades flashing. I bet in her younger days she could have convinced even you to fly under the black flag. Pity all she has to look forward to now is a short drop followed by a quick stop." He mimicked the pull of the noose on his neck.

"Shut up, Ducky." James splashed a bit more brandy in his glass.

"You're in a fine mood. I would have thought you'd be happy capturing one of the top five wanted ships and crews. You're set, old man. A brilliant future. The career of your choosing. You'll make admiral for this."

James emptied his glass before dropping into his chair and pushing the glass away. Frowning, he rubbed a finger across his upper lip and rested his head in his hand. "Oh, yes, I'm bloody ecstatic."

"What is it?" Ducky lifted James's glass and sniffed. "I'm guessing this isn't a celebratory drink. What's got you so…so…uncorked?"

James lowered his hand and raised his gaze. "Captain Tupper Quinn is Alice."

"Alice?" Ducky frowned. "Alice who? You've lost me."

James was on his feet and pacing once more. "What I'm to tell you is in the strictest confidence. It can't leave this room."

"Of course, but—"

"I told you the story about the woman who fought a duke? Saved the day? Aunt Alice?"

"I remember something, yes, along with some fairy tale about heroic acts and bravery."

"Yes. *Alice*." James stretched out her name, and gave Ducky an expectant look.

It took Ducky a moment to connect all the pieces. "Oh, blimey…." He covered his mouth with a hand.

"Please." James threw up exasperated hands. "If ever there were a time to swear like a sailor, now would be it."

"Hold on." Ducky frowned. "How can you be so sure? The woman is a pirate. She lies and plunders for a living. You're mistaken. It's been years."

"Do you remember the ring my mother wears? We just spoke of it."

"Gold oval with an 'A.'"

James touched the tip of his nose and pointed to Ducky. "Well done." He paced back toward him. "Mother's ring has a twin. Captain Quinn is wearing it."

"She stole it, surely."

"That's what I thought," said James excitedly. He lifted his glass once more and found it empty. "Didn't I pour more brandy?"

Ducky snatched the bottle out of his reach. "Concentrate, James, the ring?"

"Yes, the ring. I asked her where she got it and she said...what were her exact words? 'It was given to me by the finest woman I've ever known. I believe she's your mother.' *My mother.* Her best friend is a pirate captain. And not just any captain, mind you. Tupper Bloody Quinn! It wasn't bad enough I had to seize my father's ship. No, no. I'm to be the bastard responsible for hanging the woman who saved my parents' lives. Do you realize without that breeches-wearing, pistol-smoking pirate, I wouldn't exist?"

"This is unbelievable." Ducky narrowed his eyes and pointed the bottle at James. "You're not thinking about releasing her?"

James looked at his friend as if he'd sworn the sky was green and the sun set in the north. "I'm sorry. Have we been introduced? I can't defy a direct order."

Ducky set the bottle aside and swept his forehead in relief. "Just checking. You were scaring me for a minute there."

James stopped pacing and rubbed at the back of his neck. It had turned into an oak plank. "This is a nightmare. Plus—"

"Good Lord, there's more?"

"I've given the woman my word I won't reveal her identity to my mother. I'm to let her go on believing Alice Tupper died during her crossing to the colonies."

Relief spread over Ducky's face. "Well then, your problem is solved. What are you worrying about? Deliver your prisoner as ordered, collect your well-earned promotion, go home, marry the incredibly wealthy Lady Lillian, and live a long happy life. No one ever need know about this."

"*I* will know."

Ducky threw up his hands. "So what do you propose? You can't unscramble an egg, James. What's done is done."

"Remember when you played devil's advocate? If my father's name was on the wanted list? Yours? Would I bring you to justice?"

"Yes, I remember. You said you would move heaven and earth to gain my release. What exactly do you think you could possibly do to gain that woman's release?" He pointed a sharp finger toward the door. "She has been a pirate most of her life. Signed a Letter of Marque and Reprisal, and has ignored a direct missive from the king to surrender. If anyone should hang for piracy and treason, it would be her. Don't be daft, man. When news reaches London that she's been captured.... a woman pirate, her trial will be sensationalized like none before. Obtaining a release for Captain Tupper Quinn will be just a bit harder than stealing the king's tiny cock."

"You're in uniform, man, you can't talk about the king's cock," James reprimanded.

"There you are, thinking like the James I know. Seriously, you must realize this is a ridiculous notion. There can be no pardon. Not for her." Ducky put an arm around James's shoulder. "There are times when doing the right thing and following orders takes more than most men are willing to give. This is why you are the commander of this ship and not me. You swore an oath to King and country. You'll do your duty, and the family will understand you did what you had to do."

"They will never understand this." James massaged the ache between his eyebrows. "There has to be a way."

Ducky shook his head and patted his back. "I can't see one, James, but who knows, miracles sometimes happen. I mean, look here." he stepped away from James and held his arms wide. "Who'd have ever thought I'd be the sober, rational one in the room?"

A quick knock on the door brought news his surgeon, Oliver Taylor, known to all as 'Stitch,' urgently needed him below.

Entering the surgery, the tang of blood was sharp. The sights of war's indiscretion never lost its stark horror. Bodies torn apart by guns and blades being pieced back together. Naval seaman and pirate alike. An ocean of hurt and pain. Dead lined the walls, awaiting their final slip into the sea.

Over the moans and cries of the wounded, he heard Stitch call him over to a litter. A young lad lay pale under a sheet. One of the *Scarlet* crew. Hard to determine his age. His face was turned toward the wall.

Stitch wiped at the blood staining him to his elbows. "Captain, we have a situation with this one."

"Is he dead?" The lad hadn't moved. His skin was so pale it almost appeared blue.

"No." Stitch moved the boy's hair aside to show him an angry purple knot on the base of the patient's skull. "Unconscious. Took a serious slash to the hip. Forty sutures. Lost a good deal of blood, but unless infection sets into the wound, stands a fair chance."

"I'm not seeing the problem. It seems cruel to save him only to bring him to trial, but—"

Stitch leaned closer and lowered his voice. "What I need to tell you, is this *lad* is missing some necessary equipment."

"What are you talking about? I don't have time—"

"Look for yourself." Stitch gave a quick scan of those around them before lifting the sheet of the boy. The large, angry wound on the lad's hip still weeped bright blood. "If my medical training is correct, a lad should also come equipped with a cock and a pair of bollocks."

James's eyes darted to the normal location for such things. He shot Stitch a questioning glare. "What the hell?"

Stitch lowered the sheet and scratched at his jaw. "Her chest was bound tight, I'm surprised she could breath." He kept his voice low. "Something else."

"I don't know if I can handle anything else." James closed his eyes and shook his head. "Proceed. Tell me."

Stitch lifted the sheet and tipped the body slightly. "See here," He pointed to an area where the girl's skin was slightly discolored. "And here. Old bruising. Whoever this is, she took quite a beating not too long ago. I examined her, and other than her present wounds, she was in sound health, but there's no question, someone used more than their fists on this woman."

"Son of a bitch." Disgust flooded him, followed close by anger. James was almost grateful for the slap of reality this poor woman's injuries provided. It reminded him that Tupper Quinn and her vile crew were lowly, vicious pirates. Nothing more. Alice Tupper may wear his mother's ring, but that was where any resemblance to the woman who showed such bravery all those years ago ended.

"I swear to you I'll get to the bottom of this and hang the man...or woman responsible, myself. I'll start in the brig."

As James turned to leave, Stitch stopped him. "What do you want me to do with her?" He jerked his head toward the patient. "I can't put her in with the rest. She won't survive the brig. Bad enough we've got one female on this ship...if the men find out there's two..."

James wanted answers about this girl now, and Tupper was going to be the one to answer them. He didn't have time to debate sleeping arrangements and blurted out the first thing to come to mind. "Move her into my cabin. I'll bunk with the officers and put a guard on her until I decide what to do."

"A wounded criminal in the captain's bed? Isn't that going to be a little hard to explain?"

"Do you have another suggestion?" James snapped.

A moan from the litter had both men shifting their attention. The woman in question turned toward them, grimaced, and tried to move before going still once more.

"She's coming around. That's a good sign. We can find out who the hell she be. May still be gone for a few hours yet. I won't give her any laudanum for her pain 'til she wakes."

James heard Stitch's voice as if it came from under water. The blood rushed in his ears. What did the man say? All James could do was nod. He could be agreeing to anything, but nothing else mattered. Stunned, he wasn't sure if he still breathed. He pulled a deliberate breath into his lungs.

Good God! It was her. But how? "We don't need to wait. Her name is Samantha."

Chapter 13

"What kind of game are you playing?" James demanded. His fists curled around the bars of Tupper Quinn's cell door. She sat on the straw-strewn floor against the back wall.

Tupper raised the brim of her hat and frowned at him before rising to her feet. "I have no idea what you're talking about."

"I'll make it simple. Samantha Christian," he snapped. Rage coursed through him. He slammed the heel of his palm against the bar.

Tupper glanced over to her men. "Could we discuss this in your quarters?"

"No. We'll discuss this here. Now."

"She's alive then?" Tupper lowered her voice, sending another nervous look toward the other cell.

James followed her gaze. The men paid them no attention. "Yes, she's alive, no thanks to you."

"Hey." Tupper held her hands out to her sides. "I sent her below. Forbid her from joining the fray. Told her it wasn't her fight. It was her mule-headed self who wandered into a battle with a blasted empty gun."

"Empty gun?"

"Yes. Fool never checked." Tupper leaned closer. "Misdirected loyalty to me was all it was. I told her she should hide until your people found her. Claim she was a prisoner of the *Scarlet Night* and plead her innocence."

"Was she a prisoner?"

Tupper shook her head. "No, of course not. She was my cabin boy."

James's knuckles whitened as his fists curled around the bars once more. "You're in the habit of beating your cabin boys?"

Tupper jerked back as if struck. "What? I never touched her. Cut her hair, yes, but—"

"Then which one of your men is responsible?" He looked back over his shoulder.

"If I wasn't so fond of your mother, I'd be insulted." She crossed her arms over her chest. "Perhaps you should talk to Samantha before you start throwing around accusations."

"I will if she regains consciousness. Until then you'll be the one to answer me."

"Your father was just as demanding and stubborn at your age." She suddenly stopped the damning comparison, narrowed her gaze, and tipped her head. "Wait a minute... If she's unconscious, how do you know her name?"

She kissed me one night on a veranda... "It doesn't matter. I want to know how she got here and who used her as a whipping post."

Tupper sighed. "Fine. A short time ago, I was contacted by an acquaintance in Virginia asking for my help. Samantha was a friend. Secured a position as governess at a plantation nearby. However, her employer had a nasty habit of raping and beating her whenever he fancied. I freed her from the situation. At no small expense to me, I might add. But fearing my crew would be less than welcoming, I cut her hair, bound her chest, and disguised her as a lad before bringing her aboard. Only my first mate knows the truth, and I'd appreciate it if we could keep it that way."

She shrugged. "We were on course to England, where I was planning to drop her at our first landing. Like I said, when we saw the *Lion* bearing down on us, I sent her below. Told her to play the part of hostage, after which you and your crew could see her safely back to her family."

James recalled the fury in Damian Wessler's eyes the night of the ball. He did a quick accounting in his head. Samantha's bruises could definitely have been delivered that night. Why would she have provoked him knowing what he'd do? *Forgive me.*

"Why didn't you tell me this before?"

"We were a little busy discussing other things, and the rum was sweet..." She shrugged again. "I saw her fall. For all I knew she was dead."

"I'm beginning to wish I were." James rubbed a weary hand over his eyes. "Tell me, was she or was she not a member of your crew?"

"As a ruse, yes."

A feeling of dread curled around his throat. "Did she put her mark to the Ship's Articles?"

Tupper sighed again, shaking her head. By the look on her face, she knew the gravity of her answer. "Yes."

He closed his eyes. His stomach twisted, but he straightened his shoulders. "If she signed the Articles, she is an official member of your crew. As such, she is under arrest and charged along with the rest. When she wakes, she will be processed accordingly. Her wounds have been tended and private accommodations are being made for her during her recovery. As soon as she is able, she will join you in this cell."

"Sam is guiltless in all this, James."

"She is a signed member of your crew. In battle she raised a pistol against a member of the British Navy."

"An *empty* pistol. Her scribbled signature doesn't make her a pirate. She's no traitor. I'm telling you, Samantha's harmless. You saw her bruises. If she hadn't come with me aboard the *Scarlet Night*, she would have died by that bastard's fists. You can't condemn her from one death to another."

"I must turn her over to the magistrate. Once they listen to her story, if it is as you've told me, she'll be released."

Tupper rolled her eyes and barked a short laugh. "You don't know any such thing."

"I have to follow the proper procedure."

"Right, proper procedure. Do what's *proper.* I'll tell her not to worry. Innocent people never hang do they?" she mocked.

Bile rose in James's throat. It was bad enough he'd carry the death of Alice on his head for the rest of his days. If they killed Samantha, he wouldn't be able to live with the guilt. "I'll do my best to protect her."

"I would hope so, and I would do what you can to keep her identity a secret." She dipped her head and whispered. "My crew does not know I've deceived them. They wouldn't care why I did it. Your bars wouldn't be able to contain their anger. Neither the girl nor I would be safe from them." She lifted a hand toward him. "And you've a crew of hundreds. Do you truly want them to know there's a tempting young woman aboard? She could be in serious jeopardy if you exposed her to them."

"My men know they'd be shot if they did what you're suggesting."

Tupper snorted. "And we've both been around long enough to know death is hardly a deterrent to some."

"Pirates, perhaps. Not members of the British Navy." He held his hand up to stop her denial. "My first duty is to see Samantha survives her injuries. I won't hide who she is. I can handle my crew. You decide how you'll tell yours the truth." He glanced over his shoulder at the men in question. The remaining crew of the *Scarlet Night* sat along the walls of the cell or lay out on the floor. Less than twenty in number, they were broken, defeated. "Not much of a threat now, are they?"

Tupper narrowed her eyes at him. "Don't get cocky. There's nothing more dangerous than angry men with nothing to lose."

* * * *

As James returned to his quarters, a man exited quickly carrying a litter. He gave James a proper if not hasty salute as he flew past.

Samantha was in his bed. Stitch checked her wound as James nodded toward the door. "What did you tell him?"

"I covered her face and told him the patient might have the pox. Needed to be quarantined." Stitch laughed. "Think the greenhorn held his breath the whole way up here."

"How is she?"

"Surviving." He straightened. "I got six more men who need my attention more than her, however. I can't stay. She's going to need tending, and I've got my hands full. May have to confide in another man for help here."

James planted his hands on his hips and tucked his chin. "I'll see to her."

"You're already being more than generous giving up your bed. Now you want to play nursemaid? You're obviously acquainted. How well do you know this woman?"

Forgive me. James shook his head at the memory. "We shared a dance once."

"Must have been one hell of a dance." Stitch laid out a half-dozen rolls of bandages, a small brown bottle, and a shallow basin. He held up the bottle. "After she wakes, two drops in a cup of water for the pain. Every four bells. No more." He stretched his back. "I'll drop in from time to time. I want to keep her wound as clean as possible."

"I can change the dressing if needed." Samantha looked impossibly pale lying there. His earlier anger ebbed into a consuming worry and fear for her.

"If you insist. All you'll need is here. Send a man to fetch me if you need help, or if she becomes feverish."

It was crazy taking it on himself—there was no denying it—but he couldn't bear the thought of anyone else close to her. "I think I can handle it."

"I don't doubt it." He gave James a grin. "My curiosity would love to know why you'd want to."

James crossed his arms over his chest. He wasn't sure he could explain it himself. "That's my business."

"Aye, aye, Captain." Stitch flipped him a haphazard salute.

James hadn't known Stitch Taylor for long, but recognized a good man when he saw one. "I'll send for you if I need to. Thank you for your discretion."

After Stitch left, James pulled a chair over to sit beside his bed. Samantha was as white as the sheet covering her. Her beautiful hair had been cut into a ragged cap. The shattered ends seemed to race in a hundred different directions. Lying there, she reminded him of a doll his sister Alicia had as a child made of fragile bisque porcelain. Alicia used their mother's needlework scissors to hack off the doll's hair, believing in her childish mind that it would grow back again.

James reached out to brush at her cheek, expecting she might be cold and rough as the doll's porcelain face, but his fingertips met warm satin. Thick, dark lashes swept her cheeks. Her lips curved into a gentle pink bow. How had anyone mistaken her for a lad? Was the crew of the *Scarlet Night* blind? The length of her hair only accentuated the lovely sweep of her jaw and gentle curve of her cheek. He tucked her hair behind one ear.

Tupper's men were nothing if not loyal. They probably never raised any question when their captain brought a new cabin "boy" aboard. Fools.

And none a bigger fool than he.

James covered Samantha with one of his blankets and left her to rest. Returning to his desk, he withdrew the ship's log. It would make a fine novel one day, considering all that transpired in the last few hours. Had he not lived it, he would not have believed it. If this were some test of his steadfast resolve…

Resolve, indeed. He lifted his gaze to the woman in his bed. *A woman in his bed.* It had been more than a year since he said those words. His relationship with Lillian was chaste. It would be his wedding night before he was allowed to unwrap his proper lace-and-satined wife. For the first time in near a week, he thought of Lillian. He couldn't image what her reaction would be to this, even if the reasoning were purely innocent. Or was it?

It wasn't the first pang of guilt he'd experienced regarding Samantha Christian. Since the night of the Whitmore's ball, he had struggled to get her out of his head. And now, here she was. As desperate as her situation, as hideous as the events that brought her to this place, past all the worry, a small part of him was elated. He feared he would never see her again.

Never learn what prompted her to kiss him and cause him to question and relive that single moment over and over again.

It was wrong to compare Lillian to Samantha. Completely unfair. But he couldn't help but think if their two lives reversed somehow, Lillian wouldn't have survived the trials Samantha had lived through and would continue to endure. The future for Samantha would not include endless debates over the color of shoes, or an elaborate wedding with a dozen attendants and more guests than this ship would hold.

No. Samantha had made it here through some miracle and faced a future of pain and uncertainty. Once more, she would be fighting for her life. He wouldn't abandon her and allow her to walk alone into hell, as he had unknowingly done the night of the ball. She deserved someone to defend her. Tupper had risked a great deal to help her. It was only right for him to do the same.

Chapter 14

Samantha struggled to swim to the surface of a dark, fathomless sea. Her head pounded. Pain sliced through her when she tried to move. Opening her eyes, whispers of panic tickled up her spine. *Where am I?* The last thing she remembered...what was the last thing she remembered? The throbbing in her head made thinking near impossible. She moaned and covered her eyes.

Deep breaths began to clear away the cobwebs hanging in the corners of her mind. Peeking beneath her hand, she tried in vain to recognize something—anything—to give her a clue as to where she might be and what happened.

"Samantha?" A gentle hand moved hers away from her eyes.

"Thank goodness," she sighed, smiling. "I know you. Your handsome face. I shouldn't be so bold to say, but you have the most beautiful eyes..." Hers closed. Their lids weighing more than she could lift. She remembered where she was at least. The Whitmore estate. The harvest ball. "Has the orchestra stopped playing? I-I don't hear the music."

"Samantha, open your eyes."

"I can't. I'm so sorry. I'm afraid you'll have to dance with someone else, Captain Steele." She laid a hand on his shoulder. "James..." she sighed. She brushed her fingers across her lips, remembering the feel of his against them as they kissed. Why were hers so dry? Parched?

"I don't wish to dance with anyone else."

His voice was gentle. She smiled, then gasped as she tried to move and a shock of pain burned across her hip. "Why does it hurt so badly?" She gripped his sleeve. "Did Wessler...?"

"You were injured in a battle. Do you remember? You were fighting against my men on the *Scarlet Night.*"

The Scarlet Night? Her eyes flew open as the memories flooded into her consciousness. The battle. Noise and smoke and... "British soldiers and cannons. There were so many men. And blood everywhere. Tupper? Is she okay? How...? My mind is muddled. My head is splitting." She frowned at him. "James... It is you, isn't it? How is it you?"

"Aye. Lie still. I'll bring you something for the pain."

She closed her eyes, trying to piece everything together. A moment later, he held a glass to her lips. "Here, drink this. It will ease your discomfort."

The liquid tasted bitter, but if it would take away this excruciating throbbing, she would drink it willingly. She finished the cup and thanked him. When he leaned to set the mug aside, she saw past him to the rich appointments of the room. "We're not on the *Scarlet Night.*"

"No, you're on my ship, the *HMS Lion.*"

Samantha clutched at the blankets. "You...you captured the *Night.*"

"Yes. You were injured during the battle."

"Tupper. Is she alive? Bump?"

"Tupper is alive. I'm afraid I don't know anyone named Bump."

"That's not his real name.... I know it.... I can't remember." She rubbed a hand over her eyes.

"I'll see if I can find out for you, but you need to rest now."

"What will you do to them? Tupper and the rest? Don't hurt her. Please." Sam tried to sit, but the searing pain made her cry out.

He laid a firm, yet gentle, hand on her shoulder. "You must lie still."

"You don't know her as I do. She's brave and kind. Don't judge her too harshly." She tugged on his sleeve. "Please. You must understand. I owe her my life. Bump, too."

"You'll tear your stitches if you don't lie still." He eased her back.

She didn't know what he'd given her to drink, but it was making things haze around the edges of her vision. "I...please..."

Sitting next to her, he held her shoulder with a warm hand, keeping her from shifting again. "You need to rest. We'll talk more later."

Some of her anxiety eased. His voice and his touch wrapping her in a comforting cocoon. She could feel herself slipping back into sleep. "But she's unharmed?"

"Aye. I give you my word." He cupped her cheek.

* * * *

James stroked the outline of her lower lip with his thumb as the laudanum pulled her back into a dreamless sleep. How could his heart fill upon hearing her whisper his name, only to shatter when reality slammed into the middle of his fantasy?

She was here. With him. He was touching her lovely face. And the next time she awoke, he would have to tell her the truth. James closed his eyes to the ache and utter frustration.

Samantha had looked up to him with such pleasure upon recognizing him. She thought they were still dance partners. Then pleading with those eyes, imploring him to help. He didn't want to imagine how she would look upon him when he had to read the charges against her.

This was impossible. He wasn't made of stone. Yes, he had a responsibility and a duty, and he would see it carried through, but Tupper was right. This girl was guiltless, a victim of circumstance. She was gray in a sea of black and white.

He would defend her position with his dying breath if need be. She would rest and recover from her wounds and he would build a case in her favor. By the time they reached the mouth of the Thames, she would be free to...to....

James stood and looked back at her. She would be free to pursue her life and return to her family. Without him. He could have no possible claim to her. Either way, he would lose her. But somehow he could live with the hurt that came with such a realization. What was important was she could live her life however she chose.

Samantha breathed deeply. James guessed she would be asleep for hours. The processing of this prisoner could wait forever if he had his way, but now would be the time. He moved to his desk and gathered the necessary articles. Never before had he been mired in such conflicting emotions where his duties lie, but one duty was clear. The prisoners below could wait no longer.

James drew to his full height. He would deal with each thing in turn. Order and efficiency had always served him, and now was no exception. He was facing challenges beyond his wildest imaginings, but he would face them one after the next, and see them to their right and proper conclusion. If the outcome was not to his liking, he could find solace in knowing he'd done in this as he had always done...his best.

James closed his eyes with a grimace as he screamed within his own mind. *What a load of steaming horse droppings.*

* * * *

A table had been set up outside the brig. Four guards stood two abreast, flanking the door behind him in case the prisoners decided to become foolish.

The first captive to be processed would be the captain of this pirate crew. James kept his eyes averted. Desperate to remember his place. Follow proper protocol. Do his duty with necessary precision.

"State your name."

Tupper dipped over the table. "Sweetheart, you know my name."

He lifted his eyes to hers. "Please. This is difficult enough…."

Tupper straightened and snapped to attention. "Of course, sir. Forgive my impertinence."

James slammed his hand upon the table. "Do you think this is some kind of a joke?"

"Frankly, yes." She waved her hand over the desk before her. "Do we need all this pomp and parchment? Hang me and be done. Or throw me over the rail with the dead. I'd much rather die with sea water in my lungs than hemp burns around my neck." She stroked at her throat.

"If she be going in the drink, shove me over as well." A large Scotsman standing behind Tupper added. "'Course, if ye could wait till we get a bit farther north, save the cannonballs. Surely, I'll float. Maybe I'll wash ashore closer te home."

"No one is going in the water," insisted James. The muscle in his jaw clenched. "State. Your. Name."

"Tupper Quinn. Oh, sorry, Alice Tupper Quinn." She leaned forward to inspect his writing. "Wait…shouldn't that be Captain Alice Tupper Quinn. Or, Alice Louise is my full given name. Okay." She stood at attention. "My name is Captain Alice Louise Tupper Quinn." She turned back to the Scotsman. "That's a three-ink dipper, that is."

"Wait 'til ye git a load of my moniker. Da was shiteface pissed when he landed me with my string."

James took a deep breath. "Captain Quinn. Do you understand the charges against you?"

"Of course. Save your breath. I'm guilty as the sea is wide." She leaned over again. "Where do you want me to sign?"

"You have nothing to say in your defense?"

"I did what you say I did. And a good deal more. I'm only surprised it took you this long to catch up to me."

James shook his head and marked that the prisoner denied making a statement. When he lifted his gaze, Tupper's grin had disappeared. She captured James's gaze and held it firm. Bravado gone, she spoke just to him. "There is little I regret, and nothing that can be changed. This was to be my fate with or without you. Understand?" She plucked the quill from his hand. "Where do I sign?"

Spinning the parchment, he indicated where her mark needed to go. Tupper never lowered her eyes from his as she scribbled her signature. She handed the quill back to him and smiled before stepping aside.

The Scotsman now faced James. Tupper lingered to the side. James scanned the other prisoners. The first mate they'd discussed earlier hung toward the back of the group, if her description of the man was correct.

"I'll hear this man's statement before I take care of your first mate."

Tupper nodded and crossed her arms over her chest.

"Your full name?" James asked the unkempt kilted beast before him.

The man scratched at his beard. "Malcolm Fergus Francis Eugene MacDougal MacDonald MacTavish."

"Bloody hell," Tupper snorted.

The man, MacTavish puffed his chest and pointed. "Got ye beat… mine's a five dipper."

James finished writing the man's name. "Your rank."

"Aw, fuk. Battling is strenuous work." He lifted an arm and sniffed beneath. "Did ye expect me te smell like a garden o' roses?"

James ran a weary hand over his eyes while several men, his own included, laughed loudly.

"I was asking about your position on the ship, sir." James glared at his men to stop. "Not commenting on your body's pungent odor."

"Oh, beg pardon." The man stood proud. "I be Master Gunner."

"Do you understand you are being charged with piracy and treason?"

"Aye." He shook his head. Braids in his beard danced.

James waited. "And did you wish to defend yourself?"

"Nay." MacTavish scratched at his jaw. "Been a pirate all me life." He shrugged. "Well, 'cept fer that month I spent in bed wit a fine English lass. Right a'fore I signed on te the *Scarlet*. Bonny lass she was. Priscilla be her name. Hair like spun honey. A smile te rival the sun. She hated her pa. He hated me more. Paid me a fair quid to pack up me tartan and quit soiling his daughter or he'd rid me of certain bits of me manhood I was fair fond of, if ye gather me meaning. Week later, I sign on wit Captain Quinn. Gavin be a fair man. Fought wit two rogue crews 'fore finding my place wit this lot."

James narrowed his eyes. "So your answer is 'no.'"

"Aye…no."

James groaned to himself. If every man told him his life's story, he'd be at this for a week. "Here." He pointed to the parchment. "Make your mark."

Malcolm whatever-his-ridiculous-name MacTavish signed his warrant.

"I'll see to the first mate."

Tupper got the man's attention and beckoned him over. He was tall, broad through his shoulders with hair hanging past them in long, twisted hanks. A line of fresh stitches closed the flesh above one eye nearly swollen shut.

"State your name." The man stared at him with oddly light eyes given his Jamaican heritage.

Tupper made a few quick moves with her hands. "He's known as Bump, but his given name is William."

Bump. This was the man Samantha expressed concerned about. James wrote the name "William" on the order. "His surname?"

Tupper translated. The man shook his head before Tupper interceded. "His last name is Quinn." As she repeated herself using her hands, Bump gave her a look of surprise.

He wasn't the only one to be surprised. James looked to her. "Is this man your son?"

"As far as I'm concerned, he is." Tupper held Bump's gaze as she answered. Her hands moved quickly. "I didn't carry him in my belly, but he's as close to my son as any being alive."

"It is important he understand the charges levied against him."

Tupper shot a glare back toward James. "His brain works just fine. It's his ears he's got problems with."

"Just make sure he understands, and ask him if he'd like to make a statement at this time."

Tupper finished signing. Bump set his jaw and signed back. Tupper snorted. "He understands perfectly, and would like you to tell the king and his magistrate that they can kiss his pretty arse."

Grabbing the quill from James, the man called Bump signed his petition clearly and distinctly *William B. Quinn* in a large sweeping hand. Tupper watched with almost a bittersweet grin upon her face. When he finished, she traced under the man's signature with a gentle fingertip.

Bump tapped Tupper's sleeve to regain her attention. His hands moved in the same quick manner. Tupper frowned, then nodded. "He's concerned about the girl. He saw Samantha taken from the surgery draped in a sheet. Did she die from her wounds?"

"She's fine." James added a few notes to William Quinn's statement.

A soft grumble filtered through the other prisoners. Tupper lowered her voice, "Then where is she?"

"We couldn't exactly have her bedded with the men, now could we?" He met Tupper's frown with his own. "She's not fit to join you." Why was it all of a sudden difficult for him to tell Tupper that at this moment

Samantha was in his bed? "I've made the necessary arrangements to keep her from harm while she recovers."

Tupper tipped her head in Bump's direction. "Doesn't answer his question."

James met the man's stare before shifting his gaze back to Tupper. "She was brought to my quarters."

Chapter 15

Tupper blinked in shock at James. "She's where?" she hissed. The rumbling of the crew behind her grew louder.

"At the time, I believed the safest place for her was in private quarters. How many of those do you believe there to be on a warship?"

Tupper crossed her arms over her chest. She was having a hard time believing what she was hearing. "Have you told her you intend to hang her?"

The muscle in James's cheek pulsed. "Leave it to you to simplify the most complicated situation. No, but I will. She's only just regained consciousness. When the time is right, I'll break the news to her." He went back to his work. "I'm personally supervising her care. It only made sense to put in her in my bed. I just left her, and she's resting comfort—"

"*Your* bed?" Tupper rubbed her ear. They say the hearing is the first thing to go when you get old. She couldn't have heard him right.

Bump tapped on her arm, asking her what the Englishman had said. It didn't take a mind reader to know what was going on behind Bump's concerned scowl. Tupper was one of the few people who could read his emotions like a book. Bump cared for Sam. He cared deeply. By the look in his eye, too deeply. When the hell had this happened? They spent a total of two minutes together. Dammit. This was all her fault. She had asked for Bump's help; pushed them together. She couldn't have guessed he'd fall for the girl. Not this damn quick.

And now, hearing James, he'd given up his bed? Or was he joining her there? Hadn't he said he'd known Sam before? He'd been angry... and vague. How well had they been acquainted? Had they been lovers? *Bloody hell*. Was Samantha Christian some kind of siren? A silkie in breeches? The woman had both these men rushing to care for her, making allowances, risking their lives and reputations for her. Wanting to rescue her, each in their own suit of shining armor.

If it weren't so futile, it would all be extremely chivalrous, but the truth of it all was neither Bump nor James could save Sam from the fate awaiting her.

James glanced at Bump. "Assure him she's being well cared for."

She relayed the message, mumbling. "I doubt knowing where she is receiving that care will assure him in the least."

Tupper returned to her cell after James was finished with Bump. The rest of the crew processed easily. None had anything to say in their defense. These men held little stock in living long, healthy lives. None had family or loved ones who would likely stand and weep over their bodies. Of course, like her, she'd wager they'd rather have met their end in battle. Seemed more honorable than being dipped in hot tar and hung in a gibbet.

When James and his men left, one of the crew, Chester Allan, called over to her from their cell. "Capt'n? The men and me got a question burnin' holes through us."

Tupper was tired. She'd stretched out on the floor and pulled her hat down over her eyes. "Can it wait?"

Another man raised his voice. "It bloody well can't."

She pushed the brim of her hat off her nose. A thread of unease circled up her spine. "Butler, is that you griping?"

"Aye, ye lied te us." He slammed a fist on the bars.

Tupper got to her feet and looked toward the men's cell. A small group had gathered at the front. "Yer sober. Ye don't know what yer saying. Go sit down."

"I'm sober all right. Ain't been so clear-headed in six months, but it's got me hearin' things pretty damn clear too. Things I ne're thought te hear."

"Shut yer hole, Butler," MacTavish grumbled. He sat with his eyes closed and his beefy arms folded over his chest. "Some of us be needin' our beauty sleep."

"Don't ye want te hear how she's tricked us?" piped Allan.

Tupper shook her head. "What are you babbling on about?"

Butler pressed his face through the bars. "New lad ye dragged aboard in te middle of the night. He ain't a he. Is he?"

Blast. Tupper waved his suggestion away. "Are ye sure yer sober there, Butler? Sure be talkin' like a watered sot."

He pointed toward the table where James had sat. "Just heard ye wit that fancy capt'n. I ain't deef like Bump, ye know."

"I heard it, too," Allan added, nodding like an albatross.

"Explains why were sittin' here waitin' fer a noose." Butler shook at the door. His voice raising. "Ye cursed us! Bitches be bad luck, and ye dragged one aboard under our noses te doom the whole stinkin' lot of us."

Tupper yelled back, "*I'm* a bitch, ye great superstitious fool."

Allan kept nodding, spurring Butler on. "Maybe been pressing our luck this whole time trustin' a woman te our fate, and one more of yer like pushed us off the edge."

"Luck or no, ain't the point. Tupper lied to us." Butler pointed an accusing finger through the bars at her. "Don't be denyin' it." He turned back to the others. "All these years and this is how she plants a blade in our backs."

"I didn't stab any of ye in the back," Tupper countered. "The girl was in trouble. Be dead if she didn't get away from Virginia."

Another man, Peters, stood up along with the others. "An' now we all be dead, 'cause of 'er."

Tupper shook her head. She needed to defuse this before the lot of them turned on her. "The *Lion* was on our tail before Sam came aboard. She didn't cause any of this."

MacTavish stood up, planting his hands on his hips and scowling at her. Friend or no, she'd deceived him too. His anger simmered below the surface. "Why didn't ye put it te a vote?" The look on his face asked another question. *Why didn't ye trust me?*

"There wasn't time. I made a decision. Right or wrong, it's done. I didn't want to hide it from you, but I feared for the girl."

Allan continued to stir up the waters. "Bump knew. Didn't he? He was part of that there conversation." He waggled a finger toward her.

"You two 'ave always been in thick as thieves," Peters added.

MacTavish shoved him. "We're all thieves, ye dumb fuk."

"Can't trust neither of 'em," Butler grumbled.

Bump sat resting in the rear of the cell, eyes closed. He'd never had a problem defending himself, but a band of angry men was a dangerous powder keg. If Tupper didn't keep their anger directed at her, Bump could be in trouble. "Listen to me. Bump didn't know anything 'til we were well on our way. He figured it out on his own, but by then it was too late to turn back. He had nothing to do with any of it. It was me. Ye've a right to be sore at me. I take full responsibility for my actions. If we ever see ourselves back aboard the *Night,* ye can vote me off. I'll split my share among the lot of ye as compensation."

Butler crossed his arms over his chest. "Like we're e'er gonna see that day."

"Ye're lucky you an' her ain't in here wit us. That's all I'm sayin,'" puffed Allan.

"Lass took a blade in te fight," pointed out MacTavish. He'd turned away from Tupper, but still defended the girl. "Seems te me, she already gave her due."

"Not from where I'm standin,'" glared Butler.

Chapter 16

James crossed paths with Ducky on his way back to his quarters. He was anxious to check on Samantha. The laudanum should have kept her sleeping, but his business in the brig had taken longer than he anticipated.

"Processing go well?" Ducky fell into step with James.

"Too bloody long." James repositioned the parchments and logs he carried under his arm. "I know more about the lot of them now than I ever wanted—or needed—to know. One of them told me the reason he became a pirate was to get away from his nagging wife. Another had a name longer than my arm."

"And the lovely Captain Quinn? Did ye learn anything new about her?"

"Only that she can speak to the deaf and is determined to die."

Ducky struggled to keep pace. "What has you in such a rush?"

James could dodge Ducky. Make some excuse, but in that instant he couldn't think of a plausible one. Better to come clean. He stopped short and turned to his startled friend. "There's something I need to confess, and I need your utmost discretion."

Ducky's eyes widened. "Should I be calling for the priest?"

James righted the shifting parchments and moved past. "I'd hoped you could behave seriously for once."

"James, old man, what is it? I realize having Captain Quinn turn out to be—"

Juggling his armload, James freed a hand to wipe at the sweat rolling into his eyes. "It's not about Captain Quinn."

"Everything appears right with our crew?"

"The crew is more efficient than even I'd hoped. I doubt if they'd miss me if I fell overboard." He began walking toward his quarters and stopped again. "Perhaps tossing myself over the rail wouldn't be a bad idea."

Ducky grabbed at his arm. "Tell me your confidence, for goodness' sakes."

"It might be best to show you."

James beat Ducky to his quarters by several strides. He fiddled with the key to his door.

"Since when do you lock your door?" Ducky panted. He scooped the items out of James's arms.

"Since now." James looked over Ducky's shoulder to make sure they were alone. He released the lock and pushed into his quarters. "Dear God!"

Samantha was on the floor, tangled in a bloody blanket. He rushed to her. The stitches holding her wound had torn, explaining the blood, but how had she gotten on the floor?

"What in the hell? Who—"

"Get Stitch Taylor. Now." He disentangled her from the ruined blanket. Heat radiated from her. She was limp in his arms. "She's burning up with fever."

"She? But who?"

"Get him now!"

Ducky scrambled out, slamming the door behind him. James lifted Samantha back into his bed. Her blood stained his uniform. He rushed to gather water and drying cloths, threw them into a basin, and doused them in water from the pitcher on his washstand. After wringing the water from them, he laid cooling towels along her skin.

The shock of the chilled clothes brought her around with a start. She began thrashing wildly, flailing against him and shoving at his chest.

"Samantha, lie still, please…"

"Stop." she screamed. "Get your hands off me."

"You have a fever. I have to cool you down."

She scratched at his arm. "You rutting bastard, get off me!"

"I won't hurt you, I swear." James struggled to hold her down. "The doctor is coming."

Samantha's screeches withered to tearful pleas. "You have no right… Please, not again… I'll mind my tongue…" She crossed her arms over her face in protection. "Please, stop…please…"

Bloody hell, she thinks I'm Wessler. "Samantha, it's me, James. No one is going to hurt you. I swear." He gently eased her arms away from her face. "You're safe. Darling, can you understand me?"

Her head dropped back. Her body went limp once more. "Oh dear God... Samantha? Open your eyes. Can you hear me? Answer me, please." He shot a panicked glance toward the door. "Where the hell is the doctor?"

James continued to bathe her burning skin, laying cooling clothes over her forehead and along her neck. He could feel the beating of her heart beneath his fingertips and prayed it kept beating.

Stitch was at James's side before he realized they had returned.

"Shit." He used his thumb to raise one of Sam's eyelids. "This is what I was afraid of." Stitch fingered the weeping wound at her side. "How did she tear her sutures?"

"She must have fallen out of bed. I found her on the floor."

"I thought you were tending her?" He pressed a cloth to her wound.

"She woke. I gave her laudanum. She was resting well, and I assumed she'd be asleep for hours. I had business I needed to attend."

"Get him out of here, and take yourself with him." Stitch jerked a chin toward Ducky.

"Will she recover?"

"Doubt it." He bent over Samantha, placing his ear to her chest. "Go on. Give me room to work."

Ducky didn't need to be told twice. He grabbed at the back of James's coat and tugged him toward the door.

As soon as it closed behind them, Ducky spun on him. "Who the hell was that woman?"

James started to cover his face with his hands before realizing they were covered in Samantha's blood. *I have her blood on my hands. How fitting.*

Ducky pulled a fine linen square from his pocket and pushed it into James's hands. "Answer me, damn it."

"I'm sorry. This was what I needed to tell you earlier. Don't you recognize her?"

"Recognize her?" He looked at James as if he'd gone mad. Perhaps he had. His head pounded. Is this what madness felt like?

Ducky grabbed his lapels and shook him. "James. Who is the woman in your bed?"

"Samantha Christian."

"That's impossible. How—?"

"I know it sounds like insanity, but I swear to you it's the truth. She was on the *Scarlet Night*, passing as a cabin boy."

Ducky pointed toward the closed door. "And why is she naked in your bed?"

James rubbed at his forehead. "Please tell me you noticed the gaping wound at her hip, or did the sight of bared breasts render you senseless? The woman is busy dying. Where else would you like me to put her?" James looked back at the door. He should be with her.

"There was no report of another woman."

"Stitch and I wanted to keep word of it to ourselves. Needless to say, he noticed she wasn't a he. No need having the men informed. Superstitions still run high. It's bad enough to have Tupper Quinn aboard. My only thought was keeping her away from the men. I hadn't thought beyond that. Then I saw her face."

"However did you recognize her? She looks nothing like I remember."

"You remember little from the ball beyond the pleasures of Justine Whatever-her-name's overflowing bodice." James dropped his head back against the doorframe. "I danced with Samantha, spoke with her." *Kissed her in the shadows.* He stared at the ceiling. If asked, he could describe which shade of brown matched her lovely eyes. "She was rather unforgettable."

Ducky stood alongside him and mimicked his stance. "Bloody hell, James, could the capturing of the *Scarlet Night* be any more of a bane to your existence?"

James closed his eyes. "She could have been carrying plague."

"Ever the optimist."

He shook his head and opened his eyes, giving Ducky a guilty glance. "I have another confession."

Ducky shot a worried glare toward him. "Pray, tell me it has nothing to do with Samantha Christian."

"When I saw her, I swear my heart tried to leap out of my chest."

Ducky nodded in sympathy. "In panic."

"No. Joy." James stepped away from the doorframe and faced him. A frown knitted his brows together. "I spent mere moments with her, less than an hour, and yet, I haven't been able to get her out of my mind since." He rubbed his hand over his jaw. "I've never experienced anything remotely similar when I see Lillian." James groaned. "Even speaking her name now fills me with shame. She should be with a man who feels joy when he sees her."

"Whoa." Ducky held his hands up in surrender. "You can't be thinking of passing over Lillian for some woman you barely know who is currently bleeding all over your quarters. Are you daft? You're forgetting several important points. Several hundreds of thousands of points."

"I'm not marrying Lillian for her fortune."

"It isn't for her warmth and passionate nature," Ducky muttered. Before James could defend her, he added, "And what about the small matter of Samantha Christian's warrant for piracy?"

"She's innocent." James stared back at the door, willing it to open and for Stitch to tell him she'd live.

"So she didn't sign on to the *Scarlet Night* crew?"

James shrugged. "She did, but there are circumstances—"

"Circumstances like you have feelings for the woman?"

"Someone has to step up and be her champion."

Ducky's eyebrows pushed toward his hairline. "Strong feelings, then?"

"You don't know the whole story."

"I don't need to. You're the prince of black and white. She signed the Articles." Ducky ticked off one finger. "She served on the crew in some capacity." He raised two fingers. "She didn't get that little cut on her side shaving, which tells me she battled against a British Naval vessel. Our man wouldn't have struck with such force unless she was armed. Am I correct?"

James ran an anxious hand over his hair. "The pistol wasn't loaded."

"Doesn't matter." Ducky held up three fingers. "All it takes is one to make her guilty."

Before James could respond, Stitch emerged, wiping his hands. "How is she?"

"Alive for now. If the fever doesn't break soon, there's no hope for her. I re-sewed the wound. Gave her more laudanum. If she survives the night, she may just live." Stitch started to leave. "I'll send up one of my men to stay with her."

"That won't be necessary."

Stitch spun on him. "You said the same thing before."

"I made a mistake. It will not happen again."

Stitch planted his hands on his hips. "She has to be bathed to keep her temperature down, and kept quiet."

"I said I would tend to her."

"Suit yourself, Captain, but if she rips those sutures, again, there's little I can do."

"She won't."

"I'll be back later." Stitch gave James a weary salute and left.

Ducky shook his head. "This is not a good idea."

James shot him an impatient look. "Do you have a better one?"

Ducky waved a hand at the door. "You're too involved. You're not being objective."

James threw his hands wide. "I'm being as objective as I can be, given the circumstances. I didn't foresee any of this, but I can't deny my overwhelming desire to protect Samantha. She's been to hell and back already. If any member of the *Scarlet Night* crew has a defense, it's her." James slapped Ducky on the shoulder. "I'm grateful for your counsel, but let's see if she survives the next twenty-four hours."

Chapter 17

James stayed by Samantha's side. His fingertips resembled pale dried fruit as he rinsed and wrung cooling cloths to lie upon Sam's heated body. After four hours, he gave her another dose of laudanum. Still the fever raged through her.

Stitch returned shortly before tea. He laid a hand to her forehead. "Her temperature is still dangerously high. We may be fighting too strong a foe on this one."

James rinsed another cloth. "I'm not done fighting, and neither is she."

"Why not let me take over? It looks like it's going to be a long night. You should get some food in your belly."

James shook his head. "I'm not hungry."

"Let me bring you something."

"I'm fine," he snapped.

Stitch brought him a mug of watered ale. "Drink, then, and see if you can get some into her. With a fever this high, she'll get dehydrated easily."

After he left, James spooned a bit of liquid into Samantha's mouth. He wiped a stray drop from her lip and sighed. "When I watched you leave the Whitmore's ball with that man, I knew you were in some kind of trouble. I should have followed. Trusted my instincts. Had I, I wonder if you'd be here now? A day has not passed where you haven't crossed my mind. I tried to push such thoughts away, but you sparked something in me with your kiss." He slipped the spoon once more between her lips. "More than anything I wish you would open your eyes and let me kiss you all over again."

He set the mug aside. "You asked me to forgive you. I only hope you can be the one to forgive me." James brushed at the damp hair clinging to her temples. One perfect dark curl caught at his finger. "Open your eyes, Samantha."

James lost track of the hours, but some time before the gray blush of dawn announced the start of another day, the fever's hold on Samantha broke. He did his best to change the bedding and slip her into a dry shirt of his.

Stitch stopped by again after dawn. "I'm shocked. I wouldn't have bet two bits on her. On you either, for that matter. If you ever want to give up your commission as captain and join us down in the surgery..."

James held up a weary hand. "No, thank you. One patient is more than enough." He stood and stretched out his back. "What's to be done now?"

"Now you go get some sleep. I can stay, if you'd like."

James shook his head. He wasn't going anywhere. "Not necessary."

"Let her rest. Try to get more liquid into her. I'll send down some broth from the galley to build her strength. And breakfast for you. Don't even think about arguing with me." Stitch covered the patient. "Last thing I need is to be playing nursemaid to you."

True to his word, a tray of food and broth arrived a short time later. James managed to get Samantha to swallow a few more spoons of weak ale. She was still far too pale, but at least her skin was cool and dry.

He slipped her hand in his, unwilling to let a little thing like utter exhaustion break their connection. Sweeping a gentle touch across the backs of her fingers, he finally allowed himself the luxury of closing his eyes for a moment or two.

"James?"

He jerked awake. The sun was high. How long had he been asleep? He shot a glance at Samantha and nearly shouted with joy. Her lovely eyes were open. Had he ever seen a more beautiful sight?

"Samantha." He kissed the back of her hand still held by him. "Thank you, God."

"W-what happened?" She rubbed at her eyes. "I remember asking you about Tupper..." She plucked at her sleeve. "My memory is so fuzzy, but I know I'm on your ship." Samantha tried shifting. "Oh, God...it hurts." She grimaced.

James held her still. "What hurts?"

"I think everything," she whimpered.

"That doesn't surprise me. You've had a rough time of it, but you're alive and that's the important thing." He brought her the broth. "Doctor's orders." James held the small bowl to her mouth, but she took it from his hands. "Let me try and fill some of the holes in your memory."

He told her of the last forty-eight hours, assuring her Tupper and the man they call Bump were alive, how sick she'd been, and how relieved he'd been when her fever broke.

"You've stayed with me this whole time?"

"Aye."

"I'm grateful, but," she frowned, "I can't help wondering why."

James didn't answer.

"You captured our ship. Aren't I your prisoner?"

"It's more complicated than that."

"I'm afraid my mind is too jumbled to make sense of it all." She winced again as she tried to move.

"We've plenty of time to straighten it all out, I promise you. You're safe and under my protection." He handed her another dose of laudanum. "The only thing you need worry about is resting and gaining back your strength."

Samantha met his gaze over the rim of her cup. "I chose the most handsome man in the Whitmore's ballroom to dance with the night of the ball. Who could have guessed our paths would cross again like this?"

"Some might call it fate."

Samantha's eyes slid closed. "Or in your case, Captain...perhaps I'm just a bit of bad luck."

* * * *

Two days passed. Little by little, Samantha got stronger.... as did James's feelings for her. She was still sleeping for long stretches. The laudanum saw to that. James was able to leave her for small spans of time to see to his other duties, but she was never far from his thoughts.

Stitch came less now, pleased with her progress. "Give her another few days, and she'll be well enough to join the others."

As the *Lion* roared over the waves toward London, James knew his days with Samantha were numbered. He had yet to formally charge her with her crimes, claiming her health was more important. But the truth was, once the words were said, it made everything official. The hourglass of the fates would be turned. He hadn't come up with a solid plan to resolve things for Samantha or Tupper. The horrifying prospect of what was to come circled the perimeter of his thoughts and kept him awake through the long hours of the night.

His prisoners below were sullen but compliant. James considered their recent request for some air time above deck. He had the manpower to keep them contained, but with prisoners it was wise to be wary.

When he returned to his cabin late that afternoon, the sight of Samantha awake and sitting up filled him at once with equal parts of delight and distress.

"I feel as if I should say 'good morning,' but the sunlight tells me I'm too late."

James hung his hat and heavy uniform coat. "Aye, I'm afraid it's past six bells."

She gave a small shrug and tucked an errant curl of her hair behind her ear. "I never know what all the bells mean."

"And you claim to be a sailor." He grinned as he loosened his neckcloth. "Six bells means it's three o'clock. It's rung at each three, seven, and eleven."

"Why wouldn't you just ring the bells three, seven, and eleven times?"

"Fair question." He sat near her and studied her lovely face. Her eyes were bright. A slight blush warmed her cheeks. James laid the back of his fingers against the pinked cheek. It was cool. "The official answer is quite boring, but I was always told it's less confusing this way."

She grinned. "Not to me."

"My father still clocks the day with bells. It makes Mother cringe, but the staff doesn't seem to mind."

"We had to rely on the church bells in the village."

"The one with the impossibly tall spire at the east edge of town?"

"Yes. You do know South Oxbridge as well as you claim." Samantha lowered her gaze and fiddled with the folds of her blanket. "It seems a lifetime ago since I was there."

"Why did you leave?"

She gave him a small sad smile. "I was a silly girl with fanciful dreams. I went off to meet my true love, save my family from poverty and hardship, and live an idyllic life full of promise." Samantha tucked her chin. "But the promises were empty ones, and there was nothing true about the love."

"Wessler." James hated saying the bastard's name.

Samantha turned to look away. "I'd rather not talk about him."

"But there is something I need to know. After the night we met... how did you get from there to passing as a cabin boy on the *Scarlet Night*?"

It took her a long moment to answer him while she worried her lower lip. "Isabelle and Rebecca Whitmore. They knew his sons, and witnessed some of Wessler's cruelty. They reached out to me in friendship and sympathy. They were my lifeline, but Damian hated them. He refused to allow me to visit or even speak with them after a while. We became quite clever in getting messages to one another, but things were growing worse by the day. They were afraid for me."

She twisted the edging of her blanket. "The night of the ball, I was told a savior was coming to rescue me," she continued. "Tupper. I had to make sure Damian's punishments would include him locking me away in my room." Samantha lifted her eyes to his. "That's where you came into the story. I'm ashamed to say I used you."

Her gaze locked with his. "Which is why you asked me to forgive you."

She nodded, her throat working against the sudden welling of tears in her eyes. "I danced with you so he would see me. Led you onto the veranda knowing he would have to follow and find us...me...in a compromised position. That's why I kissed you." She covered her eyes. "I didn't think it through, however. I never imagined Wessler would turn some of his anger toward you. That's why I feigned drunkenness. To aim it all back on me."

The image of her bruises returned to his mind. "Your plan worked."

She nodded. "Wessler...he reacted as I knew he would. Tupper arrived two days later. I don't know what I would have done had she not come." Tears shimmered in her eyes. She blinked them back. "I should have listened to her and stayed below during the battle, but she'd risked so much to come for me. I couldn't sit hiding while she was captured or killed. I couldn't. But something went wrong with the pistol. I've been over it in my mind a dozen times. I don't understand what I did incorrectly. I clicked back the part holding the flint twice, like she showed me."

Samantha shrugged. "I squeezed the trigger. Then everything slowed down, got quiet, as if the battle had somehow concentrated on what was happening just with me. The gun didn't fire. A huge man swung his sword, and the world went black." She shook her head and looked back at him. "The next thing I saw was you. I thought for a moment I was still at the Whitmore's."

"It was a shock for me as well, finding you amongst the wounded. Gave our surgeon a shock as well, discovering you weren't a lad." He tucked the same stubborn curl behind her ear again. "Why didn't you tell me you were in trouble at the ball? I could have helped you."

Samantha's eyes widened. "What would I have said to you? 'Would you dance with me, Captain Steele, and save me from a mad man? Please, before we have punch?' I was a stranger dressed like a rotted plum. You're heroic and gallant, but even you would have run as far from me as you could."

"Well, if you'd put it like that..." He lifted her hand, turning it over to trace his thumb along her palm. He started to promise her all would be well, that he would somehow keep her safe from what lay ahead, but he couldn't make such a lie. "I am far from heroic or gallant. I have no right, but all I want to do is wrap my arms around you."

"Before we have punch?"

He smiled, smoothing his hand over the back of hers before lifting it to his mouth for a kiss. Meeting her eyes, he gave in to the desire he'd had since their first kiss ended so abruptly. He stood and crooked his finger to catch beneath her chin, lifting her face as he lowered his to capture her mouth.

Chapter 18

Samantha slipped her hand around the back of his neck as the kiss deepened. Their first kiss had rumbled through her like summer thunder. This kiss was lightning. Bright hot, it lit up her entire being. His finger, tipping her chin, stroked down the front of her throat as he urged her lips to part. Shamelessly, she opened them to the sweep of his tongue, angled her mouth, and kissed him soundly in return. More lightning.

She should end this, push him away. But every inch of her wanted to pull him closer. She ached to feel his arms around her, his hands on her. Somehow she knew he'd love her with a slow, earth-shattering gentleness.

The bite of her wound was her saving grace. Shifting her knee sent a sharp-edged reminder. At her gasp, James broke the connection with a start. The blue of his gaze held hers a moment longer. Their breathing matched, coming fast and hard, his fanning the hair curling at her cheek.

"Forgive me," he murmured before pulling away. Before she could answer, he doned his woolen coat and left.

Samantha dropped her head back against the pillow with a groan. Her body pulsed with a mixture of need and shame. He was promised to another. A wedding awaited him for goodness sakes. His future was bright and set. Hers was a shambles. She covered her eyes. What was she thinking, kissing him like that?

She was thinking she'd never known such kindness or caring from a man. Was she confusing desire with a deep sense of gratitude? No, it was much much more. Samantha brushed her swollen lips with her fingertips. She could still feel his there. Passion drove his kiss. Desire. She could still taste it. It was like honey to someone who had only tasted bitterness, and she wanted more.

"You've overstep your boundaries," she scolded herself. "Wanting someone you can never have. Craving what you don't deserve."

She was his prisoner and his patient. Any feelings of caring came from his sense of compassion. It was foolish for her to spin it in spun sugar and see it for anything more. He was promised to another...another finer and far better matched than her. Did his betrothed love him? Did he love her?

"Aaahhh." Samantha groaned at the paneled ceiling. *Stop this now, before it goes too far.* He's simply a man—a polite, caring, handsome, compassionate man. She'd built him up into something else in her weeks of daydreams since kissing him at the ball. Something more than what he was. He was a fantasy that swept her away on a dance floor. A steeded champion to a damsel in distress. A strapping figure wrapped in a uniform. What woman could resist a man in uniform? How ridiculous. It was clothing. A woolen coat trimmed in gold. Nothing more. Worn by a man....

A man whose kisses stole her breathe. Whose eyes reminded Samantha of a clear summer morn. A man who didn't sleep for two days while he nursed her, bathed her, dressed her in his shirt, and gave up his bed for her.

"I'm a hopeless fool."

Still recovering, she slept fitfully through the day. James had left the laudanum nearby if she needed it, but she chose to bear the pain. The drug muddled her mind as it dragged her into a dark pool of sleep. She hated the grogginess when she woke. No, she'd rather feel the pull of her stitches and be alert when James returned. If he returned.

As the day melted into night, Samantha grew more and more agitated. She'd done little else but watch the damn door and practice how she'd apologize to him.

She had questions, too, about what was to happen next. To her. To Tupper and the rest. What would happen to Bump? She eyed the laudanum. Perhaps muddled wasn't the worst thing.

It was late when Samantha heard the door open. Low lanterns dimly lit the room. She'd decided against the drug, but had fallen asleep once more without it. Before she could speak to James, another man entered.

"How is she?"

Samantha was quick to close her eyes and lay quiet. "Sleeping still, but she's out of the woods."

"And sailing smack into the middle of a bloody forest."

"Shh, you'll wake her." James lowered his voice. Samantha strained to hear, "Don't remind me," he sighed. "I've yet to tell her."

"You haven't issued the petition? What are you waiting for?"

"I thought I'd let her regain consciousness first." A drawer opened.

Samantha heard the sound of glass hitting glass. They were drinking James's brandy.

"Are you sure that's all?"

James groaned. "I beg you, I'm in no mood."

"Have you slept since they moved her in here? I know you haven't visited the officer's quarters."

"Not much. Exhaustion has nothing to do with this, however. For the first time in days, I've come to some realizations. I've been pacing the decks for hours, and while I might not be able to prevent Tupper Quinn from hanging alongside her crew, I refuse to hang an innocent woman. I finally have all the pieces to the puzzle, and I'm convinced the only thing Samantha Christian is guilty of is being an idealist and believing the lies of some sick bastard in Virginia. The only reason she was on the *Scarlet Night* was to escape him. She was in a desperate situation, and Tupper Quinn was her way out. Samantha would have followed Tupper into hell to get away."

Samantha's stomach pitched. Fear crept along her spine. Tupper and Bump were being taken to their execution. Her neck was in the noose as well, even if James believed her innocence.

"She was an active member of the crew." The man with James argued his point.

He was right... There was no denying it.

"I'll borrow Tupper's lie. Samantha Christian was a hostage. Dragged aboard against her will."

"She freely signed the Articles. How do you plan on erasing her name?"

"The Articles were lost. Burned in a fire. Blown overboard in a storm."

"Listen to yourself, James. You're not talking sense. Without the Articles, the rest of them sail away free. Along with your career, and your future. You've worked too hard to achieve the rank of captain and this commission, and you're ready to throw away the last ten years? Your life is steps away from being golden. Think, man. What about Lillian?"

At the mention of her name, Samantha gave a silent groan. The man was right. It was all too much.

"What about her?" James countered.

"Are you considering her at all?"

"Of course I am. I'm considering telling her she'd be far better off with a man who isn't in love with someone else."

Samantha bit her lip to keep from gasping. Did he say—

"Be serious. You don't love Samantha Christian. You don't even know her."

"I do know her. It may not have been for months and years, but each moment I'm with her, I learn a bit more and fall a little bit harder. I know I can't get her out of my mind, and how I feel when I'm with her, kissing her. How the thought of losing—"

"Hold on. Kissing her? When did this happen?"

"Doesn't matter, Ducky. I'm telling you, I'm in love with her."

Samantha's heart skidded in her chest.

"James, I'm your best mate. I'm also your first lieutenant. Please hear me. You may love her, but all the love in the world isn't enough to save her."

The two men were silent for a long moment. Samantha trembled with a flood of battling emotions. James loved her. As the words struck her heart, she knew at once she loved him in return. It made no sense. James's friend *was* right. They barely knew one another. But who could explain love? Was there a more unpredictable emotion? It was not something you could choose, or control. It struck... like...lightning.

Samantha wanted to shout for joy and curl into a ball and weep all at the same time. The man, Ducky, was correct on another count. None of this made any difference. She was to be counted amongst the crew of the *Scarlet Night*. When they landed in London, it would be the end of them. All James's love and position and influence could not change the outcome, and she wasn't about to let him ruin the rest of his life by lying for her.

She stifled another moan. Why were the fates so brutally cruel? Why lead her to her true love, only to rip her from him? Why show her heaven, but deliver her to hell?

"I can't lose her now that I've found her." James's words echoed the ache in her heart.

The sound of glass meeting glass sounded again. "All I can say is, we're not in London yet. It may all crash in on you once we arrive, but if you truly love her, then love her well in the time you have." Ducky's voice was muffled, as if he spoke into his glass.

"And Lillian?"

"She doesn't wear your ring yet. You've certainly not consummated your relationship, or kissed more than a hand or a powdered cheek. Has she mentioned the word love? No. Your marriage to Lillian is a business negotiation, not a courtship. Until you stand in front of a priest and say, 'I do,' you are not legally bound to her. Now, I'm all for fidelity and monogamy after you're joined. I'm a confirmed cad, but I do have some scruples. But if you still choose a life with her, after this is all over, you can go to her with your eyes open, if not your heart."

"I won't lie to her."

"So don't lie. Not to Lillian, not to Samantha, and most of all, my good man, not to yourself."

There was another pause in the men's conversation. Samantha tucked her chin and brushed away silent tears.

"Any chance we won't reach London?" James voice carried his exhaustion.

"We could sail into the eye of a hurricane and be lost at sea. Cross paths with the entire Spanish fleet and be blown out of the water. Or perhaps we'll be caught by a kraken and dragged down into the briny deep."

"Ah, at last, something to hope for."

Chapter 19

Ducky left James to his drink and his thoughts. James put the stopper back into the neck of the brandy carafe. Exhaustion hung on him like a heavy, wet cloak. He pulled at the tight cue of his hair, releasing it, and pushed his hands through the strands to hold his aching head.

He didn't want to think any more. Please, someone shut off his blasted mind. Cease the endless loop of his musings. Let him be blissfully ignorant for an hour or two.

Dragging a deep breath into his lungs, he opened his eyes and surveyed the trappings of his office. Logbooks, navigation charts, arrest petitions… Nay, ignorance for him was not an option. He was captain. There were duties to perform. A ship to run. Three hundred men to command. Three hundred men…and two women.

James pushed the brandy aside, slid the logbooks before him, and rolled up the sleeves of his shirt. Raising the wick of his lantern, he glanced at Samantha, not wanting the light to wake her.

Instead, the warmth of her gaze greeted him.

"Samantha… I didn't mean to wake you. I'm sorry."

She shook her head. "No, I was awake."

Sitting behind his desk, he felt too far from her. He stood and moved to sit on the side of the bed. "How are you feeling?" The urge to touch her was too strong. He ran the back of his finger along her cheek.

"I'm well." She captured his hand and held his gaze.

"About earlier…after I kissed you. When I left so abruptly…"

"You don't need to explain."

"But I do. There's so much we need to talk about. Things you need to be made aware of."

"I know," she whispered.

She looked at him with such trust, it made his stomach twist to have to tell her, but he could not continue to lie to her. Protecting her from the truth wasn't protecting her any longer. It was only delaying the inevitable. "I pray I find the right words."

"James...I wasn't asleep." She studied his hand. "I heard you and your friend talking. I didn't mean to eavesdrop, but..."

"How much did you hear?"

"Everything." She lifted her eyes to his. "I heard every word."

"So you know I have no choice. Now that you're stronger, I can't put it off. I must formally arrest you." He squeezed her hand. "When we reach London, I'll not leave your side. We'll go directly to my supervisors, tell them your story. They must—"

"You love me."

The words flooded his chest. "Aye." He swallowed the sudden lump in his throat. "I would have liked to have said the words to you first, and not to a man named after a blasted water fowl, but yes."

"Then say them to me now."

"It makes no sense. A month ago I didn't know your name, and there couldn't be a worse time or situation to declare my feelings, but I can't seem to help them even if I wanted to."

Samantha put her fingers over his rambling mouth to stop the inane prattle. "Say the words." She lifted her fingers away from his lips.

"I love you, Samantha. Inexplicably, completely, hopelessly."

"And I inexplicably, completely, hopelessly love you as well."

It was as if the sun rose in his chest. "You do?"

"Yes, I do."

He leaned in close and kissed her, the words still bittersweet on his tongue. She loved him. She rained sweet kisses over his lips, cheeks, and his closed eyes until he pulled her mouth back to his. Holding her face, he slanted his mouth and fully captured hers. Claiming her. Pouring his heart into that single heated kiss.

He rested his forehead on hers. Eyes closed, he brushed the tip of her nose with his. "Good Lord, woman, what do we do now?"

"Stop the clocks? Slow the movement of the sun? Chart a course to London taking a more westerly route?"

He pulled back to look her in the eye. "Don't joke."

She stroked his cheek. "Your friend may be named after a mallard, but he made a few good points."

"Such as?"

"We are not in London yet."

James shook his head. "But we can't ignore it."

"Tonight we can." She toyed with the neck of his shirt.

"Samantha..." She couldn't possibly be suggesting what he imagined. Her body was still healing. He pulled away before he forgot himself and hurt her.

She caught his arm. "Lie with me. Sleep in your bed rather than your awful chair. Hold me. Let me hold you. Kiss me good night. That's all. Your surgeon would never forgive us if we attempted more. Just lie with me." Samantha gave him a small smile. "We may not have any more time than we have right now. Once we reach London...neither of us can know what's to come." She stroked his arm. "I don't want to waste a single moment."

She gingerly moved to the far side of the bed to give him room. Offering him the solace of a simple night in her arms to share the intimacy of sleep, to relish every moment they had together. After the days and nights of worry and strain, it sounded like a small bit of heaven wrapped in silk.

"I think a night cradled in your arms sounds like a wonderful idea." He turned and began pulling off his boots.

Samantha rested a hand on his back. "Could you help me take off your shirt?"

"You don't need to undress me. I can manage." He grinned and pulled the shirt from his trousers, then lifted it over his head, casting it aside.

Her hand returned to his back. This time her fingers splayed across his skin, smoothing the muscle, sending tiny ripples of pleasure across his flesh.

"I wasn't talking about the one *you* were wearing."

Heat surged through him. He shot a glance over his shoulder. She shrugged hers. "It's not as if you haven't seen me naked before."

"That was different. You were burning up with fever." He knew how she'd felt. Any moment now, he was sure to burst into flames.

"I'm still a bit warm." Her fingertips sparked paths across his skin.

"And you were weak."

She gave him a small grin. "I'm stronger now."

He bit back a note of laughter. "I'm not." What was she trying to do? Drive him mad?

She ran her hands over his shoulder again, following the sweep with her gaze. "I trust you."

"I don't. I wouldn't trust me for a second." The pulse of his erection was proof of that. Lie with her and not touch her? Find some way to take her without hurting her? She couldn't know what she was suggesting.

"I want to feel your skin next to mine. That's all."

That's all? "I thought you were offering me rest. It's sounding more like a test of my resolve. One I'm sure to lose."

"You've misunderstood. I'm not trying to catch you in a web. I've never seduced a man before."

James bit out another short laugh. "You're doing a fine job of it."

"Help me get rid of this shirt, and I'll stop. I'll say no more and lie beside you quiet as a lamb."

"There is nothing quiet about naked. Naked is the exact opposite of quiet. In fact, two nakeds together practically scream."

"You can leave your hat on," she suggested, blinking up at him with wide innocent eyes.

"And my pants," he insisted.

"I have no pants," she whispered against his shoulder.

He closed his eyes and groaned. "You're getting loud again."

"Would kissing me make me quiet?"

"No. It would only stop you from talking."

With great care, he slipped his shirt from her, gathered her close, and stopped her from speaking while his body howled with restrained need.

Samantha wound an arm about his neck, arching into a gentle curve against him. The soft warmth of her breasts pressed into his chest. The satin sensation of her skin on his was almost more than he could bear as her heat penetrated along his entire length.

"Have I mentioned that I love you?"

"Not in the last ten minutes."

"I'll order myself keelhauled at first light." He kissed her lightly again.

"What's 'keelhauled?'"

"Well, you take a long length of rope, tie it around a man, toss him overboard, and drag him across the keel of the ship."

Samantha smoothed a hand over his chest, tracing around the rim of his nipple. "But there are barnacles down there. It sounds painful."

"Very." Although at that moment, he could think of something almost as painful. He tried shifting the position of his trapped cock. Any more of this "quiet" discussion and he might split his trousers.

"Are you uncomfortable?"

Very. "I'll survive."

"Are you sure you wouldn't rest better without your trousers?"

He narrowed his eyes at her. "You're sure you've never seduced a man before?"

"Never."

James kissed her once more. "Then you're a bloody natural."

Chapter 20

James strolled along the bustling upper decks of the *Lion* the next morning no more rested than he'd been before he slipped into bed beside Samantha last night. They'd kissed and whispered in the dark half the night. The other half he spent trying to ignore the pale tipped peaks of her breasts he desperately wanted to taste, or the way her navel dipped into a tiny spiral, or the silken feel of her hair against his shoulder as she slept against him.

"Good morning, Captain." Stitch met him standing at the bow. The sun already burned bright over the waves. James had only just noticed.

"How long can a man survive without sleep?" Perhaps a better question would be how long could a man walk around with a wooden cock in his breeches.

"About eleven days. Why?"

"Curiosity." He turned away and began another sweep.

"Have you tried counting sheep?" he suggested.

I'll lay beside you as quiet as a lamb. "No, but I'll give it a try."

"I could give you something to help."

He shifted the ache in his trousers. "I'll be fine."

"How's the patient?"

Still naked in my bed. "Doing well. I think she's in a lot less pain."

"Good. Her stitches can come out soon, then it should be safe for her to resume regular activity. Slowly at first."

"Slowly?" Lusty images ran through James's mind…slowly.

"Right," Stitch continued. "Being impatient and rushing these things is always a great concern."

"I couldn't agree with you more." He slapped Stitch on the shoulder and checked to make sure his waistcoat covered his impatient erection.

"Could be as early as tomorrow. I'll stop by your quarters later and check on things."

"Make sure you knock," he muttered under his breath.

Ducky fell into step. "What happened to you last night? I thought you were finally going to get some sleep after you finished with the logs."

"Decided to stretch out somewhere else."

"Least you got some rest." He leaned closer and lowered his voice. "Did you get a chance to talk to Samantha?"

No, I was too consumed with keeping her quiet. "Some."

"Good, good. Speaking of prisoners, I've just come from the brig. Tensions are running a bit high down there. I'm not sure what's happened. They're quiet, but there's something in the air, and it isn't the stench of unwashed bodies. Although there's one Scotsman…man would make your eyes water." Ducky ran a finger under his nose. "They've made another request for some deck time. Might be a good idea to air them out a bit."

"Don't see what harm it would do. Gather enough men to discourage any unruliness."

"Shackles?"

It was bad enough to see Tupper sitting in a cell. Clapping her in irons seemed unnecessary. None of her men fought their arrests. Hadn't she mentioned the man, Bump, would be seriously affected by shackles? "Let's see how it goes without. Just see there are three men to their one. No one takes their eyes off them for a second."

"Aye, aye." Ducky frowned. "Are you sure you got some sleep? You still look like shit, old man."

"Maybe I could use a little more time in the sack. Stitch thought counting sheep might work for me."

"A bit of physical activity might help, as well. Couldn't hurt. The strain is written all over your face." He swept a hand. "Everything is running smooth throughout. Go. Take a few hours. Do a few pushups, and you'll sleep like a baby."

Entering his quarters, James found Samantha as he'd left her—asleep and bare beneath the sheets. He stripped down to nothing but his breeches, considered another moment, before removing them as well before climbing in alongside her.

At his touch, she started, shrunk back and cried out in pain and fright. A look of utter panic crossed her face before instinct had her cowering and covering her face.

"Samantha, it's me. Oh, God, I'm an idiot. I'm sorry."

"Oh…James…I-I thought." She held a shaking hand over her heart. The other reached out to touch him, as if to assure herself he was real or keep him at arm's length, he wasn't sure which. She pulled the blanket up to cover her naked breasts.

"Samantha, I'm sorry." He watched her throat work as she tried to still the panic that raced through her and pulsed visibly at the notch of her throat.

"No, I'm the one to-to be sorry." She closed her eyes and pulled a deep breath into her lungs. "Y-you surprised me is all."

James reached out a tentative hand. He smoothed his palm over the curve of her shoulder. Beneath his touch, she trembled. "I didn't think. I'm sorry. Are you all right?"

She gave a quick nod, but he could tell she was lying.

"You have to believe I would never hurt you."

She nodded again. This time it wasn't a lie.

James didn't move, giving her time to gather herself. Inside, he recoiled in disgust and white-hot anger. What had that monster done to her? He wanted to turn around this instant and sail back to Virginia for the sole purpose of beating the life out of one Damian Wessler. Of course, that would come after he finished beating up on himself for being an insensitive bastard.

He didn't know all the gory details of what she'd endured, but he knew enough. Bloody hell, the evidence still shook in his bed.

"I'm sorry." Wide eyes captured his before she forced a small smile. "I startle far too easily."

"I'm the one who's sorry. Would it be all right if I held you?"

She pulled in a shaky breath. "Of course."

He moved nearer, ready to retreat should she begin to panic again. Slipping his arms around her, he tucked her beneath his chin and kissed the top of her head. He held her close but not as tight as he would have liked. He was afraid if he tried, she'd shatter like crystal.

After a while, she softened in his arms and leaned her head against his chest. He stroked her back and reclined, still holding her firmly to him. James pulled a blanket over them both and slowly counted the beats of her heart.

* * * *

The sun kissed Tupper's face for the first time in days. She pulled in great gulps of fresh air as she and the rest of the *Scarlet Night* crew were given a short respite. Their request for a bit of deck time had been granted. Her once fearsome crew stood squinting in the bright sunlight like a labor of motley moles.

Armed British sailors flanked an open area, giving them no question as to what would happen if any of the crew were to make a misstep.

Allan and Butler glared in her direction. Several others joined in their superstitious grumblings. Let them. She'd explained herself once; she wouldn't do it again. If they needed someone to blame for the state they were in, she might as well be the scapegoat. It wouldn't change a damn thing, and she couldn't give a rat's arse.

Tupper skirted around them and found Bump. She signed the words, "Are you all right?"

He nodded.

She pointed to her head, asking about his injury. He nodded again, but was distracted, scanning the ship in both directions. A frown darkened his glare. Tupper tapped his arm to get his attention. "What is it?"

'S.' 'A.' 'M.' He made the sign of a question.

Tupper shrugged and shook her head. "I don't know. Last I heard she was alive." With thumbs up, she tapped her waist, then her chest, with her fists. "I would have heard if something happened to her."

Bump moved away. Tupper watched his retreating back. She sat in the shade of one of the masts. Twice. In the entire lifetime she had spent with Bump, she had never lied to him, and now she'd done so twice in as many weeks. The reasons now were as valid as the reasons then. All she wanted was to keep him safe. Shield him from the ire of the crew for being her accomplice in bringing Samantha aboard, and now she wanted to protect his misguided heart. Wherever Samantha was, Tupper was sure James Steele was close by her side. What faced them at the end of this journey was enough. Bump shouldn't have to meet his maker with a shattered heart.

"He's been as chatty as ever." MacTavish dropped down beside her and jerked his head toward Bump.

Tupper sent him a side glance. "I didn't think you were speaking to me."

"I wasn't."

"Just my luck," she snorted. "You've forgiven me."

"I ken why ye lied." He shrugged, knocking his shoulder against hers. "Ye could'a told me the truth, ye ken."

"So then they'd be hatin' you now." She jerked a chin toward Butler and Allan. "Best not spread their joy around. I was the captain. The biggest share comes with the biggest risk. I knew I was taking a chance. Better it be all on my head."

"Still. I thought we were mates."

"We are, ye hairy troll."

They were both quiet for a moment. MacTavish broke the silence. "Ye ken the worst part in all this?"

"Beside the hanging?"

"Aye, there's that. Nay, it be too much time te think." He scratched at his chest. "I ain't had so much time te woolgather in me whole life."

"Sorting through regrets?"

"I got none o' those. Nay, it's the 'whatif's.' Wondering if ye'd stepped wit yer left foot one day instead of yer right, would ye still have reached where ye sittin.' Not regrets, really, but if ye said 'yes' instead of 'no,' 'no' instead of 'yes.'" He dropped his head back against the mast. "Where would ye be now?"

"Maybe it's a good thing ye never know. Not like ye can go back and do it over again."

He turned to look at her. "Anything you'd do different?"

Tupper shook her head, then stopped and shrugged. "There was that week-long bender a few years back, where I ended waking up face down twenty miles from where I started, with Gavin's name entwined with roses tattooed on my arse."

MacTavish snorted. "I remember it well. Tuk four days te find ye. Coulda been worse. Coulda been my name on yer arse."

"Both halves and down one leg." She laughed.

"Ye had a good man there. Tattoo or no."

Tupper nodded. "I've been thinking about him a lot the last few days. I'm glad he ain't a part of this."

"Ye did 'im proud, taking over like ye did. Ye can't think ye didna have a good run of it."

Her hands swept the deck. "We're still sitting here with these tea swillers waiting to swing."

MacTavish knocked against her again. "But blast an' go blind, ye bloody stripe-haired bitch, admit it, we've had one hell of a ride."

Chapter 21

Sometime after six bells—Samantha's new but limited bell knowledge had become a tiny source of pride with her. The only occasions when she was positive about the time were at three, seven, and eleven o'clock.

It was a bit after those six bells next morning when the surgeon James referred to as Stitch returned to remove the sutures from Samantha's hip.

"Looks well healed. A miracle considering the infection, but there'll be no helping the scar." He finished quickly. "You can be moving about a might freer now. The rest of the prisoners have been allowed to spend time on deck. Might do you some good, as well. Clean air and sunshine is the best medicine, but take it slow. Your legs will feel like pudding for a few days still."

Stitch covered her once more with the sheet. "Course you'll be needing some breeches. I had to cut away the ones you came with when they first carried you into the surgery." He turned to James, who'd been working and watching from his desk. "I could scrounge her up a pair."

"Thank you. That would be helpful. She's not going on deck wearing nothing but my best shirt."

Samantha smiled as she fussed with the cuffs. In the last few days, she'd been out of his best shirt more than she'd been in. She thanked the doctor and waited until the door closed behind him before she swung her legs out of bed and took her first official stroll.

It was fourteen steps over dangerous terrain of smooth polished wood and thick wool rugs to reach her final destination--James's lap. The doctor was right. Her legs were as watery as the sea. Grasping the edges of the desk, she reached her goal. Her reward was the feel of his arms circling her.

"Well done." He kissed her.

"I'll be climbing the center mast before you know it."

"I'd wait for the breeches." He trailed a finger up her thigh.

Samantha shivered out of a sudden rush of anticipation, but James was quick to pull his hand away as if he'd done something wrong. The scene from yesterday morning continued to hang heavy between them. She behaved irrationally, but at the time, coming from a sound sleep, she had little control over her reaction to him coming into the bed. Still, James didn't deserve the reception he received. He'd been nothing but kind and loving. He'd shown incredible restraint and patience. To panic like that... without cause... She was embarrassed and angry with herself, and more angry at the man whose ugliness still tainted her.

Her fearful reaction to James's had been born out of months having to defending herself on those horrible nights Wessler chose to visit her bed. She'd been trained to expect the worst. She hated that Wessler's poison still had a hold upon her, and she wished she could come up with the words to try and explain it to James.

Reaching out to take his hand, she returned it brazenly to where it had been on her thigh. She looked into his summer-sky eyes. "If I trembled, it was because now I'm free to be as *loud* as I wish in your bed."

He dropped his forehead to hers. "I hate that I frightened you."

"I hate it too, but not for the reasons you think." She wound her arms around James's neck and kissed him. "I'm sorry for yesterday. You are *nothing* like him. Not in the tiniest way. I despise the shadow he's cast across what is only good and wonderful between us. He may have stolen a piece of my soul, but I won't allow him to touch the piece that belongs to you. It's hard to find the words to explain. It isn't like a wound you can stitch back together. I'm not sure if I'll ever fully heal from what's happened, but it's unfair to you—to us—to have it ruin a single second."

"Nothing is ruined," he assured her in a whisper, smoothing the hair away from her cheek.

She whispered back. "It is if you're afraid to touch me."

He held her gaze and allowed his hand to move higher. "I love you. I'll never hurt—"

Samantha stopped his words with a fingertip. "You can stop with 'I love you.' It's all you ever need say to me." With her other hand she guided his touch higher still. "Or better yet, you could show me."

When his fingers slipped between the folds of her sex, she gave a small gasp. He sucked the tip of her silencing finger into his mouth as he urged her to open for him. Delicious tremors raced along her limbs. His touch was achingly slow.

Samantha moved upon his fingers with tiny shifts of her hips and whimpered. James angled a line of kisses down the side of her throat. He paused to nip at the sensitive bend where her neck curved into the line of her shoulder. The combination of sensations was magical. She pulled the leather thong holding his hair allowing her to bury her hands in its rich thickness and pulling him to her. James murmured his approval against her skin. The timber of his voice rumbled through her.

His feather-light strokes soothed while igniting an unknown urgency inside her. She arched into him. "James...please."

He lifted his head, captured her lips, and stopped his intimate caresses only long enough to scoop her into his arms and carry her back those fourteen steps—he made them in eight—to lay her on the bed.

She smiled up at him. "I could have walked."

"You need to save your strength," he grinned, hovering over her before dipping his head and pulling the tip of her breast into his mouth. He hadn't even bothered to remove his best shirt, but sucked at her nipple through the fabric in his haste, dampening the fine linen.

"Take it off me," she insisted, backing away from his impatient mouth. She needed to feel that impatience on her skin. With one simple tug, she was naked, where James was still dressed all the way to his perfectly knotted neckcloth.

"You truly are beautiful." He made a slow study of her, from the tips of her toes to the cap of her unruly hair. He grazed the angry pink of her scar with a fingertip.

It embarrassed her to see its ugliness. "All except there." She covered it, but James pulled away her hand.

"Don't hide it. It's part of you. A sign of bravery and—"

"Utter foolishness," she countered.

"No." He leaned down and kissed the injured skin. "Not many women would have rushed into a battle to fight for a friend. You're brave and noble." From her hip, he laid a tender kiss on the flat of her belly, the dip at the juncture of her ribs. The muscles in her abdomen shimmered with pleasure. Her heart fluttered like a trapped bird.

Samantha's breath raced in anticipation as he concentrated his attention on her left breast. Cupping it, he teased the tight tip with his thumb before taking it between his lips. A wave of pleasure crashed over her. It was almost more than she could bear.

"James...please..." She begged him again, for what she couldn't have said. Samantha could no longer offer him her innocence, but every cherished feeling, each tender sensation felt new, unknown, undiscovered. In all ways but one, she was still a virgin.

She tugged at his shirtsleeve. James gave a final swirl of his tongue around the edge of her swollen nipple before lifting his heavy-lidded gaze to her. When he licked his lips and smiled like a cat who'd stolen the cream, part of her dissolved into molten honey.

Samantha began tugging the buttons of his waistcoat from their holes, one after the other. "I-I need to see you. Touch you." Her fingers fumbled with the normally easy task, but he had her shaking with want.

Even in undressing, he deliberately took his time, carefully removing each piece of clothing with excruciating care. "Are you trying to torture me?" she sighed.

He pulled the shirt from his trousers and tossed it to one side. "No. I want to savor you."

"Or tease me until I become nothing but a trembling pool of desire?" She fingered the defined muscles of his stomach. James took her hand and lowered it to rest on the solid ridge of his erection trapped within the confines of his trousers. When she curled her fingers over the swollen shaft, she could feel the heat of him radiating through the fabric. He closed his eyes and pulled in a great breath before opening them again. "Then I'll drown in your arms a very happy man."

He was quicker removing his boots, and finally his trousers, but to Samantha's impatient sense, it took far too long. But then he stood before her. Strong. Defined. Aroused.

"I chose the most handsome man at the dance," she murmured.

Samantha left the bed to stand before him. Wrapping her arms around his neck, she aligned her body along the solid length of him before lifting her mouth to his.

James ran his hands down her back and over the curve of her bottom, hauling her tight to him. "I much prefer this outfit on you." His hands smoothed over her skin, fanning the embers into flames once more. Gently, he raised one of her knees and lifted it to rest high upon his hip. The positioning of her moist sex against him made her plead with him once more to hurry.

"Please..."

He backed her toward the bed. In one exquisite move, he had her on her back and positioned himself between her thighs. The strength and power of him surrounded her.

A sudden wave of panic crashed over Samantha. Instinct wove a past thread of fear to tangle with the heat of her current desire. Her body tensed in preparation for an assault. But none came.

James made love to her. Gently. Slowly. With his whole self. Kissing and stroking every inch of her with such profound tenderness, it made her weep. With each touch, he erased all any fear.

When he finally pushed into her, filled her with the solid length of his cock, she shuddered around him. Her body surged into a swell of release that took her breath and left her trembling beneath him.

He found a rhythm, slow, strong, fervent. Each press of his hips burying him deeper. Filling her, fusing him to her like none other, reaching a place within her she had never known.

A new urgency built within her. She ignored the dull pull of her wound and began to move with him, clutching at the slick skin of his back and buttocks. Pulling him deeper, she lifted her hips to meet the strength of his. She sighed his name, urging him faster.

Samantha cried out at the sheer pleasure of sensations racing through her. In response, James moaned deep in his chest, as he was somehow able to fit an arm beneath her and lift her hips into a new position. The new angle of his thrusts undid her. Curling over her, he ground out her name, "Samantha...sweet God, I love you..."

Arching her back, she bucked beneath him as her body soared straight into the sun.

Chapter 22

Lying on his back, James struggled to catch his breath. His heart rushed faster than waves passed the hull as he pulled Samantha tight to him. She laid her head on his shoulder, her body molding to the contours of his. Their skin damp and flushed. He buried his face in the softness of the curls crowing her head and filled his lungs with her scent. She smelled vaguely like cinnamon and strongly of him.

"Give me the words," she murmured against his chest.

"Words?" She was asking him to think? Speak coherently? Given the intensity of what they shared, he was sure walking would take him a moment or two to re-master. Talking? Linking one word successfully to the next? "Not yet."

"But I don't know how to describe…"

He stroked her from her waist to her shoulder and back. Nothing could compare to the feel of her in his arms. "The way you just called out my name, described it well enough."

She snuggled closer. Kissed his chest, brushing her lips across the flat of his nipple, sending another heated shot across his proverbial bow. His body surprised him by responding when he was fully prepared to raise a white flag to her insatiable charms.

"Are you trying to ruin me?"

She smiled against his skin. "Quite the opposite."

He pulled her on top him, lifting her mouth to an urgent kiss, aligning her body to lie along his, pinning himself beneath the delicious weight of her.

"Is it your plan to keep me in my bed all day? Distract me from my duties?"

She nodded and brushed her lips over his. "Just until my new breeches arrive."

He smiled against her kiss. "And after that?"

"I would love to stroll along the decks. I want to see the *Lion* in all her power, catching every inch of wind. And fill my lungs with that breeze myself before it's too late."

"It's not even eight bells. The day is young." He tucked her hair behind her ear and smiled. He loved her delicate ear—the sweep and swirl of its tender lobe, the tiny shiver she made when he ran his tongue along its edge. *Dear God, he was spellbound.* Next, he'd be writing sonnets to the sweetness of her perfect breasts.

Samantha broke through the mist of his indecent thoughts. "But before we head deck side, you have one more duty." Her gaze focused on his mouth before lifting to meet his.

He stretched both hands lower to cup the rounds of her behind, grinding against her. "I wouldn't call such a tempting proposal a duty."

"You've waited long enough—"

Between them, his erection pulsed in anticipation. "Demanding vixen... I'd never have imagined—"

"—to officially arrest me."

Icy seawater could not have cooled his ardor quicker. "I-I..."

She shrugged one bare shoulder. "You were waiting until I got stronger. I'm stronger."

He frowned. "I know, but—"

"I heard the conversation with Ducky, remember? You have no choice in this." She held his gaze with the soft brown of hers.

"I may not have a choice in the *what*, but I damn well have a choice as to the *when*." He moved her off him and propped himself up on one elbow to look down at her. "And I don't think minutes after I've made love to you is quite the time to charge you with treason."

Samantha traced a hand down his chest. "I don't want you to confuse the two."

"How on earth would I do that?" His brows drew together.

Samantha sat and pulled a blanket to cover her nakedness. "I want there to be no question as to...to what we just did."

James sat back himself, willing some of the blood back to his brain so he could make sense of what she was trying to say. "Okay, now I am confused. What are you talking about?"

She set her chin. "I'm fully prepared to take responsibility for my actions, no matter the outcome. I don't want you to ever doubt my feelings, or my reasons for wanting to be with you. I didn't lie with you to help my cause. I used you once, the night of the dance. I need you to know I'll not do it again."

His frown deepened. "I'd never think that."

"No, but others might if they found out. I don't want there to be a moment's doubt in your mind. And I don't want you to bear any guilt in doing your duty. Or take any blame for what befalls me."

"Samantha…"

She touched his chest to quiet him. "No, please. I love you. I'll love you for as much and as long as I am able, but that won't change things. At some point, I have to face my future on my own."

James lifted her hand and placed a kiss within its palm. "First, you're not on your own. You have me."

She drew a deep breath and pulled back her hand. "But I can't have you. That's what I'm trying to tell you. You're such a wonderful man. Beautiful and loving. You deserve so much…much more than someone like me. I won't let you risk your happiness or your career for me. I'm not worth it."

He shook his head. The need to defend her, even to herself, ran hot through him. "Of course you're worth it. I love you."

"And I love you. Which is why I won't let you jeopardize your life when I have none."

James jumped out of bed and back into his trousers. Anger and fear pushing him. He wouldn't listen to any more. "Don't talk like that," he snapped.

"You have to promise me." She stood, dragging the blanket with her. "If you love me, when the time comes, you'll let me go. Walk away. Don't get dragged down with me. You're too good…too important. I'm noth—"

"Stop." He bit out the word. "I won't stand here and let you call yourself nothing. How dare you minimize who you are and how we feel? I have *no* intention of walking away from you. Not for a second. Is that understood?" He grabbed her by her upper arms. Her eyes went wide. Dear God, he'd frightened her again. He reined in his anger and lowered his voice. "You and I. We love one another. We are together now and forever."

"James—"

"*Nothing* is going to prevent us from being together," he insisted. "You're innocent, and I intend on speaking to everyone from the admiral to the magistrate and all the way to King George if I have to, in order to get the charges facing you dropped. I don't want a future without you. I refuse to even contemplate such a thing."

Samantha lowered her chin and whispered, "But Lillian."

James kissed her forehead and sighed. "She doesn't have my heart, and I certainly don't have hers. Lillian is a business arrangement. The merging of two households. A tidy bank account and some fine property. A life of loveless leisure. You and I together will be ten times richer." He cradled her face. "We're ten times richer standing here now."

She blinked at him with wide tear-washed eyes. "You promise not to jeopardize your career over us?"

"No...I swear to you on my mother's eyes, I won't endanger my commission."

Samantha held his gaze for a long moment before giving him a watery nod. "Good." She took a deep breath. "Then arrest me."

He shook his head and teased. "I have extremely strict standards, Mistress Christian. It is not my practice to arrest anyone not wearing trousers."

"Oh," She gave a quick bite to her lower lip. "Then we'll have to wait."

"Indeed." He ran a fingertip over the line of her collarbone and down the center of her chest to the shadowy valley of her cleavage, hooking his finger into the top of her blanket. "I wonder what we might do to pass the time."

"I could put this cover back where it belongs." Samantha began to back toward the bed.

"Let me help you with that." He snatched the blanket from her in one clean jerk and tossed it to the side.

* * * *

"It's huge."

"Not monstrous, but good sized. Gets the job done." James recovered slightly. Stood a wee bit taller. It was a proud moment, seeing his ship through Samantha's eyes.

"I've never seen so many sails. She sits so tall, it feels as if the masts could catch the clouds." She took a few steps ahead of him, looking skyward.

His gaze lowered. He'd never appreciated the vision of a woman in breeches before. Even if they did bring with them his promise to do his sworn duty and arrest her officially.

Samantha had insisted on being treated as he had the others. Earlier, she stood before his desk as he read the charges against her and asked her to state her full name and rank.

"My name is Samantha Ruth Christian. I was Captain Quinn's cabin boy."

Yes, she understood the charges. They both understood. It made James sick to think about the precarious implications.

"You plead innocent." In his notes, he included all the extenuating circumstances that had brought her to the *Scarlet Night*. After he was finished, he pulled her back into his lap and reiterated, "If anyone else asks your plea, you're innocent. Understand?"

She pulled his mouth to hers. "I'm not feeling very innocent at the moment."

Watching the sway of her hips and the way her new trousers hugged her thighs, he wasn't feeling innocent either.

"Your ship is truly impressive, James." She turned with a smile.

Bringing her on deck had caused a minor ripple throughout the crew. If there were concerns or comments regarding a second woman aboard, the men they passed had the good sense and manners to keep it to themselves. His officers would let him know if there were any grumblings below later.

James purposely kept to the front of the ship. Samantha's stamina was in no way restored, and Stitch had warned them both about overdoing things. And they'd already overdone this morning…three times.

He took a step back and watched her lift her beautiful face to the sun, run her hand down the polished wide railing of the ship's gunwales, comment on the miles of thick rigging. *He loved her.* There was a good chance he'd loved her from the beginning and not been clever enough to realize it. It filled him with such warmth simply to look at her. And when she opened herself to him in bed…. She trusted him—even after all she'd been through in the past. To be that generous in her lovemaking, that honest…. It made him fall in love with her all over again.

Their conversations kept circling in his mind. The growing need to protect her continued to overwhelm him. He'd keep his promises, but she was his. There was no way he would let her stand alone in this. He was prepared to walk through fire for her if need be.

James scanned the length of the decks, as was his habit. He caught sight of Ducky with his company of men supervising the prisoners of the *Scarlet Night*.

"Let's show Tupper something more impressive than this ship. You. Walking, talking, vertical. She's been concerned."

"I should be moving to the brig soon. Isn't that where I should be?"

James wanted to pull her back into his arms and argue his selfish need to keep her with him, but he knew to keep his hands to himself while they were on deck. "You're still recovering."

She looked at him over her shoulder. "I was recovered enough earlier."

He lowered his voice so only she could hear. "And I selfishly need to have you recuperate completely before I'm ready to let you go." James eyed the prisoners once more. His stomach churned at the thought of her with them. She didn't belong there. She wasn't one of their crew. "Aye, a few more days."

As they moved closer to Tupper and her crew, the men began to take notice. The first one to see her was the *Scarlet Night's* first mate. William Quinn—the one they called Bump. When he saw them, he leapt to his feet. His abrupt movement caused Ducky's men to pull their pistols. He made no other move, however, but stared at Samantha with a slightly unnerving intensity before shifting the same concentrated gaze on James. He forgot his original intention not to touch Samantha while on deck and instinctively took her arm and slowly moved her tight to his side.

Bump's stare triggered others to follow his gaze. Two more men stood to watch their approach. The larger of the two pointed, "There's the unlucky bitch now!"

Samantha stopped walking and shot James a nervous glance. Ducky's men ordered the three to sit back down. "Stand down, the lot of you!" Pistols were slid from holsters.

The two that could hear the order did as they were told, but continued to complain and spit more insults in her direction.

"Be more then limpin' if I had me way."

"Give me five minutes wit her...make hangin' worth the rope."

By this time, Tupper took command. "When are you two going to quit acting like a couple of great arses? Keep it up and I'll ask them to hang ye sorry bastards right here." Using hand signals, she told Bump to return to his place. He did so, but never took his eyes off Samantha.

Tupper and the other two continued to exchange barbs until Ducky put an end to it all. "I'm done listening to you bastards bitch. Take them below!"

Amid the grumbles, the crew was rousted. Bump's gaze lingered on Samantha until he was moved away.

"What was all that about?" Samantha looked to James in question.

A nagging worry tripped up James's spine as he watched the prisoners. Ducky had mentioned the tension within the brig. Seemed it was more than simple friction. He'd give the order to double the guard. Turning back to Samantha, he ran a reassuring hand down her sleeve. "I don't know, but I mean to find out. And I've just decided you'll stay with me until I do."

Chapter 23

The guards were quick to move them all back into their respective cells. After the fresh air and brightness of the day, coming back below was like entering a rotting cave. Tupper couldn't see. Too bad it didn't dull her hearing.

Butler and Allan were still spewing their love and joy throughout the rest of the crew. It was the same old argument. Tupper lied to them, she'd lied to them for years. Evidently every time she opened her mouth, another lie spilled out. They'd seen the cabin "boy." This was all Sam's fault. They'd been cursed. All bitches were bad luck, blah, blah, blah.

Tupper did her best to ignore them. What she couldn't ignore was Bump. At first, she was happy to see Samantha. Other than a slight limp, the girl looked good. She was healthy and obviously well cared for. Watching the interaction between her and James, the way he'd pulled her close. She couldn't help but think perhaps Sam was being a little too well cared for. Tupper wasn't the only one to think that, either. She'd caught the look on Bump's face seconds before the young, fair-haired lieutenant had ordered their removal.

Tupper had tried to "talk" to Bump on the way back down to the brig, but the stairway narrowed them to single file, and he'd gotten ahead of her. If the others would settle down, perhaps she could get his attention. There had always been one major advantage to communicating with Bump the way she did—they could "speak" to one another from opposite sides of a crowded deck, "hear" in the midst of a raging battle, even "whisper" secrets at a distance. She was counting on that advantage now. She'd have to bide her time and be patient. Not one of her strong suits.

It wasn't until hours later and several miles of pacing in her cell that she was able to whisper to Bump through the bars. Most of the others were asleep. She managed to get Bump's attention, and he moved to where they could see each another.

'Will you talk to me? About Sam?'

'Nothing to say.'

Tupper gave a sharp shake to her head. *'Bullshit.'*

Bump crossed his arms over the broad span of his chest and set his jaw. It was a favorite sign of his from when he was younger; his version of the silent treatment. At least he hadn't turned his back. He might be refusing to "talk," but he was still "listening." It was something, at least.

'Will you cease worrying about her now?'

Bump cross his wrists as if they were shackled, his hands in fists, and pulled them apart. *'Is she free? Safe?'*

Tupper shrugged. She tapped her shoulder with bent fingers. *'Captain Steele will help her. I want someone to help you.'*

He shook his head and pulled his thumb out of a closed fist before pointing to his chest. Tupper was quick to respond. *'I give a shit what happens to you.'*

'Don't.' Bump lowered his gaze to the floor, his hands still by his sides. He drew in a deep breath and raised his eyes. *'Better this way.'*

Tupper frowned. She didn't like the look of defeat on his face. If he retreated, she'd lose him. That was the last thing she wanted. *'Better what way?'*

'I'm deaf not blind. She loves him. I'm happy. She deserves a good man. Better than me.'

Tupper signed 'bullshit' again. *'None are better than you.'*

It was his turn to sign *'bullshit.'*

She held his gaze. *'She'd be lucky to have you.'*

Bump swept his hands wide before signing, *'For the hour before I hang?'*

'Don't remind me.' Tupper put a hand over the sudden ache in her heart.

'I'm not a child, Tupper.'

'Don't remind me,' she repeated sadly.

He stood quiet for a long moment before lifting his hands. *'I want to say thank you.'*

'For what, getting you charged with t-r-e-a-s-o-n?' She didn't know a sign for that and had to spell out the word.

Bump shook his head and fixed her with the fathomless gaze he'd given her from the time he was a wee lad of four. He'd been new to the ship and scared to death. All alone in a strange life. They'd bonded like duck and duckling.

He tapped two fingers together. *'My name. Thank you for my name.'*

* * * *

The next morning, Tupper had a surprise visitor. "Captain Steele." She held her arms wide and did a sweep of the cell, smoothing the straw that lined the floor and collected in the corners. "I'd offer you a drink, but we're a might dry in this part of the ship." She checked his hands. "Don't suppose you brought along anything to wet my whistle and brighten my day."

He grinned, but shook his head. "It's a bit early for brandy."

Tupper scoffed. "It's never too early for rum. To what do I owe this honor?"

"My lieutenant tells me you're having some problems with your men down here. I witnessed a bit of it on deck yesterday. "

She cocked her head. "Nothing I can't handle. Lot of hot air being passed around. They like to bitch and complain, especially when they're stone cold sober and fixin' to hang. Ye'll have to forgive them. They're not too fond of your British hospitality."

James narrowed his eyes. "Is that all?"

Tupper shrugged and narrowed her eyes. "Tell me about Samantha Christian."

James frowned and folded his arms, appraising her. "You saw her. She's doing well."

"Have you changed your mind about charging her?"

"No. She's been charged."

Tupper jerked back. "Well, I'll be damned." She was impressed. He'd done it. She had an odd flush of pride. Not that she had any reason. Annalise and Jaxon should be the ones to be proud. They raised an honorable man. His sense of duty was unquestionable...but there was still that one thing burning a hole in her mind. "If she's a prisoner, then why is she still in your bed?"

To his credit, James didn't flinch. "Her health and safety are my personal concerns. I don't believe it's safe for her down here. Your men are angry at you, but they blame her for their current predicament."

Tupper lifted a shoulder again. "They like to flap their jaws."

"You aren't denying it. Samantha Christian has been charged, although I'm convinced now more than ever she's innocent of any wrongdoing."

She gave him a smug look. "I told you this all along. I'm guessing you have a plan for how to resolve this?"

Lisa A. Olech

"I'll accompany her personally once we reach London. Keep her safely in my custody. Talk directly to the admiral. Explain the situation. Vouch for her character."

"A solid plan."

James planted his hands on his hips. "Given the attitude of your men, she'll stay with me until we reach London."

Tupper gave him a long hard stare. "You love her."

"I do." Damn it if he still hadn't flinched.

"And what if you can't convince your supervisors of her innocence?"

"I'm prepared to go all the way to the king if I need to."

Tupper settled back and folded her arms over her chest. James was a good man. She was proud of him. She liked him. If he weren't a British officer bringing her to hang, he'd be bloody nigh perfect. "I'm glad she has you to fight for her."

"What about you? Have you given any more thought to letting me help you?"

Tupper waved the suggestion away. "I told you. You can't help me."

James tipped his head. "I could try. I could plead on your behalf as well as Samantha's. At least try to get you a lighter sentence."

"Why? Because I'm a woman?" she sniffed.

"No." He held a hand out toward her. "Because you're Alice. *Aunt* Alice."

Tupper laughed and rolled her eyes. "Ah, yes. Aunt Alice." She held up a finger. "Let me tell you a little bit about her. It's time you heard the part of the tale you don't know." Tupper took a dramatic pause. "A long time ago, your Aunt Alice killed a man. The story tells how brave and heroic she was. She saved your parents. In truth, there was nothing heroic about it."

She pointed to the floor. "The moment I took that life, part of me changed. Went cold as winter, as if a shard of ice had pierced my heart." She gave him a stern stare, shaking her head.

"I didn't kill him to save anyone. He'd been stopped. I stopped him. The threat was over. It was done." She brushed a bit of straw from her breeches. "But did I stop? No. I *chose* to kill the vile bastard and drew the sword to do it. I could have just as easily left it in its scabbard. But I didn't. I stepped over a line, which could never be uncrossed. It's haunted my every step to this day. Stained my soul. I should have hanged for the crime back then.

"Instead," she held her arms wide. "I tried to run and fell headlong into this life. I became a pirate. Not what I'd imagined in my wildest dreams. But damn if I wasn't good at it. Wasn't a bad life either. I've lived a good long time. Known a great love, suffered a great lost, fought battles, won wars. I have seen both sides of this fathomless ocean more times than I can count and watched the sun rise and set into her blue waters for more years than I deserved. I've survived days I had no right to survive and looked into the face of death thousands of times. She doesn't scare me."

Tupper sniffed and looked away. "You heard my name in a bedtime fairy tale you were told as a babe. You believe you know who I am, that I'm somehow linked to you and your beautiful mother. I'm not. I stopped being that woman a long time ago. Alice doesn't exist." She looked back at James. "Aunt Alice died in a cave on the north side of Jamaica when she pulled a sword out of a scabbard and raised it over her head. Do not misplace your loyalty, James. I've done nothing to deserve it."

Chapter 24

As the weeks passed and the *Lion* moved closer to the English coast, James and Samantha spent as much time together as possible. The tensions below in the brig reinforced his decision to keep her with him. At least that was what he told Ducky, Stitch, or anyone else who should mention it.

They made a habit of walking the decks at night, when they would have little chance of seeing the rest of the *Scarlet Night's* crew. They took long walks in the quiet of the dark, surrounded by the endless stars above dipping down to dance on the surface of the bottomless sea below, as the moon smudged her light across the waves.

Listening to the sounds of the ship without the distraction of the crew, they could hear the deep creak of the wood and the hum of the rigging. A moment of peace for them both within the chaos of all that was looming.

It was their time, a respite from the daily bustle of duties and activities, away from the scores of questioning eyes that seemed to follow him these days. The night's watch came to know their routine and, after a few evenings, paid them no mind.

And following their strolls through the dark, he would take her to his bed. Their lovemaking was never rushed, no mad impatient tearing at one another. Instead, it was an unhurried voyage of discovery and breathtaking delight. He learned every inch of her. Discovered where a simple kiss could make her whimper with pleasure. Where a swirling touch could cause her body to arch and writhe like a sensuous wave. He came to know each and every delicious way to bring her to climax.

Samantha studied him as well. She found new ways to drive him mad with wanting. Gave herself to him without reservation. Trusted him. Loved him with her whole self.

James came in late last night after his final round of the *Lion*. The sight of Samantha curled up warm in his bed brought its own rush of emotions, from elation to fear and back to loving desire. He poured himself a brandy and, for once, ignored his precious logbooks and charts and instead heeded the incessant need to slip into his bed and hold her close.

His clothing fell where it may, before he eased himself in beside her.

Samantha moved against him, snuggling tight to his side, she touched her lips to his shoulder. "You forgot to hang up your uniform."

"To hell with my uniform." James swept his hand over the heated curve of her naked hip. "I didn't mean to wake you."

"I wasn't asleep." She kissed the side of his neck before lifting her knee to drape her leg over his. The rush to his already rigid cock made him fist the sheets with his free hand. Would his body ever have enough of her?

Samantha raised herself on her elbow before lowering her mouth to his. "You taste like brandy." She moved like water over the hull and straddled his hips. Her wet heat pressed along his erection. "And salt air." She licked at his lips.

"What are you doing to me?" James clutched at her thighs as she trailed a line of kisses down his throat.

"Seducing you." She tipped her hips to slide her sex along the length of him. "Didn't you tell me I was a natural?"

It was all he could do not to toss her onto her back and plunge blindly into her.

"Aye..." The word wrenched from his throat. He held himself still. Stone still. Everywhere she touched him, stroked him, pressed her lips to him, ignited into a consuming flame. "Dear God..."

"I may not get another chance," she murmured against his chest, "to show you how much I've come to love you."

Her words pierced through the sexual fog. James stopped her hand before ending her kisses by tipping her chin. "Is that what this is?" He cupped her cheek. "Are you afraid this is our last time together?"

She didn't answer; didn't have to. The words were written in her eyes. "Unless you've come from steering your ship in a great circle, we're running out of time."

He shook his head before pulling her mouth to his. "You and I have the rest of our lives to be together."

"Suppose the rest of my life is counted in days." She lowered her gaze and traced the lower edge of his lip. "If something goes wrong, and all your plans don't—"

"Nothing is going to go wrong." He tipped her chin again. "I swear to you. I love you."

Samantha gave him a small smile as he tucked a shining curl behind her ear. "Does that mean you want me to stop seducing you?" She moved his hand to her breast and pressed into it.

"Only if you want the rest of *my* life to be counted in minutes." He surged his hips upward to emphasize his life-threatening condition. "If you don't take me now, I'm going to burst."

* * * *

But Samantha wasn't wrong in thinking their journey was close to an end. The time to bury themselves in a protective ignorance was indeed over, but whatever happened, they would face it together.

The *Lion* had reached the Thames.

James held her once more in his arms that morning. "You remember what I've told you."

"Yes. We've been over it a thousand times."

"There's bound to be a great deal of disorder moving the prisoners off ship. I don't want you to get caught up in the commotion and lose sight of what's to come."

Samantha smiled patiently and repeated what he'd instructed, "I will join the *Scarlet* crew at the last moment to leave the *Lion*. Tupper and I will hold back and remain separate from the rest. I'll stay with her as we're moved to board the prisoner barges into the tower. You'll be waiting for me there."

"Exactly. I'll have secured your release from the tower guards. You'll never board the barge or pass through Traitor's Gate. I'll have spoken to Admiral Marcus, and you'll be released under my authority and custody. Together we'll proceed to a direct audience with the admiral to have the charges against you removed." He kissed the top of her head. "By tonight, this will all be over, and once that is done, I can put into place the plan to keep Tupper's neck, if not out of the tower, at least out of the noose."

Samantha lifted her chin to look at him. "Do you think you can get her sentence reduced?"

"I mean to try, regardless of what she says. No woman has ever hanged for piracy in London before. If I have anything to do with it, Tupper Quinn will not be the first."

* * * *

A few hours later, they'd arrived. James and Samantha stepped out into the brilliant sunlight. Ducky and his company had already brought the prisoners on deck. James scanned the group. Not all appeared as calmly resigned to their fate as their captain.

As the anchor dropped, the order was given to shackle the pirates and make ready for the transfer. James leaned close to Samantha. "I'm sorry it has to be this way. You'll only wear them for a short time." He held her gaze as he himself locked the irons around her wrists. He leaned closer and whispered, "Don't lose faith. It will all be over soon."

He watched her throat work as the second band locked over her delicate wrist. No sooner had it snapped into place than a man within the crowd of prisoners shrieked. "I'll kill ye, ye bloody bitch." He broke away from the others, followed by another. They knocked one of the guards down, rendering him unconscious. The first man stole the guard's pistol and headed straight for Samantha. Around them James's men drew their weapons and screamed for the prisoners to halt and stand down.

In the ensuing chaos, the man, Bump, wrenched away from his guard, one shackle swinging from his wrist. He rushed toward James and Samantha.

James pulled Samantha behind him. Before he could draw his pistol, all hell erupted around them as Ducky's men still screamed their commands for immediate order. "Halt." "Everyone down!" "Stop that man!" "Halt or I'll shoot."

The scene moved in slow motion after that. James stepped between Samantha and the charging prisoners, shielding her. Three men fired. The lead man with the stolen pistol was killed on the spot. Two other men dropped within the swirling smoke as shots ripped into them from behind. Bump was one of them. His body jerked and lurched forward with the first impact. He went down hard to the deck after the second shot hit him.

Tupper flew toward her first mate with a high-pitched screech. The huge Scotsman in the red tartan caught her around the waist and knocked her aside as another series of shots rang out.

When the smoke cleared, five men lay dead or wounded on the deck. Ducky's men had quickly subdued the rest of the prisoners, pinning them to the decking. "Get them all below!" ordered James over the shouts and screams.

Tupper wailed with an inhuman keening James had never heard before, crying out for Bump. Her guard struggled to keep hold of her. James pulled a shaking Samantha into his arms. She buried her face in James's chest at the sight before her. "No. Not Bump..." She started to cry.

Tupper screamed at the top of her lungs to be released, "Let me go, you bastards. "You bloody bastards. You killed him! You fucking killed him." She fought them wildly. It took three men to haul her away. "You... fucking...killed him..."

Samantha watched Tupper be dragged off deck. "Oh, God, let me go with her."

James wiped at Samantha's tears. "Yes, go. This only delays us. Understand? I'll see to these men." He removed her shackles. "Go, stay below with Tupper. Our plan is still the same."

"Plan?" Samantha sniffed, looking lost.

He held her face. "Yes, darling, don't forget. I'll be waiting at the gate."

All she could do was nod before James handed her over to one of his men as bodies were carried from the decks.

* * * *

Samantha rushed to Tupper's side. She lay in a ball on the straw covering the floor of the cell, wailing. When Samantha tried to wrap her arm around her, Tupper shoved her away. She glared at her before wiping her nose on the back of her wrist.

"They were fucking *right*. Butler and Allan. You're bad luck. I never should have brought you aboard my damn ship." She jumped to her feet and screamed at the ceiling. "Ahhhhhhh."

"You said that was a silly superstition. How is this my fault?" Samantha backed away. "Those men wanted to kill me."

"He *loved* you." Tupper spit the words before covering her eyes and curling into herself once more. "Bump loved you. He was rushing to protect *you*."

Samantha gasped as if she'd been punched. She covered the sudden profound ache in her heart with her hand. "I-I didn't know."

"Of course you didn't know, you foolish girl. How was he supposed to tell you?"

As Tupper reminded her, realization crashed over Sam. "Oh, God...he never heard them. When they ordered him to stop..."

Tupper screwed her eyes shut and growled. "They shot a deaf man in the back."

Tears ran down Samantha's face as her mind tried to make sense of it all. "They didn't know. Everything happened so fast. They couldn't have known."

"Makes no difference now, does it? Makes no difference at all." Bitter anger infused Tupper's misery. "One less rope to tie." She moaned. "Or two...does MacTavish live? He pushed me out of the way and took the shot meant for me."

"They hurried us below. I couldn't tell who was alive and who wasn't."

"Tell them to come take me now. I don't care anymore." She sobbed with such anguish, it broke Sam's heart. Tupper yelled to her guards, "Do it now. Hang me, shoot me, wrap your bastard fingers around my throat and squeeze the life from me. Just kill me now!"

Samantha wanted to go to her, hold her, and somehow ease her grief. She felt helpless to do anything but bear witness to her suffering. "Tupper, I'm so sorry...."

She turned anguished eyes toward her. "What do you care?"

"I cared about Bump. He was a friend. For the short time I knew him, he was one of the few allies I had on the *Scarlet Night*. Him...and you."

"I told you before, I'm not your friend." Tupper curled herself back into a corner. "Why are you here? Leave me alone."

Samantha wasn't sure what to do. She brushed at her wet cheeks. Bump loved her? Had she mislead him somehow? Her mind reeled. Images past and present raced through her mind. She wanted to be back in James's arms where things were safe. "I didn't know MacTavish well, and I had no idea Bump had feelings for me. But he was a good man. Strong, smart. It was obvious how much he cared for you."

A sob wrenched out of Tupper's throat. "I beg you...if you aren't going to end my miserable life, then leave me the hell alone...."

Chapter 25

"What the hell happened?" demanded James.

Ducky shook his head. "Three dead. They took one of my men. Two more wounded."

"Bloody hell." The smoke still clung to the decks, as did the pools of bright blood running between the deck boards. James watched as the last body was carried away. "The bastards were intent on killing Samantha."

"They didn't succeed." Ducky indicated the blood smears on James's uniform. "You can be thankful none of that is hers."

"Did you have any notion this was coming?"

"No." Ducky shook his head. "Must have been a last desperate attempt to escape now that we're so close to land. A slow anger has been building for weeks. I thought it had settled down. Things had been quiet for days. I thought they'd finally resigned themselves to their fate."

Men swirled around them, clearing away any evidence of the skirmish. James again marveled at the rate of efficiency among his men. "We obviously gave them more freedom than prudent. When the tower officials arrive, unload them one at a time. Shackle them below. Two guards on each."

"Aye, Captain," Ducky nodded. "And what about Mistress Christian?"

"I'm taking a dispatch to the office of the admiral now. I'm asking that she be remanded into my custody. She knows she'll be unloaded from the *Lion* with the rest, but she'll be placed into my care before they can sail through Traitor's Gate."

"And Captain Quinn?"

"She's stubborn as a mule, but you saw her. Her spirit is broken. Maybe she'll listen to reason now. While I'm with the admiral, I'll suggest the possibility of a reduced sentence. Once I'm back with Samantha, I'll ride to Weatherington."

Ducky cocked his head. "I seem to remember a promise made to the stubborn Captain Quinn. You weren't to mention finding her to your mother."

"Aye, and I won't." He gave Ducky a small grin. "When have you ever known me to go back on a promise? I did pledge not to speak to my mother about Alice Tupper Quinn. However, I made no such oath regarding my father."

* * * *

James boarded the small transfer skiff with four other men who made quick work of getting him to shore. His time was short. He had to get Admiral Marcus to agree to waive Samantha's imprisonment in the Tower of London before the prisoners were transferred into the hands of the tower guards.

James rushed into Marcus's quarters. He removed his hat and tucked it beneath his arm. A large hank of hair had pulled from the cue and fell across his face. He pushed it back. With blood still staining his uniform, he was far from his orderly self, but there was no time for either pleasantries nor polish.

"Captain James Steele, *HMS Lion*. I need to see the Admiral on a matter of the highest urgency." He headed toward the wide, ornate doors behind the greeting officer.

A spindly lieutenant manning the admiral's outer office stood to block James's entrance. "I'm sorry, Captain, but the adm—"

"Will see me." He stared down at the man. "That is what you were about to say. Am I correct, lieutenant?"

"No, sir. I was about to say the admiral is preparing to leave momentarily for a pressing social engagement. I can make an appointment for you to meet with him first thing tomorrow morning."

James straightened his jacket and stood to his full height. "Does it look like I can wait until first thing tomorrow morning? If the admiral is preparing to leave, then he has not already left. Which means he is right behind those doors." James moved to skirt past the infuriating man.

"But, Captain…." He stepped in front of James once more.

James clenched his jaw so tightly, his back teeth were in danger of being ground into powder. He took a step back from the man and drew his sword from its scabbard. "Step aside, lieutenant. That is an order."

The soldier's face went a lighter shade of pale before he did as he was bid.

James pushed into the inner office.

"What the bloody hell?"

"I tried to stop him, Admir—" James turned back and slammed the door in the lieutenant's face.

"Just who the hell are you, Captain? What is the meaning of this?" Admiral Jonathan Marcus finished donning his bedecked and beribboned coat. His valet draped it over his shoulders and adjusted the tails of the admiral's wig. "Put away your weapon, sir, unless you've come to run me through. In which case, could you take down my valet *after* he's finished dressing me?" The valet peered over the aging admiral's shoulder with wide, panicked eyes.

"I beg your pardon, Admiral." James sheathed his sword. "Captain Steele, James Steele, *HMS Lion*, sir. I need a moment of your time."

"You have less than a moment, Captain. I'm late for an appointment."

"Then I'll make it brief. I have captured and returned with the ship known as the *Scarlet Night* and her crew."

"The *Scarlet Night*? Good show. Well done. You'll receive a fine bonus for such a catch."

"Thank you, sir, but there is a far more important issue with one of the crew." James showed Samantha's signed petition to the admiral and quickly explained the situation. "The woman is clearly innocent of these charges, admiral. I see no reason why she should be imprisoned in the tower. Samantha Christian is no threat. She is no pirate. I'm asking she be placed in my custody for the period of time it takes to clear up this unfortunate matter."

"She signed the petition of charges?"

"Yes, but only because her name appeared on the Ship's Articles, and by order, the charges had to be read and agreed."

"Indeed."

James's hand swept the documents laid before the admiral. "As you can see, procedure has been followed to the letter, but in this case, an exception must be made."

Admiral Marcus rolled the parchment and handed it back to James. "And procedure will continue to be followed, Captain. I'm afraid the wheels are already turning. I believe you think this Mistress Christian is innocent. Quite a compelling story...*if* it is true. And when she stands before the magistrate and pleads her innocence, she will be heard accordingly." The valet continued to add sashes and baldrics to the paunchy admiral. "However, until that time, our hands are tied. The moment she leaves your ship, Captain, she is a prisoner of the courts. It's procedure."

"But surely—"

"You have done your duty well, Captain Steele. With honor. You and your crew should be proud. This will all play out as it should, in an orderly time and manner. The best I can do is see to it Mistress Christian gets a cell to herself."

"But, Admiral—"

Marcus shook a finger at James. "I advise you, strongly, to continue following proper protocol in this manner, unless you truly dislike your new commission. I've heard only glowing reports about you, Captain, but I'm beginning to cast doubt upon them. I warn you, if your performance and roughshod appearance here today is any indication of your true character, heed me well. *Any* interference of any kind with Mistress Christian's handling will find you in a cell not too far from hers." Admiral Marcus pushed a perfumed, lace-trimmed handkerchief into the end of his sleeve.

"There is also the matter of Captain Tupper Quinn. She is another issue entirely, but I was hoping to plead upon your honor to find a way to reduce the full measure of charges against her."

"Fear not," the Admiral scoffed. "I highly doubt the courts would see a woman hang, in either case."

"But there is a strong chance, and I—"

"I wouldn't test my patience any further, Captain Steele. We are done. You're dismissed."

* * * *

When James raced back to the *Lion*, he was too late. The prisoners were already being led away from the ship. Ducky rushed to join him. "Cutting it close, don't you think?"

James could do nothing but stand there and watch. Blood pulsed in his ears. Frustration, fear, and impatience threatened to tear him apart. "The admiral denied my request."

"Why? What happened?"

James explained the scene with the admiral. "I'm to do nothing to interfere. I can't even talk to her to explain what's happening." He saw Samantha then, marched in a line with the others. Every fiber of his being wanted to go to her, tell her to stay strong, give her hope, and try to calm her fears. Instead he had to stand there, hands in fists by his side, unable to even call out to her. He prayed that somehow she would come to understand and forgive him.

He met her panicked gaze. It broke his heart. "Oh, God, I have to—"

Ducky grabbed tight to his arm and held him back. "Steady, man. You'll do her no good from your own prison cell. Let her go. They won't even allow you in to see her today. Tomorrow, go to her and explain everything."

The sight of her tore at him. "Can you see the way she's looking at me?"

"I can see. Stay strong. All will be well."

Across the crowded dock, all James could do was watch the horrendous scene unfold. Samantha tried to take a step away from the proceedings and was yanked back into line. Two guards struggled to move her forward. When they lowered Samantha into the waiting barge, she looked back once more and cried out his name. Over the din, he couldn't hear her cry, but he saw it. Felt it reach into his chest and tear at his heart.

"Dear God..." Ducky strengthened his hold as James pulled against his friend's restraint. "Let me go."

"You can't help her now." Ducky jerked him back. "Tomorrow will come."

James wanted to scream. Then he saw Tupper and his heart tore once again. Gone was the brash bravado, the cocky swagger the fearless posture. She looked utterly defeated. Beaten. Old.

He buried his face in his hands. What the hell had he done? *Bloody hell!* This was a nightmare.

The barges sailed off, along with the shreds of his heart. James turned to Ducky, a rush of determination firing through him. "Tomorrow. That should give us just enough time."

Ducky frowned at him. "To do what?"

"Get our asses to Weatherington and back."

"Weathington?"

"I need another Captain Steele in the mix. Time to tell my father, I found his ship."

Chapter 26

Two pairs of strong hands grabbed for Samantha and pulled her toward the waiting barge. Pure panic surged through her. *Wait, this wasn't the plan. What was he doing?* "James!"

He stood there. Stone still. Ducky at his side. Were they speaking? From this distance, she couldn't tell. Her heart started to pound. She pulled against the rough hands tugging on her. Any second James would march forward, part the sea of uniforms between them, and take her away from this madness.

But he didn't move, not an inch. The cold truth slapped her across the face. Terror clawed its way up her spine. She pleaded silently with him. Her gaze locked with his across the space. *Please, move. Say something. Stop them.*

"Oh, God, he lied...." The cold truth punched the air from her lungs. James had no intention of stopping her transfer to the tower. He was going to stand there and watch it happen. *Let it happen.* The edges of her vision hazed. "He lied...." A buzz in her ears drowned out the sounds around her. The world went gray.

Two guards held tight to her upper arms, otherwise, she would have fallen into the feted water of the Thames. Instead, they carried—or dragged— her to one of the waiting barges, shoved her in, then carried her through the arched water gate known to all as Traitor's Gate before delivering her into the hands of her jailors.

They led her through a maze of tight stone corridors and narrow curved staircases until finally unshackling her wrists before pushing her into a small cramped cell and slamming the thick wooden door behind her.

A narrow slit of a window sat high in the far wall, allowing only a weak shaft of light into the dank space. The area in front of the window bore the evidence of the cell's past inhabitants. Stones removed, in perhaps a vain attempt at escape, had created a makeshift seat in the thick outer wall. Over the years, the seat had been smoothed and worn by prisoners clinging to the faint sliver of light that struggled through the window. It was a fragile hold on the outside world while they awaited their fate.

Samantha tried to climb the slick stones. She couldn't breathe. The smell inside the cell was indescribable. Filth crept up the stones of the walls and darkened the corners. She didn't dare think about what else occupied her cell within the lumps of rotting straw.

Pulling her knees to her chest, Samantha curled into the window seat. From this vantage point she could see a tiny corner of sky. Trembling with a mixture of shock, and fright, she hung on to that little triangle of cloudless blue in a world gone dark and tried to make sense out of what had happened.

She'd been betrayed. That was what had happened. James had stood there, staring. He hadn't moved or spoken. All his promises and endless planning—what had they been for? How many times had he gone over them? Made sure she repeated them to assure she fully understood. Why would he have gone to all the trouble? What was it all for?

An elaborate ruse to keep her in his bed? Sick entertainment to fill the hours? It made no sense. But there she stood on that accused dock, like some naïve fool believing he would sweep in and rescue her again. How many times did she have to face the cold reality that no one could save her. Not even herself.

She'd committed the ultimate sin. Wanting and reaching for more than she deserved. Coveting another life. She should have been content to stay in South Oxbridge and marry a farm boy, raise another crop of farm boys, and die old, worn, and empty. No, she had wanted to sail to a new land, to a promise of wealth and privilege. Be the bright star in her family's lives. Relieve their burden. Pull them back from the brink of poverty. Share her good fortune.

Instead, she chose to ignore the wee small voice in the back of her head warning her of Wessler's lies. She wanted so much to believe them, she had sailed across an entire ocean and into hell itself. It was only by grace her family didn't lose everything waiting for her to shower them with riches.

And now, she had done it again. Reached for something beyond her grasp. Fallen in love with a man she had no right to and believed another clever set of lies. Yet another host of empty promises. But even as the thought filtered through her mind, her heart fought against it.

James loved her. How many times had he pledged himself to her? Taken her into his bed and shown her a tenderness and loving passion that made her love him more as each day passed? Was it all a sick hoax?

He'd deceived her... used her... lied to her.

No! Samantha wrapped her arms around herself and held tight. *Not James.* Not the man who nursed her back from her wound, fed her broth, bathed her skin through a fever. Not the man who loved her, touched her the way he did, kissed her on the decks at night, whispered tender endearments while surrounded by starlight.

He couldn't have lied. But here she sat, hanging on to a speck of sky the color of his eyes.

Samantha covered her mouth as the tears wrenched from her soul began to fall. *He couldn't have....* The image of him standing in the sunlight, coldly watching as she was dragged onto the prison barge, would forever be etched in her mind. A sob wracked though her body.

Oh, God, he did.

She pulled the tail of her shirt to wipe at her eyes. *His best shirt.* Anger and grief welled and crashed over her. Grabbing a fist full of snowy linen sleeve, she ripped it to hang from its shoulder seam. Samantha tugged at the neckline, tearing the ties holding it closed at her throat.

With her chest pumping like hearth bellows, the paleness of her breasts stopped her from shredding the garment. She covered her face, destined to wear the shirt of her ill-fated love when they ended her ill-fated life.

* * * *

"This is not the way to Weatherington." Ducky raced behind James.

"Did you think I planned to walk there?"

"No, but where—"

James kept up his long strides. Time was wasting. He could almost hear the tick of the clock in his head. "Lillian's."

Ducky grabbed at his sleeve and dragged him to a stop. "Have you lost your mind? You can't see her now."

James pulled away and kept walking. "Why not?"

Ducky rushed to keep up. "And say what? 'Oh hello, darling, I've been gone for months, but the only reason I'm here is for your carriage. I must rush home to get my parents to help me save the woman I am terribly in love with. You don't mind, do you?' She'll bat those ice-jade eyes of hers and reply, 'Of course not, my dearest, take my carriage. As that's surely the last possession of mine you'll ever touch. Enjoy... kiss kiss.'"

"Lillian never says, 'kiss kiss.'" James quickened his pace. "Besides, there's a good chance we'll not see Lillian. She's not much of a homebody. I will leave a note with her maid, and when I return, I'll speak to her about the rest."

"The rest," Ducky scoffed. "As in, you've fallen in love with someone else, the marriage is off, she is going to be a social laughing stock? *That* rest?"

James shot him a glance over his shoulder. "You do have the annoying habit of pointing out the obvious."

"Someone has to keep their wits about them. I'm still shocked it's me," Ducky panted.

Soon they reached the Waterford's grand London home. Set back from the street, large ornate iron gates guarded the entrance. James took the wide front stairs two at a time. He'd been there a hundred times and refused to stand on ceremony. He let himself in and came face to face with Lillian's butler. The man's eyebrows nearly parted his hair.

James handed off his hat. "Basil."

He'd completely flustered the man, but he had the impeccable training not to show it. However, he couldn't stop his wide forehead from starting to sweat. "Captain Steele, sir. We were not expecting you until later this week." He took Ducky's hat as well.

James pushed past and peered into the library. It was empty. "Winds were with me. Is Lillian at home?"

"Yes, however Lady Waterford is with... a... caller at present. If you and your companion will wait here, I will announce—"

"Since when do I need to be announced? Is she in the parlor? Never mind, I'll find her." He gave the man's shoulder a quick pat.

Basil rushed to step in front of him. "I am afraid I must insist, Captain Steele. Lady Waterford is not prepared to greet you, if you will kindly wait—"

"So sorry, Basil, but we're in rather a rush." James paused by the parlor doors and turned back to him. "In fact, if you would be a good chap and get word to the groom, I'll need Lady Waterford's carriage readied as quickly as possible."

Opening the double doors, he discovered the cause of Basil's damp forehead and urgent insistence. Lillian and her "caller" scrambled to right themselves. No small feat with yards of skirt pushed clear to her waist and one pale breast freed from the confines of its corset.

The man valiantly tried to shield Lillian while she shot to her feet. Turning her back on them, she attempted to repair her appearance. He was tall and broad through the shoulders. Course clothing. Smelled of horses.

Ducky chuckled. "Ah, looks like you'll be able to inform the groom yourself."

Lillian spun back around, frantically smoothing her platinum hair. "James, you're back."

James raised an eyebrow. "You don't look... pleased."

Her corset was still alarmingly askew. Red flushed her chest and brightened her cheeks. "This isn't what it looks like."

"It looks like you're getting private riding lessons from your groom."

"And losing another groom in the process," chuckled Ducky.

James glared at him. "Shut up, Dunbar."

Ducky leaned toward the flustered stable master. "Captain Steele wants a carriage horsed and ready. I trust you're properly motivated to make haste in providing that?"

The man didn't need a second invitation to leave. With a quick exchange of glances between he and Lillian, she nodded and he gathered his jacket and left.

"Ducky, oversee the carriage, won't you?" James jerked his head toward the gaping parlor doors.

"Certainly. Come, Basil, scandal always makes me ravenous, and I'm guessing Captain Steele will be requiring some stiff refreshments for our trip. We'll raid the kitchens first, then find what's hiding in the brandy closet."

As soon as the doors shut behind them, Lillian's composure crumbled. "James, I can explain."

He shook his head. "There's no need, Lillian. My eyesight is perfect."

With each panicked breath, her milky right breast threatened to escape its confines. She fluffed at her wrinkled hems before notching her chin. "You don't seem the least bit upset. You're not angry, or even unnerved."

He lifted a hand. The observation didn't surprise him quite as much as it did her. "I'm none of those things actually."

She planted her hands on her hips. A hank of silvery blonde hair fell from her elaborate hairstyle onto her shoulder. "Then what are you?"

"Frankly, Lillian, I'm relieved. Over the last few weeks, I have been regretting our arrangement, and now we can both make a clean break of it. Truth be told, I'm happy for you and...and..." He waved a hand toward the doors.

"Gerald," she replied sheepishly.

"Yes," he smiled. "Gerald. I hope you two are well suited."

Lillian narrowed her eyes at him. "Why are you being so gracious?"

"I wish I had time to explain it to you, but as you've gathered, I'm in a quite a hurry to get to Weatherington."

She dropped the hands from her hips. "Weatherington? Is someone ill? Your parents? Alicia?" Two flushed spots heightened the color on her cheeks.

"Your concern is touching. No, as far as I know, my parents are fine. Alicia is well. I have urgent information I must deliver, however." He bent to kiss her cheek just as her breast escaped its hasty prison. "I'll explain all another time. In the meanwhile, my darling, you may need some help from your maid reining in your chest... and I believe there's horse shit on your carpet."

* * * *

Leaving the city, the horses were given free rein. The coach raced north.

Ducky roared with laughter. "The bloody groom?"

"Better him than me." James took a swallow of his drink. He couldn't think about Lillian right now. His mind had only one thought—get to Weatherington as quickly as possible. He hadn't even thought about what he would say to his father. *'Oh by the way, I found the Scarlet Night. Aunt Alice is due to hang in the next few days. Don't mention it to Mother, will you.'*

He refilled his glass. Perhaps more brandy would erase the scene forever branded in his mind. The look of pure terror on Samantha's face as she cried out his name. The men lowering her into the barge. And worse than the fear, her face as she coped with the pain of his perceived betrayal. Nothing tore at him more than knowing how deeply he'd hurt her.

Hours later, he nudged Ducky out of his brandy-induced slumber. "We're here."

The coach turned in to the long cypress-lined lane leading up to his parents' grand estate. Wide, rolling fields of brilliant green stretched on as far as the eye could see in both directions. His father once described it as trading a blue rolling sea for a green one.

The house, while modest in scale of grand estates, was still impressive. Built of stone, it replaced the old manor that was destroyed by fire shortly before his parents met. They'd matched the old-world details of the original—stone archways and full gables lining the roof, but at less than forty years old, the estate was still regarded as new.

James was out of the coach before it stopped rolling and took the stairs two at a time. Bursting into the wide marbled foyer, he called out,

"Father?" He flung open the heavy doors leading into his father's study. His wide leather desk chair sat empty.

Back in the foyer, he called up the sweeping staircase, "Father? Mother?"

His sister appeared at the top of the stairs, "James, is it you?" Lifting her skirts, she rushed down the stairs and leapt into his waiting arms. "What are you doing here?" She kissed his cheeks. "The letter announcing your commission arrived day before last. We're all so proud, but we didn't expect to see you until the wedding. Wait until you see my new dress. Mother and I have been with the dressmaker all week."

James hugged her and spun her about. "You'll have to cancel the new wardrobe. I'm afraid the wedding is off." He lowered her to her feet in front of a grinning Ducky.

The man looked as if he'd woken from a year's nap. "Alicia..." He breathed her name.

"Hello, Goose." She batted her eyelashes at him. The two had a playful, sibling-like relationship. Yet there seemed a new appreciation in Ducky's eye. They hadn't seen each other in near two years. However, James neither had the time to analyze it, nor to ship Alicia away to a convent.

"Wait." She spun back to James. "The wedding is off? Why?"

"Lillian preferred steed over Steele, I'm afraid," quipped Ducky.

"What?" Wide blue eyes blinked at both of them.

"Don't listen to him. It's complicated, but right now I need to speak to Father."

"You've missed them. Both Mother and Father have gone to London."

"Bloody hell," cursed Ducky, earning a disapproving raised eyebrow from Alicia.

James tugged her sleeve to pull her attention back to him. "When?"

She shrugged one shoulder. "First light this morning."

"We must have passed them going the other way," Ducky noted.

"Why were they headed to London?"

Alicia held out her hands, palms up. "I'm not sure. We were sitting at breakfast when the Robbins arrived."

"Robbins?" James searched his memory.

"Yes, Ric and his wife, Jo Beau. She's French. Lovely dark hair."

James drew his brows together. "I don't know a Ric or Jo Beau Robbins. Who are they?"

"Mother and Father knew them. Or at least they knew Ric. Mother was so excited to see him. She called him 'Henry' at first. Tall, blond hair, a bit gray at the temples. Very handsome." She shot Ducky a coy look before continuing. "He must have had something to do with Father's days as a privateer. They'd traveled from America. Jo Beau's father was sick, and they'd just come from visiting France."

"What did they want?"

"I didn't hear all of it. Evidently, when Ric and Jo Beau returned to London, they heard something about Father's old ship being there. The captain is in trouble?" Alicia shrugged again. "All I know is, they all left in a great hurry."

"We'll need fresh horses if we're to catch up with them."

Ducky nodded before he left in search of a servant. "I'm getting good at this."

Chapter 27

"How many times do I need to tell you? I don't want to see him."

The guard dropped a basket of fresh bread. "He's a persistent sot, I'll give 'im that. Been here since dawn."

Samantha pulled her knees to her chest and huddled tighter. "I have nothing to say to him."

"Suit yerself." The door closed with a solid slam.

Her small triangle of blue sky hid behind a blanket of drizzling clouds. The dampness oozed between the rocks and leached their chill into Samantha's bones. She couldn't sleep. She'd lost all track of time. The concept of six bells was a long lost world away.

Sometime after noon, they brought her more food, but she hadn't been able to keep the vile slop down. She'd survived without food before, and she was too light headed and nauseous to care.

She thought about Tupper. Samantha hadn't seen her since they were transferred from the barge into the tower. Was she close? Had she already been brought before the magistrate? Did she still live, or had she gotten her wish for a quick end to her life? Bump's death destroyed her. It made Samantha's heart ache to think about it. Perhaps it was a better that Bump died trying to be a hero rather than swinging for being a thief and a traitor. Had she a choice, she would have picked anything over hanging. She closed a hand over her throat and fought the urge to retch.

Fear's icy fingers joined the chill of the stones. Samantha's body wracked with a fierce shudder. Closing her eyes, she pulled her knees tighter to her chest and lowered her forehead to them. Perhaps if she simply curled into herself, she would disappear.

Like Tupper, Samantha didn't care anymore. Her fate was sealed. She had been used and broken. Letting her live with the shame and an empty future would be a crueler sentence than the rope.

When James held her gaze back on the dock, pinning her with his ice-blue eyes, and didn't give the order to stop her transfer, part of her died. His silence hollowed out the space within her chest where her heart once resided, where it once fluttered at his touch. A now empty cave that had known the joy of his kisses and the passion of his lovemaking

All they had shared between them was stripped away in a single moment. Samantha hoped the hangman's noose would make quick work and end the pain of her own heart's betrayal.

She'd cried out to James. Begged for his help. But there was no help for her. He'd lied by promising amnesty when there was none. There would be no forever for them. She'd fallen for his every deception.

The scrape of the iron key in the cell's ancient lock brought Samantha out of her thoughts. Four more guards entered the tiny space.

"I told you—"

"On yer feet. Ye've a date with the magistrate, 'n he hates bein' kept waitin.'"

"A date, and me without a maid to see to my hair." Her bravado shook from her soul.

"What hair ye got. Look like a sickly lad to me. 'Course, no lad e'er had such a lovely set of breasts, aye gents?"

Samantha crossed her arms and glared at the guard. She held her tongue. Hanging would be bad enough. She didn't fancy fighting off a detail of rutting guards as well.

"Put yer hands behind yer back," ordered one.

The heavy shackles snapped over each wrist. A guard took each arm. The other two flanked her front and back. They led her down two flights of stairs and through a maze of cell-lined halls. Shouts, leers, and lurid comments sprang from each rat hole. It was dark and rank, and the smell stung at her nose. Was it because she was a woman that they'd put her in an upper cell? She never thought she'd be grateful for such a thing.

The guards marched her down yet another spiraled set of stairs to a door, which blissfully opened to the outdoors. Samantha dragged fresh air into her lungs. Walking the short distance between buildings, she passed the waiting gallows at the river's edge. Empty gibbets swung in the damp, fetid breeze as they awaited new occupants. Sleek-headed ravens pecked with thick beaks through the green stretch of lawn. They reminded her of

Leviticus. A huge clock tower nearby struck three o'clock... *six bells....* The sudden lump in Samantha's throat threatened to choke her.

Her guards escorted her into the magistrate's chamber. Tiered rows filled with wigged officials whispered, gestured, and rudely pointed in her direction as she was brought before the robed members of the judicial parliament. The guards pushed her into a tiny cage to stand before the men who would ultimately seal her fate.

Her shirt gapped in the front and hung off her shoulder where she'd torn it. She wished she wasn't shackled and could at least cover herself. She'd never felt this exposed. Vulnerable. Defenseless.

The room buzzed with conversation. Her heart pounded over the din. Try as she might, Samantha could not help but scan the gallery. Wigs in various shades of gray and beige sat atop each head in the sea of faces staring down at her.

Then she saw him.

His head was unburdened by any wig, with russet hair kissed light in streaks by the sun, and a hauntingly familiar pair of blue eyes. Once again, he was the most noticeable man in the room. He held her gaze. The hollow space in her chest echoed with a crippling ache. She closed her eyes as a fresh wave of pain crashed over her.

Turning away, the pounding of a gavel startled her. A stern, dark-browed man stood and unfurled an elaborate scroll.

"Samantha Christian, you have been charged with piracy upon the high seas in direct disregard of the laws of this land. The defiance of the crown's order of surrender adds the second charge of treason. Both charges are subject to a sentence of death by hanging. Do you understand the charges?"

"Y..." The word stuck in her throat. "Yes," she croaked.

"What plead ye?" His voice boomed in the silent room.

Samantha struggled to stay standing. Her knees shook. "I am guilty, Your Honor."

The crowded room sprang to life. The noise hit her like a fist. Repetitive raps of the gavel attempted to regain order to the proceedings.

"Do you realize what you're saying, Mistress Christian?" the magistrate addressed her. "By pleading guilty, you leave this court no choice but to bring the full sentence down upon you. Is it your wish to sign your death warrant today?"

"I am certain as to the outcome of these proceedings, sir. I would think my expediting matters would be seen as favorable to you." She lifted her chin. "Today is as good as any other to die, don't you agree?"

The uproar was once again brought to a halt by the pounding of the gavel. "Do you not have anything to say in your defense?"

"I have no defense. I was thrown into a series of circumstances I could never have imagined, nor prevented. I did what I needed to do to survive. I am grateful to Captain Tupper Quinn for saving me. It would be my only wish to do the same for her in return."

She tipped her chin. "You see only the surface of our offenses, sir, and care little as to the cause of what drove us to commit them. I wonder if, put in the same position, you fine gentlemen would not find yourselves fighting for your life and livelihood behind the barrel of a pistol or the swing of a sword."

"*We* are not standing trial, Mistress Christian."

"Yes, sir, and as I said, I am guilty. Let us be done with this."

"If that is your wish, so be it. Samantha Christian, you have pled guilty to piracy and treason against the king. You shall be held in the Tower of London until such time as this court issues its sentence upon you. At that time, you will be given the opportunity to make one final plea for your life. I would suggest you think long and hard before discarding that final opportunity."

The guards dragged Samantha away amid the shouts and protests of the crowd. They marched her silently back to her tower cell.

Chapter 28

James stood in shock as he watched Samantha being led away. *Guilty?* Foolish, foolish woman. Didn't she realize her stubborn pride would end with her swinging in the gallows? She hadn't tried to explain how she came to be part of the crew of the *Scarlet Night*. Her desperation to leave Virginia, nor a word of Tupper's hand in what happened.

What had she done? He'd told her to plead her innocence. More than a dozen times. Had she heard none of it?

He dropped into a chair and held his head. How had everything gone so horribly wrong? Marcus had deceived him. He had followed procedure as ordered. *'No woman would hang for piracy.'* The trial would be a formality. James did as he was ordered, and handed Samantha and Tupper over. He'd saved his commission and his future, all the while ripping his heart from his chest.

But then they had kept Samantha from him. He'd tried to see her the next day, but he'd been denied access to her or to Tupper. The order came directly from Marcus. He'd been tricked. Admiral Marcus knew full well there would be no leniency shown to either woman. James had to resort to bribing Samantha's guards to gain access to her only to have her refuse to talk to him.

When Samantha first stood in the defendant's cage and looked up at him, he could read her thoughts as easily as he had always done. She was lost, without hope. Who or what had torn at her clothes? She looked beaten. Crushed by his betrayal. After all they had shared, how could she believe he would deceive her? He must find a way to reach her. Push past the wall of her hurt. If only he could talk to her, even for just a moment.

He had to make her understand before it was too late. He wouldn't watch her hang. Not for the crime of signing her damned name.

He and Ducky had left Weatherington and raced back to London. It took more than a day to track down his parents. James found them leaving the Tower of London as he was about to enter.

"Father!"

"James, my son." His father slapped a wide hand to his shoulder.

His mother hugged him and cupped his cheek. "Darling."

James looked between the two. They were his guideposts through his entire life. He owed his strength and sense of honor to them both. But standing in the shadow of the Tower with his future locked in a cell within its thick walls, he needed their guidance and wisdom more than ever before.

"Have you seen her?" James asked.

"Looks rough as hell. Did you have to be so bloody hard on her?" His father planted his hands on his hips and scowled.

"He's not talking about your damn ship, Jaxon," his mother chided. "I believe he was asking if we've seen Alice." She turned back to James. "And the answer to your question is no. They've denied us any access to her. We can't even get her a message."

James shook his head. "The entire situation is in chaos. Finding Alice and returning the *Scarlet Night* is only part of it. What you don't know is somewhere along the way, I've lost my heart." He told them about Samantha. "If ever I needed your guidance...."

"Not sure we can help anyone." His father scrubbed at his jaw. "I've appealed to everyone I can talk to. I've pulled every string I can think of, greased every palm, but I'm getting nowhere. Even if I could get to Tupper before she's led to the gallows, my reach wouldn't extend to Mistress Christian."

"There has to be something we can do." The muscle in James's jaw turned to stone.

His mother gazed at him with sorrow in her eyes.

James took her hand. "I'm sorry. The last thing Alice wanted was to hurt you."

"I only hope I can see her once more."

"I want more than that with Samantha. I want what you two have. A lifetime."

After watching her plead guilty, he doubted he'd ever know that kind of life, but he had one final card to play. He would need to wait a little while longer. When they issued her sentence, he could file the proper petition. But the waiting was torture, and there was no guarantee the appeal would be granted.

If only she would see him. James refused to give up. He went to her every day, twice a day, asking to see her. Each time she would deny him, telling her guards she didn't want to see him. He wrote letters, notes. Each one was returned to him unopened.

He brought her fresh food and water, and a blanket to keep the chill from her. He paid a high price to the guards to deliver each item. Later they would jibe him, joking he should save his money. She'd be dead soon one way or the other. She refused to eat. Threw up anything she tried. No one had seen her sleep.

That made two of them. James hadn't slept in days. When he did manage to drop into a fitful sleep out of pure exhaustion, he'd see Samantha in his dreams. They were twisted, disjointed dreams where he'd begin reliving the tender moments of their time together on the *Lion*. Nursing her back to health. Bathing her. Tending her. Then the pleasures of lying with her, tasting her kisses, stroking her skin, stirring her passion during long stolen nights.

But the dreams always ended the same horrible way, with the two of them standing on the scaffold. The crowd before them jeering and taunting Samantha before the rough loop of hemp scraped down over her haunted face. She turned to him, pleading that it had all been a mistake.

Only James himself was her hangman. As he tightened the noose about her neck, his hands seemed unattached to his body. They acted of their own volition, out of his control, moving over the lever, grasping it firmly. He could feel the firmness of the wood beneath his fingers and see the whiteness of his knuckles, but there the connection to his body's actions ended.

In his dream, muscle fought muscle as the battle between his brain and his physical movements waged. Samantha pleaded. In his mind, he is screaming, begging for her forgiveness, ordering his body to stop. But his mouth remains shut. Then his mutinous hand pulls the lever and he shuddered awake. Sweating and shaking, his fear and heartache for Samantha fresh and raw.

A few agonizing days after Samantha pled guilty, James sat once more high in the gallery. Every seat was taken. Men lined the walls. News had traveled through the city like quick fire. Samantha Christian and Tupper Quinn were two lawless, morally bankrupt, cutthroat pirates. Their executions were to be a stark warning that the crown had no tolerance for their crimes. If they broke the king's laws like men, they would hang like men.

The din surrounding him turned metallic in his head as the guards led Samantha back to the defendant's circle, hands shackled in front of her. The heavy chain rattled as they moved her into place. Her clothing hung on her gaunt frame. She looked impossibly pale and weak. He could see her body tremble. Had she continued to be ill? Had her fever returned?

The scene before him was an exact copy of the last time, with one exception. Samantha kept her eyes locked to the floor. She didn't look around. Didn't scan the gallery. Was she hoping he wasn't there? James silently willed her to lift her eyes and look at him.

Samantha flinched as the gavel struck its block. Still, she studied the boards at her feet.

"Mistress Samantha Christian." The magistrate's voice boomed over the crowd. A collective hush followed. "You have been accused and pled guilty to the charges of piracy and treason against king and country and have given up all rights to defend your action before this assembly. Do you now have anything to say to this court before we pass sentence?"

James clenched his hands into fists. The room seemed to hold its breath. Silence shimmered in the air. Samantha didn't move. Didn't lift her eyes. Refused to speak. A murmur began to encircle her. *Damn it, Samantha, say something. Defend yourself. Fight, dammit. Fight for us!*

She said nothing.

"Very well," the magistrate continued. "It is hereby decided at the hour of dawn on the morning of the eleventh day of the eleventh month, you shall be taken to the gallows and hung by the neck until dead. Your body shall then be striped, tarred, and placed in a gibbet to hang over the water of the Thames for a period of ninety days as a gruesome reminder to all who see it."

James jerked like he'd received the first whip of a cat-o'-nine-tails. Around him, the crowd surged into life. The sound of the gavel echoed the hammering of nails into Samantha's coffin. It rang in James's ears, each rap piercing his heart. Even though he anticipated this outcome, the shock of the actual proceedings threw him. Had he not held the petition of appeal in his coat, he would have leapt into the fray, seized her, and tried to battle their way out. No doubt, they both would die in the attempt, but desperation drove men to do fatal things.

The guards flanking Samantha each grabbed an arm. Samantha twitched as if a small part of her had suddenly awoke. She looked up, stunned. "Wait."

The magistrate was already on his feet, gathering parchments. "I'm sorry, you were given a chance to speak. You refused. Sentence has been passed." He waved a dismissive hand. "Take her away."

"No," she pleaded. Samantha tugged against the guard's iron grip. "No. Please. I have to speak. There something you must know." Samantha called out over the noise of the crowd. "Please."

The sharp beating of the gavel called for quiet once again. "Young woman, you're trying the patience of this court. Say what you must, and be quick about it."

"Yes, Your Honor. I did plead guilty, and I'm prepared to meet my punishment, but while I care little for my own life, I wonder if the good men of this court will sentence a woman to death and at the same time kill an innocent child."

The immediate uproar in the room was deafening as everyone leapt to their feet. Members of the gallery shouted at one another. James stood frozen to the spot. He dragged his gaze away from Samantha and watched the gavel strike six, seven, eight times yet the noise in the chamber continued. Or was it the noise in his head?

Pandemonium surrounded him, inside as well as out. He looked back at her.

In the midst of the tempest, Samantha raised her eyes to his. If he harbored even a sliver of belief that this was a clever ploy to save her neck, it was dashed the moment her eyes locked with his. She was telling the truth. He could read it in her eyes. She was carrying a child. *His child!*

A wave of emotions capsized him. Disbelief, shock, utter indescribable joy, paralyzing fear, staggering determination to see her freed once and for all, and a welling of love for her deeper than he had felt for any other being. Deeper than the widest ocean.

The pounding of the gavel finally pierced through the chaos, and the magistrate shouted over the din.

"Mistress Christian, are you telling this court you are with child?"

Samantha's eyes never left James's as tears welled up and breached the edge of her lashes to roll down her pale, dirt-smudge cheeks. She nodded.

"Yes." Samantha looked back at the magistrate. "Yes," she proclaimed louder. "Kill me. I accept my fate. I no longer care about my own life, but I beg you, save my baby. You can't kill this child." She splayed a protective hand across her belly.

Chapter 29

Shouts of the crowd followed Samantha as the guards hauled her from the gallery and dragged her back to the tower. The magistrate, after turning a brilliant shade of crimson, had stayed her execution and ordered her back to her cell. It was agreed a physician would be sent to examine her. If she told the truth and she was indeed with child, she would remain in the tower until the child was born. The baby would be taken from her and her hanging would take place immediately thereafter.

Sitting within her stone cradle, Samantha spread her hands across her belly. She didn't need the verification of a physician. She had all the indications. At first, she had discounted them. Faintness, nausea, the inability to hold down food. Certainly, mortal fear for her life would cause the same symptoms. But the calendar could not lie. She'd missed her monthly. As soon as she stopped to count days, then weeks, the truth filled her with a profound sadness.

It wasn't sadness at the prospect of carrying a child—James's child—but the thought of having a son or daughter she would never see grow. She would never see smile, take a first step, or hear the first words. She would miss it all. Their precious child maturing into an adult, finding their way in the world, watching them fall in love.

Would James claim the babe? Would he and Lillian raise her bastard? Or would they cast it aside? Send it to an orphanage? The thought churned through her. Perhaps she could write one of her sisters. Samantha buried her face in her hands. Could she bring that kind of shame to her family? Tell them the entire sordid story about Wessler and Tupper and James? For the sake of her child?

Samantha curled into her spot by the window and reached toward her scrap of blue sky. She had no answers, but thank God, she now, at least, had time.

As it had since she first spied it, the tiny bit of blue reminded her of James's eyes. He'd been shocked by her news. She could read it on his face. It still hurt to think about him and his betrayal. She couldn't look upon him with anything other than anger and humiliation, but the sharp edge of that hurt had begun to dull into a deep ache she was sure to carry with her, along with his child, for the rest of her days.

Samantha smoothed a hand over her belly. A child conceived in half the love was still better than no love at all. And she did love James. Past tense, of course. Loved. She'd laid with him freely. Given him what she'd never given any other man—her whole self. She'd believed him when he professed his love for her. Their joining had created this life, and for a few blissfully ignorant weeks she had basked in the idea of loving someone and having them love her in return.

Perhaps he had been a master manipulator. He could be the most cunning and accomplished liar she'd ever known, second to Damian Wessler, but together they'd created this child. If nothing else, she would focus only the purest love on its tiny soul.

Samantha drew up her knees and curled protectively around the baby growing inside. Closing her eyes, she imagined it was a boy. He would have chubby legs that never stopped running, a beautiful smile that lit up the world, and two pieces of the sky for his eyes.

Tears choked her. There'd been too many lies. She couldn't do it to herself as well. She still loved James. Present tense. God help her. Beyond all the hurt, there it was… She loved him and his child growing within her. Loved them both with her whole heart.

* * * *

Later, as darkness fell, her guard carried in a lantern with yet another small basket heaped with fresh food. There were fruits and hearty bread free of crawling creatures, cheese wrapped in cloth, clean water. Gifts from James again, no doubt, but she hesitated refusing it this time. It would do her and the baby well to try and eat something.

She lifted an apple and smelled its sweetness.

"Ye've a visitor," grumbled the guard.

"Don't you tire of saying that? You know my answer. Thank him for the food, but I still don't want to see him."

"It ain't the muleheaded captain brought this. Not this time. Came to his senses finally. First day he hasn't wandered the place like the blasted ravens. Nay, it's a fine lady brought the food, daring to soil her hems. Says she wants te talk."

Samantha stood. Could it be Tupper? She frowned. She didn't know if she'd describe Tupper as a "fine" lady in skirts, but who else could it be? No one else knew she was here. "Does she have dark hair, with a silver stripe? Green eyes?"

"I'm afraid not." The lady in question came in behind the guard. "I've always wished my eyes were green, however."

She lifted her skirts and moved into the cell. In the dim light, her eyes looked almost golden. Who was she? Lovely, with almost a regal air about her, she wore a cape the color of copper over a stunning gown of green.

Her hair was silvered around the edges of her gentle face, softening its bright penny coloring. She carried another bundle.

"I'd heard you were slight. I hope I guessed your size correctly." She handed Samantha the package.

Samantha took it from her outstretched hand and held it to her chest. "I don't understand. Who are you?"

"My name is Lady Annalise Steele. I believe you're carrying my first grandchild."

Samantha needed to step back. Suddenly lightheaded, she needed to sit back on her rocky ledge to keep from fainting. "L-lady Steele?" She caught the package before it fell into the muck and held it in her lap.

"Yes, my dear, are you all right?"

Samantha placed a hand over her pounding heart. "Surprised is all. Why? Why are you here?"

The lovely woman smiled. "My son asked me to do him a favor."

"What kind of favor?"

Lady Steele held up two gloved fingers. "Two actually. The first was to secure you the gown you're holding." She pointed to the package.

Samantha stared once more at the parcel in her lap. She lifted her gaze. "And the second?"

"Why, to get you to agree to open the door, of course." Annalise Steele pulled open the thick cell door that still stood ajar.

"Thank you, Mother." James kissed his mother's cheek. His gaze never left Samantha. "I can take it from here."

Annalise placed a hand on her son's chest. "Anytime, darling." She smiled back at Samantha. "I wish I could stay longer, but there is another matter needing my attention tonight and I really must rush. I hope you'll excuse me." With that, she swept out of Samantha's cell as simply as she'd swept in.

The sight of James standing in the glow of the lantern stole her breath. He wasn't in his uniform. Instead, he wore rich evening clothes. The light caught at the silver threads edging the black silk of his beautifully tailored waistcoat and shown in the polish of his tall boots. For all the anger and hurt, this was the real reason she hadn't wanted to see him. The ache of loving him and not being able to have him was more than she could bear.

"Please...I can't..."

"I have one more favor and another request." He hadn't moved.

Samantha closed her eyes to the sound of his voice. She pulled in a shuddered breath before opening them again, steeling her heart against the desperate pull of her emotions. "What's the favor?"

He held her gaze for a long moment before whispering, "Forgive me."

The air rushed out of her lungs. She covered her eyes as those two words propelled her back to their first kiss. Back to the second she fell in love with him. When the only thing good in her world was the taste of his lips and the safety she found in his arms.

James didn't wait for her to respond. He told her about his meeting with Admiral Marcus. "I couldn't reach you in time to explain. All I kept thinking was you trusted me once, I prayed you'd trust me again."

"I did trust you, and they still dragged me away. How could I have known? I was alone and scared to death. You promised me, and then you just stood there and watched them take me."

"I know, and I'm so incredibly sorry. You have to understand, I had no choice. Marcus saw to that. It was beyond my power. If I fought what was happening, they would have arrested me as well, and you'd not be standing there with a gown in your hands and an open door awaiting you."

Her head and her heart were playing tug of war. She lifted a hand to her forehead. "How does a gown and the door have anything to do with this? What are you talking about?"

"You're being released."

Samantha shook her head. "That's impossible. You were in the gallery. You heard them pronounce sentence."

"Aye, I was in the gallery. I was there when they sentenced you. I was also there when you told the world you were carrying my child."

She swallowed the sudden lump in her throat. "Then you also know I'll never be allowed to hold my baby in my arms before I'm hauled away to the gallows."

"Darling, you're not listening." He took a step toward her. "You're free to go. You and your baby. Our baby. With me."

Samantha was sure this was some kind of dream. Any moment she'd awaken and this would all have been some fanciful imagining.

"I was planning to file your appeal the second after you were sentenced, but it was you who added the perfect final argument to my case."

Samantha's head was still spinning. "What final argument? I don't understand."

"I was fully prepared to cite the fact that *you* never signed the Ship's Articles for the *Scarlet Night*."

She shook her head and stood. "But I did."

"No, Samantha Christian never signed them. *Sam* Christian signed those Articles. Sam may have existed, he may have been a member of their crew, he may have even raised a weapon against an English warship, but given the fact Sam Christian, cabin *boy*, couldn't possibly be carrying a child, they obviously had the wrong person in custody."

"You're not serious. It couldn't be that simple." She clutched the parcel she still held to her chest and started to turn away.

He pulled a parchment from his pocket. "I have your release right here."

Samantha's knees weakened. James was at her side in an instant, catching her in his arms. He held her tight, talking gently into her hair. "It was bad enough for the magistrate to face the prospect of hanging a woman, but a pregnant woman? A new mother? Leaving an infant alone in the world? Can you imagine the outcry? I knew the situation was tenuous at best. With just the right pressure on just the right person, I knew they'd agree to make this case quietly disappear."

"And you? Is that what you'd rather? That I quietly disappear?"

James tipped her chin and gazed at her. He cupped her cheek and brushed the edge of her lower lip before lowering his mouth to hers for a tender kiss. "Don't be ridiculous. I have you in my arms. I'm not about to let you go ever again." His hand slipped between them and rested on the plane of her stomach. "Not when you carry my child, as well as my heart."

"But your future? Your marriage to Lillian? If you've done this because of the baby—"

"The baby is again the perfect final argument to my case." He slipped his arm around her waist and drew her close. "I broke things off with Lillian the day we anchored. Seems she found herself another groom." He smiled. "It's you I want to spend the rest of my life with. The fact you're having my child is like blue skies *and* fair winds. A blessing on top of a blessing. I promised you I would go all the way to the king if needed to be with you. Turns out I only needed to go as far as the archbishop. That is where my request comes in."

Samantha was almost afraid to ask. Afraid to burst the bubble of joy she felt in his arms once again. "What is your request?"

He slipped the parcel from her grasp and held it up. "Put on this gown so you can marry me."

"Marry you?"

"Archbishop Tenison is elderly and his heart has softened over the years, but he is still not a patient man. He's waiting to marry us. Tonight."

Chapter 30

Tupper paced her cell. "How much longer we gonna do this?" she yelled. The stones of the walls swallowed the sound. "What's a person gotta do to get hung around here?" She pounded on the door. "Give me the damn rope, and I'll do it myself."

She slumped along the sidewall and stretched out her legs. *Bloody hell.* What was taking so long? She'd been before the magistrate. Pled guilty as charged. Told the bastards in the moldy wigs to kiss her lily-white arse and do their duty.

It had been three days. Was there some kind of debate? Maybe they were considering an alternate to hanging? Drag her through the streets, or burn her at the stake? Draw and quarter her? Tupper dropped her head back against the hard stone and closed her eyes. She didn't care how they did it, she wished they would get to it. Pacing for what seemed like hours, she felt the dangerous pull of sleep.

She jumped to her feet and scrubbed a hand over her face. No sleeping. Every time she closed her eyes, she saw it again—Bump being shot in the back. His body jerking with each hit before crashing to the deck. The gruesome scene was fated to haunt her for the rest of her days. She had prayed the "rest" would be counted on one hand.

Tupper remembered the day she lost Gavin in the earthquake that destroyed Port Royal, Jamaica, all those many years ago. She'd honestly believed that to be the worst day of her life, but she was wrong. Yes, she'd been devastated by the loss of Gavin, but she hadn't been a witness. She hadn't had to watch.

Over the years, she'd imagined the scenario in Port Royal. Gavin would have been sitting in the bar, toasting his good fortune with that drunken bastard, Fin Willie. The two men, having added the *White Witch* to the growing fleet of Gavin's ships, would have been well into their cups by the time the disaster struck.

The earthquake hit so quickly and completely, they wouldn't have had time to react before the sea reached through the land and dragged everything down to her depths. Tupper always imagined they'd have thought it a grand joke, before realizing it wasn't. It was the only sliver of comfort she could pull from that fateful day.

But Bump's death…there was no comfort to be found there. There would never be. The only comfort would be to join him. Join them both, Bump and Gavin. Of course, she could skip seeing Fin Willie again, but if he was locked with Gavin for all eternity, she'd have to deal with his obnoxious character and hideous choice of clothing.

She pounded on the door again. "Hey, I have a date with the hangman and I don't want to keep him waiting." Surprisingly, the door opened. "Finally." She held out her arms for the shackles.

"We've not come fer ye. Ye've a visitor."

"If they don't have a rope, I'm not interested." Tupper turned away from the guard. When she turned back, a huge man stood in the doorway. Satined and laced, he wore a wig and silk hose over gold buckled shoes. Tupper snorted and turned away again. "I don't need some dandy, bloody solicitor."

"Good thing I ain't one."

Hold the rudder… Tupper spun around, squinting in the gloom of the cell, not believing her eyes. She scanned the man again from powdered wig to buckled shoes.

"MacTavish?"

He held his arms wide. "Ye were expectin' the Pope?"

"You're dead. I saw ye take a bullet."

He ran a wide palm over his upper arm. "Just winged me. Damn English prigs couldn't hit water if they were settin' in the middle of the Atlantic."

"What happened to you?" She swept him from head to toe. "You're in a fucking wig. And heels no less. No beard? No tartan?" She sniffed. "Ye even smell like a bloody garden."

He lifted a sleeve and smelled himself. "Imported rose water. Think it's fukin' French."

"If ye didn't still talk like ye climbed out of a Scottish gutter, I'd not have recognized ya."

He tugged on his vest. "Don't it beat all." He adjusted his trousers. "First time in me life my balls been in dry dock. Not somethin' I'm fancyin', I tell ya."

"Then why the lace cuffs?"

"Ye recall me telling ye about that fine English woman I dallied with all those years back?"

"Father paid ye to take your hairy sporran and get the hell off his daughter."

"Aye. Priscilla." He shrugged. "Guess I left a wee bit of me sporran behind."

Tupper frowned. "A wee bit?"

"Left her with me bairn planted in her belly."

Tupper swept his appearance again. "And the father's come fer ye hide, and ye needed a disguise?"

MacTavish smooth a hand over his satin-covered chest. "I got meself a son."

"Still doesn't explain the lace."

"He be a bloody duke. Letters, and land, and rich as me Grandma's cream cake." MacTavish started to run a hand through his hair and knocked his wig askew. He tugged it back into place. "Name's Elliot. Elliot Barnes. Lives here in London. Heard the news the *Scarlet'd* been captured. Knew all about me from his mum 'n came to see if there be any news of my whereabouts. Found me in the brig nursin' my wound."

"Lucky you."

"Aye. Bought me petition without a blink of his eye. Hosed me off and stuck me in these glad rags te get me out te city."

Tupper crossed her arms over her chest. She was glad for him. Happy he was alive and would stay that way. Happy he had found family. They'd been friends for more than two dozen years. She was glad he'd finish his days well. "So ye've come to say goodbye."

"Nay, pulled a string or two te get me in here, and keep the guard's back turned for a minute or four." He jerked his head toward the door. "Let's go."

She snorted and turned away. "I'm not going anywhere."

"What? Do ye know what the blood hell yer sayin'?"

Tupper folded her arms and slid down the wall to sit once more. "I know exactly what I'm saying." She closed her eyes and leaned her head back. "It's over for me. My ship's gone. My...my... Bump's gone. I'm done. I'll sit here and wait 'til they set me swinging."

"Yer daft. Come on, time's wastin.'" He motioned toward the door.

"I don't want to go." She shook her head and crossed one foot over the other.

MacTavish pulled her up by the back of her collar. "Ye will verra much want te, ye great stubborn stripe-haired bitch, when ye see what I've got te show ye. Now move yer sorry arse."

* * * *

Draped in a satin-lined cloak, Tupper followed MacTavish past the guards and out the tower's front gate. Together they slipped into a handsome coach. A younger man sat within. As soon as the door closed behind Tupper, he wrapped on the ceiling with the silvered cap to his walking stick and the team of four perfectly matched horses took off into the night.

Tupper pushed the cloak back at MacTavish, and smoothed the hair out of her face. "Where are you takin' me?"

"Ye'll see."

"And who are you?" She jerked her chin at the other man. As soon as she asked, she noticed the resemblance. He had the same determined glint in his eye, broad shoulders and stocky build. Even sitting, the man was a mountain—a well-dressed, impeccably appointed mountain. He held out a wide hand to Tupper. "I'm Elliot MacTavish Barnes. Duke of Upton."

"And I'm Lady Codfish," she scoffed. "Where are you taking me?"

"Behave yerself. He's bloody gentry. Ye ain't captain here."

"I'm well aware." She glared at MacTavish. "Answer the question."

"Ye'll 'ave to forgive her, son. Keep her away from the stank of bilge for more than a week, she gets cranky."

Tupper cracked the tension in her neck. She wished once more for a rope. "I do apologize. Where did I leave my manners? I'm Captain Tupper Quinn. While I'm still debating whether or not I'm grateful you dragged me from my comfy prison cell, I'd be most thankful if you would tell me where we are bloody well going."

"We're almost there, Captain. I'm sorry for all the secrecy, but it's not my custom to break quite so many laws in a single night."

After ten minutes and two more turns, the coach finally began to slow. Tupper was the first to step out onto the deserted side road. MacTavish and his son soon joined her. The only light came from the side lanterns of the coach. A low fog crept across the road. Tupper reached for the hilt of her cutlass out of habit. Too bad all her weapons had been confiscated.

"Where are—"

Before she could finish her thought, four figures came out of the mist and approached the coach. Tupper straightened her spine, squinting into the dark. MacTavish wouldn't put her in danger, but a feeling of unease filtered over her none the less. She didn't care for surprises. After being the one in command for so many years, it was hard to lose her power.

"Tupper?" A man called out to her. "Is it you?"

"Who wants to know?" She folded her arms, not quite knowing what to do with her hands.

A man stepped forward into the light. Unlike MacTavish, with his shaved jaw and fancy satin trousers, this man she recognized at once. "Son of a whore, Ric Robbins."

"Tupper Quinn, glad to see your handsome face before they covered ye in tar and hung ye in a birdcage."

"What the hell are you doing here?" A smaller figure came to stand beside him. "Bloody hell, Jo Beau? I thought you two were on the other side of the Atlantic."

"Jo's father is failing, but still causing trouble. Still cursing your name." Ric shrugged. "Got mixed up with the Viscount Bolingbroke. We helped escort him to France before the British could stick him in the tower along with the Earl of Oxford. Heard you were there. We figured someone needed to save your sorry hide."

Tupper notched her chin. "Nobody asked you to."

A third figure stepped into the light. "No, but it was the least we could do. I've made it a habit to always pay my debts, and I've owed you for far too long. This should make us even."

Tupper's breath caught in her throat at the sight of him. "Jaxon? Captain Jaxon Steele." As soon as it registered who he was, Tupper's gaze slid past him to the last figure to approach. Cloaked, they hung back a few paces, but Tupper already knew who it was. "Bloody hell," she whispered. Tears pinched the backs of her eyes.

Annalise stopped and pushed back the hood of the long cloak she wore. "Alice..."

The next thing Tupper knew, the two were in each other's arms. Holding tight to a friendship that spanned decades and thousands of miles, yet somehow time and space meant nothing. *Annalise.*

"I told him not to tell you he found me," Tupper murmured into her shoulder.

"James didn't tell us. It was Ric. He showed up in Weatherington and told us you were in trouble. I'd almost given up on you being alive. Did you think we would stay away?" Tupper stepped back. Annalise cupped her cheek. The others had moved a few steps back to give the two women space to reunite. "James knows nothing of what Jaxon and I are doing here. With his new commission, the less he knows about this night the better. Besides, he's busy with his own rescue mission."

"He's a fine man you raised. You should be proud."

"We are." She stroked Tupper's arms. "Why didn't you want him to tell us about you?"

She shrugged, not quite believing the vision of her beautiful Anna standing before her. "Doesn't matter."

Annalise stroked Tupper's hair the way she used to when the two were children. It tugged at Tupper's heart. She hadn't realized how much she missed her best friend. "Of course it matters."

Tupper took Annalise's hands. Even in the dark, the difference between her hands and Tupper's was significant. "Do you remember when you thought a beautiful gown and gloves for my hands would turn me into a lady?" Tupper lifted Annalise's hands and kissed the backs of each. "You were forever calling us equals." She met her gaze and shook her head. "We were never equals. Once I made the decision to become a pirate the difference between our two lives became a chasm too broad to jump. I thought it best you didn't know what became of me. That you never knew about Alice Tupper Quinn, Pirate Captain. It was better for me to simply disappear. Let's just say I was saving you from knowing me."

"Seems you're forever saving me from something."

"I love you with all my heart. That's what friends do."

"I love you, too. That's why I'm here." Annalise waved a hand to include the rest of the group. "That's why we're all here."

Jaxon Steele came and slipped a hand around Annalise's waist. He scanned the group. "Everyone ready? We haven't much time before they change the watch."

Tupper asked once again. "Will someone please tell me what the hell we're doing?"

Jaxon slipped his other arm around Tupper's waist and pulled her along. The others fell into step behind.

"We're going to steal a ship."

Epilogue

James kissed a path starting below Samantha's left earlobe and moved with a desired determination down her neck, along her shoulder, and between the pale tender fullness of her breasts. She whimpered her approval and pushed her fingers into his hair. Her body arched into his touch as she raised one beautifully seductive knee.

Her skin was still damp from her bath and smelled of warm honey and cream. He swirled his tongue around the sensitive firmed peak of her breast before pulling it into his mouth with a gentle suck.

"James…," Samantha gave a tiny gasp before sighing into a delighted moan fisting the back of his hair and holding him to her. "I still can't believe you had Archbishop Tenison marry us in the middle of the night. Poor man had such a nasty cough. I hope he's well soon. My father nearly fell over when he realized who he was."

He raised his head. "Two things I cannot discuss while I make love to my wife are her father and the Archbishop of Canterbury's cough."

Samantha flushed pink and pulled him back for a kiss. "I'm sorry. I'm just so happy."

"That's all I ever wanted." He began his path again. Perhaps her right earlobe this time. He murmured against her skin, "Happy…." God, she smelled like a garden in the warm sun of summer. "Safe…." He cupped her breast before lowering his mouth again. "Loved…."

"I loved my gown, wasn't it beautiful?"

"Beautiful…" He rolled the tightened tip of her nipple between two fingers.

"And your parents. I adore them. I was afraid they were going to miss the ceremony. Whatever kept them?"

"Wouldn't tell me." He brushed his lips down her belly to trace her navel. "Something to do with lightening Tupper's sentence. They said I'd hear soon enough, and the less I knew, the better I'd like it." James gave an impatient nip to the inside of Samantha's thigh before abandoning ship and giving up with a groan. "I'm trying to make love to you."

"You're doing a wonderful job." She smiled and ran her fingertips over his chest.

"And yet you choose now to talk?"

"I've missed our talks." She cupped his face before kissing him. "I missed you."

James rolled to her side and gathered her in his arms, pulling her half on top of him. She stretched out along him and rested her cheek on his chest. He loved the feel of her naked skin against his. Did anything feel as good?

"You saved me. You brought my family back to me. I'm so grateful. I'll never forget it."

"That was Ducky's gift. He was the one to ride all the way back to South Oxbridge to fetch them and Alicia." As soon as he mentioned his sister's name, he knew why Ducky had been so generous with his actions. Here he'd thought him noble for making that long journey again.

Samantha traced her fingertips over his chest, leaving a trail of sparks along his skin. "You told them you met me at a ball."

"It was the truth. We did meet at a ball."

"But none of the rest. You didn't tell them the rest."

"Not my story to tell."

Samantha moved against him, lifting her knee to drape her leg across him. Desire surged through him. She raised up on one elbow. "Did I mention how happy I was?"

James tucked a stray curl behind her ear. "I do believe you did."

She sighed gently and looked about the room. "I almost miss the creak and roll of your ship."

He pulled her fully atop him, running his hands over the flair of her hips and the round firm flesh of her behind. "I'm very content to keep to dry land for a while."

Samantha kissed the place over his heart. "But you can't give up your commission for me. That's an order."

Each brush of her lips sent a rush of heat to his already impatient cock. "I thought I was the captain?"

"You are. And I'm the captain's wife." She gasped as he quickly changed their position. In one smooth move, her tossed her onto her back and settled over her, positioning himself between her thighs. Her chest rose and fell in rapid response. "I promise, no more orders. No more talking... for now. Forgive me?"

* * * *

Tupper drew a great breath of fresh sea air into her lungs. Overhead, the wind caught the sails with a snap as the last bit of canvas was dropped and the *Scarlet Night* hit open water. A dozen men borrowed into service from Ric Robbins's own crew had volunteered to man the ship. Strangers, all of them. It felt odd without the others.

MacTavish had decided to keep his balls in dry dock only until he could return safely to Scotland. He'd heard the latest political rumblings and thought the Jacobites could use another good man—to the horror of his son, the duke, of course.

And speaking of horrified sons, wouldn't she like to hear the explosion when James Steele found out his parents had a hand in her escape? It still tugged at Tupper's heart to have seen Annalise. How could two be so distant, and yet totally and completely joined? She lifted her hand and rubbed a thumb over her ring. Completely and forever.

Tupper set course with the helmsman whose name she couldn't recall. There was time enough to learn. She left the quarterdeck and made her way to her favorite spot.

Standing in the bow, she filled her lungs yet again. The moon was high. There was a lot of sea to cross before dawn's change of the guard found the *Lion's* men they'd stripped naked and tied to the dock pier.

Behind her came a soft thump, thump. Her first mate came alongside and handed her a tankard filled to the rim with the finest sweet rum she'd ever stolen. Even navigating with a new crutch, he hadn't spilled a single drop.

She lifted it to her nose and breathed in its sweet scent. How long had it been? Near a month of forced sobriety? Granted, her head had never been clearer nor her senses more sharp, but there was something to be said about the many benefits of her demon rum.

They raised their mugs and tapped the rims. Tupper tipped the mug to her lips and drank, closing her eyes as the blessed warmth spread its way clear to the tips of her worn boots.

She opened her eyes with a smile and, with a wide hand, tapped her thumb against the side of her chin before squeezing her hand twice.

Bump fixed her with a stare and repeated the sign, *'Mother's milk?'* He tapped his thumb against the side of his chin and moved his hand to cover one eye.

'Only if your mother is a pirate.'

Be sure not to miss Lisa A. Olech's sequel to *Within A Captain's Hold, Within A Captain's Treasure, Within A Captain's Fate,* and *Within A Captain's Power*:

Within A Captain's Soul

Read on for a special sneak peek of the next book in the Captains of the Scarlet Night series!

Learn more about Lisa A. Olech
http://www.kensingtonbooks.com/author.aspx/31711

Chapter 1

Madagascar
1717

William Quinn hated the dark. She'd taken the lantern when she left. He could still smell the spiced honey of her skin and the musk of their sex in the sheets. She'd been a tiger in bed. His flesh burned where her nails had raked his back. He'd lost himself for an hour or two between her smooth dark thighs. He only wished he'd learned her name.

Will lay in the bed and closed his eyes to the darkness. It was easier to visualize the layout of the room from memory this way. The door was to starboard. A three-drawer chest sat a foot to port. His pants were another matter. Where had she tossed them? She'd been in a terrible hurry to put her mouth on him. When she'd stripped him and seen his engorged cock, a smile spread across her shining face as if she'd discovered some long lost treasure. After that, she was a most eager partner.

He found his pants along with the wide blood red sash he wore about his waist. And one boot. All the while, his limited sense was still on high alert. In this darkness, it would be easy to hide and ambush him. It wasn't as if he'd hear anyone approaching, but having lost his hearing at such a young age, over his lifetime, he'd honed his other senses to razor sharp. Will lifted his nose and gave another sniff. No, he was alone.

The heat along this stretch of the world limited his choice of clothing. Bare chested, he slipped into a tooled leather vest. He patted the breast pocket. His lusty companion wasn't interested in his winnings from tonight's poker tables. As the daughter of one of the local pepper merchants, money was not what she desired most. Madagascar pepper was considered black gold along the great treasure route.

Will found his other boot, and sat on the edge of the bed to slip them on his feet. He sat there for a long moment. The girl, whoever she was, hadn't been interested in his newfound wealth or even knowing who he was. She'd only been interested in one thing. It was the same wherever he went these days. He'd become a novelty. Sex with the silent man. It wasn't as if he could brag about his conquests. Tell tales of your night in his bed. He wouldn't bore you with long stories, or shout demands. He was deaf and never learned the basic fundamentals of speech. For some reason that made women eager to spread their legs for him. At least for one night.

Making his way to the door, Will wasn't surprised to find the public rooms below still doing a brisk business. Time held no meaning to these establishments. Glancing toward the back corner, the poker game still wore on. He was tempted to add to his already bulging purse. Tonight had been too easy, but then it had always been a talent of his to read faces. Call it a lucrative byproduct of being deaf. Whether bluffing at cards or dealing with his crew. He could spot a liar at fifty yards.

Long legs carried him quickly through the dangerous dark streets. At more than six foot, Will made an imposing figure. The three-pistol baldric and side cutlass helped. As did the permanent scowl. He pulled a short knife from a leather sheath and carried it at his side. For two reasons. A handy weapon was never a bad idea, and the high polish on the blade gave him the perfect view of anyone trying to approach him from behind.

Will reached the docks without incident and was finally able to breathe easy when he dropped down upon the decks of the *Scarlet Night*. Home.

'Captain.' His first mate, Griffin tapped his shoulder to sign the word before giving Will a sharp salute.

Will returned the salute and replied with a few quick hand signals of his own. *'Are we ready to leave at first light?'*

Griffin nodded. Will scanned the deck in a slow sweep. All looked as it should. The crew was busy loading supplies of food and ale. Barrels of powder and crates of spices were all being stowed properly.

Will slapped Griffin's shoulder. He was a good man. Smart. Responsible. And a damn fine pirate. He could filet a ship with a single cannon shot down the length of their hull and fight like a man possessed. Will was happy he was on their side.

'Problems?'

His first mate shook his head. Thankfully, Griffin was quick to pick up on the basic hand signals Will had adapted over the years to help him communicate. Between the use of bells and hand signs and basic gestures, Will had been able to build a crew that followed his strict orders and knew exactly what was asked of them and when. No small feat, but after almost a year at the helm, he'd amassed a fine crew.

He recalled the day he'd become Captain of the *Scarlet Night*. He and Tupper Quinn had literally stolen their ship back from under the noses of the British Navy. They'd been captured and faced hanging for crimes against the crown, but what the wool-backed Brits hadn't counted on was the fact that not only did Tupper have friends in high places with deep pockets, but he had a hide thicker than a bull elephant. He still had the scars to prove it.

Three months after their escape, as they made their way down the west coast of Africa, skirting the British at every turn, hiding in every nook and cranny along the rugged coastline, Tupper had broken the news that she no longer wished to be Captain.

'It's yer turn now. Ye've earned it. The Scarlet Night is in yer blood. She's yer soul. Hell, ye cut yer teeth on the riggin.' It's only right to pass her on to you.'

At first, he'd laughed at her. Who ever heard of a deaf captain? But as time went on Tupper cleverly stepped back little by little. With each new crew member they acquired she planted the seeds of possibility. By giving him more responsibility, more of her power, she opened the path for him to finally take over.

It was only then he learned the real reason why Tupper Quinn was stepping aside.

He turned back to Griffin. *'How is she?'*

'In her cabin.'

Will made his way below deck to the rear of the ship. He'd swiped two bottles of her favorite rum from the galley on his way. He knocked on the thick wood of her door, but didn't wait for her to stomp on the floorboards to indicate he could enter.

The captain's quarters. Oak trimmed and impressive. While he came here daily to work the logs and charts, it was still and always would be Tupper's quarters.

He found her in the niched bed, half sitting, half reclining. When he placed the bottles on the desk, she opened her eyes.

'Bump, there you are. Where did you run off to?'

The old nickname made him smile. She was the only one to call him that anymore, and only when they were alone. He'd been given the name when he'd first come aboard. A filthy urchin from the fetid gutters of Port Royal, Jamaica. Imagine a deaf child on a pirate ship. He was always in the wrong place at the wrong time with ropes flying and blocks swinging. Needless to say, he couldn't hear anyone warning him to look out. It had taken weeks before he developed a sixth sense that something was about to cleave his skull in two. He had more knots and scrapes. Earned the name Bump. As with all nicknames, it stuck and followed him clear into adulthood.

But when Tupper made the decision to give up her commission, they agreed Captain Bump was not a fit name anymore. As it was, when Captain Gavin Quinn, Tupper's late husband, and former Captain of the *Scarlet Night* had brought Bump aboard, none knew his surname. An old woman claiming to be his grandmother had pleaded with Gavin to save him from a brutal life. She'd told him his name was William.

Against all advice, Gavin had taken him on as a fledgling cabin boy who could neither speak nor understand and who spent more time those first few days bleeding from the head as performing any duties. The man had saved his life. Will would forever regret not being able to save his. He died in the great earthquake that wiped Port Royal off the earth. Will witnessed the whole horrific event. Helpless and heartbroken. He still remembered that awful day as if it happened yesterday.

It wasn't until he and the rest of the crew had been arrested by the British that he took on the name Quinn as his own. A gift from Tupper. He'd always believed himself to be her son. She made it official.

'Pour me some rum, and tell me where you've been.' Tupper swung her legs over to hang off the side of her bed. She was looking more and more frail by the day.

Will handed her a mug. She downed the strong drink in one swallow and held her mug out for more. He refilled it. They repeated this. All the while, he eyed the charts spread out over the desk. There was no question in his mind. His original plan was not going to work.

They'd never reach China in time. He would have to risk crossing paths with the British and navigate the Indian Ocean then through the treacherous Malacca Straights past Singapore.

Tupper started to cough. Her body wracked with each bark. She covered her mouth with a handkerchief to whip the bloody spittle from her mouth. Seeing the blood, Will's stomach dropped.

He had learned about the progressive medicines now available in China. They were far ahead of western medicines. That's where they were headed. Why else would they have made the harrowing trip around the Cape of Good Hope. It had been the quickest way, and Will had found the secret to navigating the *'Cape of Good Storms'* without losing a single life.

It was good hope he was hanging on to. There was one life he was determined not to lose. If he didn't find a faster route to China, however, Tupper would soon be dead.

Meet the Author

Lisa A. Olech is an artist/writer living in her dream house nestled among the lakes in New England. She loves getting lost in a steamy book, finding the perfect pair of sexy shoes, and hearing the laughter of her men. Being an estrogen island in a sea of testosterone makes her queen. She believes in ghosts, silver linings, the power of a man in a tuxedo, and happy endings. For more information please visit lisaolech.com.